THE TOY COLLECTOR

THE TOY COLLECTOR

James Gunn

BLOOMSBURY

Published by Bloomsbury, New York and London

Distributed to the trade by St Martin's Press

A CIP catalogue record for this book is
available from the Library of Congress

ISBN 1–58234–149–4

First published in the U.S. by Bloomsbury in 2000
This paperback edition published 2001

10 9 8 7 6 5 4 3 2 1

Typeset by Hewer Text Ltd, Edinburgh
Printed in the United States of America by
R.R. Donnelley & Sons Company, Harrisonburg, Virginia

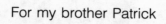

For my brother Patrick

CONTENTS

The Greatest Toy in the World

1 We acquire the toy

His real name was Trevor Forrester, but the kids in the
subdivision called him Monster because he was mean and
he was ugly and he was retarded. 'You ought to be able to
make that brat's head spin in circles, smart as you are,' my
father would say to my brother and me. But IQs didn't
help much when Monster pushed down on your chest and
squeezed your scrotum until you screamed. At night, we'd
put ice packs between our legs to stop the swelling. We
wouldn't tell our mom, didn't want her poking around
our private stuff. The old man we didn't tell much of
anything.

A good thing about Monster was he was choosy. His
father was a proctologist, he made a lot of money, and
every year at Christmas he'd buy his kid too many gifts.
Monster would pick one or two toys of which he was fond
and ignore the rest. He loved the Six Million Dollar Man
action figure, whom he called Steve and treated as a sort of
friend. There was a funny story about how one day Mr.
Forrester was drunk on the couch and Monster was
running Steve over his sleeping body and Mr. Forrester

woke up, fed up, and smashed Steve to bits on an ebony statuette of the Virgin Mary. Monster stood by yelling, 'Steve, no! No, Steve! Steve!'

When his mother had garage sales, Monster's choosiness worked to my brother's and my advantage. She was a lonely lady, had a lot of them.

The women shifted about the garage and ignored each other. They circled long tables that ran side by side, covered in old cookware and afghan rugs. Those who did talk often had funny voices; the people who lived in the boons outside Saint Louis County always sounded like that. Many of these women smelled bad from driving long distances in cars that weren't air-conditioned. 'Can I get this blouse any cheaper?' they'd ask Mrs. Forrester. 'No,' Mrs. Forrester would say. 'Priced as marked.' She didn't like the women from the boons.

Tar walked carefully. He was afraid Monster was going to show up and do stuff to us.

'He's not gonna be here,' I told my brother. 'His mom doesn't want him around, disgusting people.'

Tar made the *whew*! face, puffing up his cheeks and blowing out air. He'd collect faces from watching television. He was three.

Discounting the dust, most of the toys on the toy table looked brand new.

'A pterodactyl,' Tar said. He pointed to a box between Stratego and Chutes and Ladders. Volcanoes and prehistoric animals were on the box, and a name: Scrunch 'Em, Grow 'Em Dinosaurs. I yanked the box from between the others. Tar placed his fingers on the edge. $1.50 was scrawled in Magic Marker beneath his thumb. My mother had given both of us a dollar, which together, I was sure, added up to a lot more than a dollar fifty.

*   *   *

*Put the cubes in the Energizer Machine and WATCH
'em transform into DINOSAURS! Then scrunch 'em
up again in the DINOSAUR PIT! Endless Fun!!!*

Diagrams showed a dinosaur being squashed in a machine
and growing back to life in a clear electric dome.

Tar and I loved three things: Dinosaurs, metamorphoses, and machines. Holding this toy now was like
holding a toy designed especially for the two of us by
God. We had never seen it before in any store or on any
commercial (we later learned the FDA had banned the
machine shortly after its release). This was the toy that we
wanted, no need to look further. We moved toward Mrs.
Forrester, who was sorting pennies into neat rows on her
money table.

An old woman's hand came down upon the box, almost
knocking it from my grip. The hand had a marble-sized
diamond ring. Thick veins curled around its bones.

'I'm sorry, boys, but I just bought that,' said the old
woman attached to the hand. She had a bright orange
hairdo that swooped in a Hawaii Five-O wave. The skin
around her mouth was pleated. Her perfume surrounded
me in a thick swamp. 'I'm sorry, but it's mine,' she said. 'I
just paid for it now and now, here I was, coming over to
get it.'

'Nuh-uh,' Tar said.

'We just got it,' I told her.

'Yes, but it's mine. I've already paid for it. It's common
in garage sales to pay for the item first.' She gave a little
laugh. I wondered what the inside of her head looked like.

'Nuh-uh,' Tar said.

'This is a toy we want very much,' I told her. 'And we
have more than a dollar and fifty cents.'

The woman grabbed the box with both hands.

I whispered to my brother: 'Cry.'

Tar burst into tears. He was famous for being able to do this on command. The women in the garage looked at him.

'My brother wants this toy very much. He's crying. Look.'

'I like pterodactyls!' Tar cried.

'Let go of the box, please, son.'

'Uh-uh!' I said. I grabbed more tightly to the sides, but the woman was too strong and her perfume had weakened me. She yanked the toy up and away. She embraced it beneath her breasts. She breathed heavily.

'Now there's heaps of other toys here. Go pick one out.' She turned and walked out of the garage.

I stared at the concrete floor, panicked. I jerked my head up to see her waddling down the driveway with our toy. I chased after her. Tar followed me. He continued to cry; his sadness was becoming more real as he continued.

'We had that toy first, lady,' I said.

'Don't "lady" me, young man. I *saw* it first.'

'You're too old to have a toy.'

'It's for my grandson.'

We followed her to an olive Buick parked in front of the house. She put the box in the backseat and locked the car door. She didn't look at us as she walked back up the driveway and into the garage. Tar and I mushed our faces against the driver's side window. The toy was upside down. It was bursting with brontosauruses, pterodactyls, woolly mammoths, et cetera.

Dinosaurs. Metamorphosis. Machine.

'I hate that bitch,' Tar whispered. It was one of the phrases we had learned from our father. They were all fun to use. There were some, though, such as the C word, that didn't get even a hint of a smile from Mom.

'Yeah.'

The driver's side was locked. But I could see the stem sticking up on the passenger side. I eyed the mouth of the garage. One woman was looking over a plaid shirt for rips or stains. Another was smelling a pair of ballerina slippers. The old woman was spinning the wheel of a bicycle on the wall, one that wasn't even for sale.

'Come on,' I said to Tar. We crept, silent and careful, around to the other side of the Buick. I propped one hand on the hot metal of the car and pulled on the passenger handle with the other. The door snapped open. The victorious sound of 'eeg!' leapt from my brother's throat. I reached in. Tar gripped hard onto my T-shirt. My hands were on the box.

Let's teach that cunt a lesson she'll never forget: that was the song in my soul.

We barreled down the hill toward home. The air whistled in our ears. We giggled in random bursts, prompted by fear and its thrill. The box grew heavy in my arms. I pulled it against my chest, and we ran faster down Taylor Drive. The sun was bright; its tendrils sank fast into our skin. We turned left. Now we moved up Arblay. Wiped the sweat from my cheek with my shoulder. Then turned right on our street, Troll Court. Our two-story yellow house stood at the top of the hill and we flung ourselves toward it. My heart raced.

We collapsed against the wood of the front door and Tar threw it open. He shrieked as we plunged into air-conditioned space. We hunched over, gathering our energies, the breath being torn from our lungs in heaves, when our mother's voice dropped from upstairs: 'Did you buy anything?'

'No, there was nothing good,' I yelled.

What a lie that was! We had to put our hands over our mouths to stop the laughter.

We opened the basement door. We tumbled down the stairs. The rocking horse with the sad face, a face that wished it was real instead of plastic, stood at the bottom. I slapped it on the nose as we passed by. It bobbed.

I dropped the box on the floor. Tar peeled back the lid. Inside, a machine, dinosaurs, directions, cubes: a shred of paradise stolen.

The policeman had a pear-shaped body. He had a mouth that looked as if he were stretching his cheeks back with the palms of his hands to make a funny face. His partner, who wasn't wearing a hat, was older. They stood at the end of our hall, framed by the doorway. The hall was separated from the family room by beams; the pear-shaped cop was half covered by one. Tar and I were sitting on the floor in the family room. The best, *Ultraman*, was on TV.

The police had a conversation with my mother we couldn't hear, but we could see they were being polite. They usually would be; my father was a lawyer and most of them knew him.

Tar looked at me, his mouth cracked open a little. 'Lie,' I whispered. On the TV, Ultraman knocked over a guy in a giant bug costume and a couple cardboard buildings were squashed behind him.

'A lizard game?' my mother said.

The policemen nodded. They went on, only some things audible to my brother and me: the word *complaint*, the word *argument*, and something about the old woman's car.

My mother offered a blank stare. Some mothers get defensive, but ours knew the two of us were a special case. Something had been wrong with her ovaries. We were bad seeds. My mother told the police she'd go downstairs and root around to see if there was a lizard game somewhere. She slit her eyes at us on the way downstairs. We were her enemies.

I played with the string tie on my shorts as I stood in the doorway. The younger policeman crouched in front of me. He balanced an open notebook on his knee. The other one, who looked pissed, continued to stand. Behind them two squirrels fought on a tree limb. The darker squirrel had something brown in its mouth.

'Jimmy. We just have a couple of questions for you. First question: Did you take the lizard game from Mrs. Tolkenstein's car?'

'No.'

'You did, though, argue with her about the lizard game?'

I nodded. 'We had it first.' I stared at him. 'It's not a game.'

'And it's not lizards,' Tar said. 'Dinosaurs.'

The cop wrote something in his notebook. I looked down. *Dinosaurs.* He dotted it with a hard period and clicked his pen shut.

'She put it in her car,' I told them.

The cop clicked his pen open again.

'We know you took it,' the standing policeman said. He sighed. We were trying his patience. 'People saw you take it.'

Years later I would learn about the good-cop/bad-cop routine in more depth.

'We didn't. I swear on my dead mother's grave.'

'How old are you, Jimmy?' the younger policeman said. 'Or is it Jim? Do you like being called Jim?'

'No. I'm four.'

The policeman turned to my brother.

'Tar, a question for you. How old?'

'Three years old.'

'Did you or did your brother take the box of dinosaurs from the car? You're required to tell the truth.'

'Monster did it.'

The policemen smiled. My brother had blown the game, they thought.

'A monster took the dinosaurs, did it? Describe this monster's appearance.'

My mother's footsteps grew louder behind us.

'Monster is what the kids call Trevor Forrester,' she said. 'He goes to special school. He picks on the other children.'

The crouching policeman's smile faded slightly. He exchanged a glance with his partner.

'And there was no trace of a lizard game downstairs,' my mother said.

'Monster opened the car,' Tar said. 'He took it. Monster took it. He ran fast.'

Tar would be in the accelerated classes all through school. At the age of three he already knew there was no better scapegoat than a retarded bully.

Behind the policemen the two squirrels continued to do battle. One knocked the other from the tree limb. It fell on our front lawn. Later my brother and I went out to see if it was dead.

Our basement had a paneled corkboard ceiling. You could climb a ladder, push up the panels, and hide things in the space above them. Through the years the space housed chewing gum (my father despised the cracking sound), fireworks, smoke bombs, cigarettes, love letters from Stacey Kees, magazines with naked people, witchcraft tracts, porno videos, anarchist newsletters, condoms, a pair of handcuffs, alcohol of various grains and proofs, pills, grass, coke, a Graphix bong, a foam vagina, a .38 revolver, and many other useful items not sanctioned by the Gunn family government. The space's longest resident, though, was Scrunch 'Em, Grow 'Em Dinosaurs, known to the authorities only as The Lizard Game. Back in the early seventies my mother would probably have turned us in had we not outwitted her by hiding our contraband in the basement ceiling. She *seemed* all right, but after you had lived with her for four years you knew she'd turn rat if the circumstances were right. Due to renovation the space is now gone. Neither my brother nor I know what happened to the toy.

2. Rules of the toy

Scrunch 'Em, Grow 'Em Dinosaurs has two basic components:

(1) A boxy machine made of a sturdy red metal, and (2) Small, brightly colored square blocks. These blocks look identical to Starburst candies. Do not eat them.

A mesh circle, four and a half inches in diameter, covers much of the red machine; this circle is the heart and soul of Scrunch 'Em, Grow 'Em Dinosaurs. It is, essentially, a small oven. Plug the machine into a wall socket and watch it heat up, turning first a dim gray, then a soft pink, and, finally, a bright red. It is not necessary to wait until the mesh is red to transform the blocks. It will, however, work faster that way. A clear plastic dome with a sliding door encloses the oven. This is simply a precaution and does not facilitate the transformation process. Although an adult can only fit a few fingers through the sliding portal, a child can insert his hand with little difficulty. As an added benefit, the plastic dome is readily detachable.

When a block is placed within the dome, and the red machine is turned *on*, the block will slowly unfurl, one limb springing out and then another until it has changed into an entire dinosaur! Like the metamorphosis of a caterpillar to a butterfly or a bud to a blooming rose, this is a beautiful thing to see.

When the dinosaur is complete, the general rule is to turn *off* the machine and wait for it to cool before removing it from the dome. Without patience, blisters will occur.

A variety of creatures are included in the box, not limited to a brontosaurus, an ankylosaurus, a triceratops, a woolly mammoth, and the ever-popular pterodactyl. After a while you will be able to tell which block is which dinosaur by memorizing each animal's specific color. DO NOT put the blocks in a conventional oven; this will simply result in destroying that particular dinosaur forever.

The small bin and knob on the right side of the machine are commonly (and collectively) called a *masher*. Once a dinosaur is heated to the properly mushy consistency, place it in the bin, slide the top of the bin shut, and screw the knob. The knob will push in the metal mashing device, squashing the dinosaur back into a block shape. The masher is where Scrunch 'Em, Grow 'Em Dinosaurs has one up on all other metamorphoses, for can even nature, in all its splendor, transform the butterfly back into the caterpillar or the blooming rose back into the bud?

3. Bob and Oscar

Bob wasn't really a cowboy, he was a gunfighter and a former deputy, but he belonged to the cowboy's ilk. He was always on the ready with his pistol pointing straight. His face was harsh. It was weathered with deep grooves, trenches for tears running down his cheeks. Maybe those trenches hadn't been there before the Indians and their accomplices, the army guys, had murdered his wife and his baby daughter.

Bob was mine.

Oscar was Tar's. Oscar perpetually swung a lasso over his head. His face was similar to Bob's – in fact, many people thought they were brothers. Oscar had never been married and had never lost his family, but he had been very attached to his horse, Ernie. That psycho Bazooka Man had shot him down like a dog. Ernie knew how to fight if the fight was fair, but even he was susceptible to a smile and a carrot and a bazooka slipped suddenly beneath his muzzle.

The crunch of gravel under moccasins warned Bob. He turned in his sleeping bag and spotted the tip of an arrow between the leaves of a plant. To the right of that, a hand with a grenade rose above the beanbag chair. The Indians had surrounded their camp of snoring cowboys. Bob had that one moment of awareness before the explosion that killed half their party. Then arrows came slinging.

The battle was long. It was bloody. Bob and Oscar survived in their typical fashion – Bob picked the bastards off like flies; Oscar snapped a hundred necks with his lasso. Most the other boys were killed. The obituary column would read like a guest list to a cocktail party thrown by Bob and Oscar: Linus, Pete, Bert, Mojo, Sylvester, Handsome Dan, Gordon, Batman Jr., Willie . . . One sometimes wondered if it was worth it, this triumph, living, when surrounded by so much death.

Most of the red faces were taken alive. Bob and Oscar tied their hands behind their backs and lined them up along the Tonka tractor. Bazooka Man stuck his ugly green mug in Oscar's face.

'I'm glad I killed your horse, cowboy scum.'

Bob had to hold Oscar back from killing Bazooka Man right there.

The bowlegged cowboy without the horse was placed in charge of the prisoners.

'Okay, y'all, follow me,' he said. He led the procession of Indians and army men through the woods. They complained about the ants crawling up their legs and the chill of the night air against their bare chests. 'Y'all shoulda thought of that 'fore y'all murdered my amigos.'

They marched across the great expanse of carpet as owls and crickets cheered their passing. The cowboy ushered them up the length of Hot Wheel track and into the clear dome of the red machine. With a loud clang, the bowlegged cowboy slid the door shut behind them.

'You have no right!' the Chief shouted.

'We have all the rights we need, fucker,' Bob said. He wrapped his hands around the thick length of cord and stuffed the giant plug into the wall.

'They're burning us alive!' Bazooka Man screamed, and soon they all screamed in the worst of possible agonies. Bob's eyes spilled tears. He remembered the way he cradled his dear sweet baby daughter in his arms and hoped she now peered down from heaven with joy.

Bazooka Man futilely tried to pry his leg away from the Indian Chief's back as the two of them melted together. Orange and green merged into a sick-colored brown. Soon enough they were all melting into one huge creature of horror (which was later brought back to life by a mad scientist and attacked Bob and Oscar in revenge). The stench of his confreres' burning flesh overcame Bazooka Man and he gagged and vomited until the very moment he went to Hell.

* * *

The pipe organ blared down upon the cowboys. The little church had been converted from the old farmhouse; it still had the farmer's name, Fisher-Price, painted across the top. Bob and Oscar knelt in the pews and thanked God that they had been victorious over their enemies, that their loved ones had been avenged, and that the red machine was still in working order.

'Lamb of God, you take away the sins of the world, have mercy on us,' the priest recited on the altar. He held the holy eucharist over his head. 'Lamb of God, you take away the sins of the world. Grant us peace.'

Bob tapped Oscar on the thigh.

'Hey. I think that priest is an Indian in disguise. He just made the secret Indian symbol.'

'The Indians have a secret symbol?' Oscar asked.

The two cowboys knocked over the chalice full of wine as they pinned the priest to the altar. They dragged the old man to the clear plastic dome, where they burnt away his face. Gradually, more Indians in disguise exposed themselves through secret symbols and innuendos. The cowboys melted all of them, or turned them into freaks, or made them amputees.

Tar and I darted up the stairs. Although it was a cold fall we opened all the doors and windows in the house. The wind swept in around us, washing away the smell of burnt plastic before our mother got back home.

4. We share the secret of the toy

I once measured Gary's head from behind with a ruler. It was, in fact, quite large, just as it appeared to be. My mother had told me it was just the way he held himself.

'Mom, Gary's head is two inches and eight lines bigger than mine. And I'm taller.'

'Well, I guess Gary just needs space to fit all those novel ideas.'

Gary Bauer had a lot of those. One of his main ideas was about washing his hands, which he did as much as possible. This in tandem with his constipation problem meant he was usually in the bathroom. Also, he spoke a language he said was French.

'*Abriga!*' he said, as Tar and I met him at the bottom of Troll Court.

We stared at him. He was our best friend, which often led us to believe there was something wrong with our own lives.

'That means, "Hello, James and Tar!" *In French.*'

'Bull roar,' Tar said.

'A translation for bull roar is *blik naba.*' Gary was wearing a pirate hat he had folded from a newspaper. It was too large for his head. The brim rested atop his black horn-rimmed glasses. He was the only preschooler in the neighborhood with glasses, and we were all a little jealous of him for needing a prescription.

'Gary, there's something we want to show you,' I said.

'What?'

Tar grabbed Gary's hand. He pulled him behind him, up Troll Court and toward our house.

'Nancy!' Gary said. 'Jimmy and Tar have a *very important* thing.'

Nancy Zoomis was preoccupied with trying to make GI Joe fit in Barbie's Mansion. Her straight brown hair hung in her face. The ends were shredded from her chewing. She was Gary Bauer's other best friend, though she had just moved in.

We were behind the Delgesses' shrubs. This was where Nancy and I would later come to play house. I'll show you mine if you show me yours, one of us would say. From there it would be a race to unzip.

'I don't want to go,' she said. 'I'm playing here.'

'All right,' I told her. 'Then you'll miss out.'

I put my hands in my pockets and walked up the street. Tar and Gary followed.

'She'll be sorry!' Gary said. 'Or, as we say in France, *Ordbökon*!'

We passed the Benningtons' house. We passed the Smiths'. By the time we got to the Fitzgeralds' Nancy's sneakers could be heard scraping the street behind us.

Nancy was laughing. 'It's weird!' she shouted at Steve and Corey, the twins. Gary was picking at a scab on his arm. Steve and Corey looked at him.

'What'd they get?' Corey asked.

'You have to promise not to tell,' Gary said.

Robert and his little brother Brendan found out about it, too. At first we didn't want them to know: Brendan had a big mouth. But he's kept quiet thus far.

In secret meetings the children of the subdivision gathered: Gary, Nancy, Robert, Steve, Corey, Brendan, Tar, and me. I'd stand at the top of the ladder and push up the ceiling panel. I'd hand down the Greatest Toy in the World and it would pass from the hands of one child to the next. Tar would set it down in the center of the floor. We'd pull ourselves in around it. Blades of grass brushed against the rectangular windows at the top of the basement walls. My mother's sandaled footsteps crossed the kitchen overhead.

We'd lean in, getting closer to the machine. We'd run

our fingers over the details of the tiny beasts. I would slide open the door to the clear plastic dome. Steve would place a green block inside. In closer, Nancy's bare knee would graze against mine. Brendan's head would be nuzzled between Corey and Steve. Gary would stand, always moving. He'd beat a rhythm on the basement's hollow metal beam with a spoon. Robert would hum made-up songs. Tar's brown eyes would flood with magic. A long neck and a head would pop up from the green block. And all of us would be joined beneath the skin as we created, destroyed, created, destroyed, created.

And that is why, twenty years later, I began collecting toys.

William Sinewski III

Bill Sinewski worked the graveyard shift at Saint Dominic's Hospital near Times Square. I was hired there as an orderly the summer of '95 and Bill was asked to train me. He showed me how to adjust the oxygen and how to get a Fresca from the pop dispenser using only two quarters. Beyond that he was fairly clueless. He had worked at Saint Dominic's for two years. He and I wandered around the halls together trying out some of the strange gadgets that hospitals have. We learned a lot of things: A CPR pad will knock you to the ground, even if you just do it on your shoulder. Electrocardiographs make shitty lie detectors. No matter what the LPN tells you, catheters hurt like hell. And for God's sake don't try to work the ultrasound machine without a pass card. The bastard beeps loudly and you'll have to run.

Bill and I almost got fired for a CAT scan incident at a hospital where people never get fired. I told the tech that I knew what I was doing. I had been watching. I had been studying his moves. And, also, that Bill's brain had an ominous black spot in the frontal lobe.

'That could be something serious,' I told the tech. 'Maybe a tumor.'

Bill looked terrified. Thank God we were fucking

around with the CAT scan, he was probably thinking. Perhaps James caught it in time.

CAT scan boy told us to get the hell out of there and go do whatever it was we were supposed to be doing.

'But the spot!' I told him.

'It's just a processing thing. Now get out.'

That was a typical confrontation.

Bill Sinewski was from a lot of places, most notably Long Island, Cincinnati, and Los Angeles. His surfer dialect, however, was only from Los Angeles. His clothes were from Kmart, but he had a way of putting the cheap stuff together to form something casual and cool. I only wore vintage suits from the '50s and '60s, and the reason we were friends was that we were an interesting pair walking down the street.

Bill wasn't any taller than I, but he had more muscles. He put a lot of work into his hair, which was black and curled down one side of his forehead. He had the perfect sort of male nose, with just enough flare in the nostrils to suggest passion. His one physical fault was his skin. At adolescence he started breaking out and at twenty-four, one year younger than I was, he still hadn't stopped. Bill applied ointment to his face every night. Sometimes I'd catch him staring in the bathroom mirror with a sad look on his face, running his fingertips slowly over the bumps on his cheeks. But most the time the mirror was Bill's friend—despite his acne he was handsome and he knew it.

Even the most intelligent women seemed to melt into mawkishness around Bill and his muscles and his passionately flared nostrils. This invalidated the notion that I had been raised with, that women were innately more moral in judgment than men, especially in sexual matters. When Bill talked to a woman a new face overtook his usual one. It had a goofy grin and glassy eyes and it bobbed a bit. Any critical judgment he possessed seemed to fall away. What struck me as stupidity the nurses took as innocence and sincerity.

'Where's Bill?' they'd ask me every time I went on a run by myself.

'He's fired,' I'd tell them.

'*Fired?*' the nurses would cry, panic in their eyes, fingers to their lower lips.

'The dispatcher caught him in the bathroom,' I'd say, 'masturbating to a picture of Fabio.'

The nurses didn't like me as much as they liked Bill.

Christmas trees. Purple hearts. Black beauties. Yellow jackets, Bennies, Dexies, pinks, cartwheels, blues, jelly-beans, rainbows, reds, white crosses. Bill loved all pills, especially amphetamines.

'Why amphetamines?' I asked him.

'Uppers are prettier than downers. The guys who de-signed them were buzzing hard.'

Bill usually had a Ziploc bag of them in his gym bag or pocket.

'Here, dude,' Bill said.

It was one A.M. and I was waiting for an old Spaniard in X-ray. Bill handed me a couple dextroamphetamine cap-sules in his cupped palm.

'Thanks,' I told him. Picked them up. Tossed them down.

Bill took the space next to me on the waiting room couch.

I told him a story: 'Back in high school, my brother Tar and I, we would sneak my father's Darvon capsules out of the medicine cabinet. He had a lot of these capsules. They were for his back pain. My father is a fat man and he gets back pain from carrying around his stomach—surprising, I know, being that I'm as wiry and agile as I am, but true. Tar and I would empty out the Darvon capsules, and then we'd empty out some regular Tylenol capsules. We'd put the powder from the Darvon into the Tylenol containers and the powder from the Tylenol into the Darvon containers. Then we'd put the fake Darvon back into the medicine cabinet. My father never noticed.'

'Pla-*see*-bo,' Bill said.

'We'd take the fake Tylenols to school. We'd be so down we'd be drooling on our desks. If a girl had a headache at a party; here, have a Tylenol.'

'Cruel!' Bill said. He was laughing.

'We were geniuses.'

Bill laughed some more. The story was a payment of sorts for the free drugs he had given me.

Apples and Evian water were Bill's manna. He ate at least seven apples and drank at least three liters of Evian a day. He urinated continuously. 'If your piss is yellow that means you're dehydrated,' was one of his favorite things to say.

Apples and Evian water were two of the products on ice next to the salad bar in the hospital cafeteria. They were both easy to steal. Bill said his motto was *Healthy body, healthy mind*, but it was, more likely, *If you can get it for free, get as much of it as you can.*

Please Fill Out This Short Form

1. Education

I spent my first seventeen years in the Catholic school system in Saint Louis, Missouri. At eighteen, I came to Columbia University in New York City on an academic scholarship. A year and a half later I was walking to class, then walked past class, and then walked to a bar where I had a drink, and I thought, 'I'm living the life of my father.' I never went back to school.

As a final note on my education, Bill and I later enrolled in a boxing class at the local gym, but I got kicked out after two weeks for putting a heavy thing inside my glove.

2. Character flaws

A consistent flow of alcohol and drugs in my bloodstream; an inability to commit to anyone or anything; regret that knows no bounds; grandiosity; a belief that humans are pathetic and life is a sad, hard, lonely place; resulting melancholy; childishness; violent temper; sexual amorality; sentimentalism; I regret the loss of my past; familiar, even mundane, character flaws.

3. Character strengths

The ability to glamorize #2 for the amusement of friends; a complete and total commitment to the tumult of #2; the ability to hone in on whatever an individual feels most insecure about in himself and bring that out for the amusement of others; and, I'm not sure if it counts as a character strength, but I've never had a cavity.

4. Appearance

I have kept my looks to a fair degree, though I wake up some mornings with brown bags beneath my eyes. I put cold water on the bags, which seems to stop the swelling a bit, but not much.

My eyes are blue. I'm six feet tall, thin, wiry. My head is spattered with cowlicks, which causes my hair to sprout in different directions despite any of my interventions. I have two tattoos.

5. Appearance of your cock

My cock is longer than the average Caucasian male's, though I'm not sure by how much because I'm unsure whether you're supposed to measure it from the top or from the bottom. It's not that thick. My penis hole is exceedingly large, and I have placed various items within it for the delight and disgust of girlfriends: a penny, the butt of a lit cigarette, the first joint of a petite woman's pinkie.

Deluxe Apartment in the Sky

It was a surprise when Bill called me at my apartment. I was living on the south end of Harlem. Bill and I hadn't known each other long, and I didn't know where he had gotten my number. I was unlisted. In that way, I could tell my mother I didn't have a phone.

'What are you doing?' he said.

'Looking out the window. There are some kids down there in the alley chasing a rat with a stick. I'm rooting for the rat.'

'Hey. I was thinking you might want to come over, hang out.'

'Hang out where?'

'At my pad.'

'And do what?'

'Get drunk.'

I paused.

'You aren't like trying to fuck me or something, are you?' I asked.

'Dude, fuck. You are one paranoid fucking dude.'

'Where'd you get my number anyway?!'

'I snuck in and read some of the guys at work's files. Interesting stuff. Grabbed your number out of there.'

'Well, I ran out of money.' This was a lie I had often employed to get free booze.

'That's all right,' Bill said. 'This morning I was walking along, minding my own business, when some guys were loading crates into the liquor store. They weren't looking for a sec and I saw a crate. Nice crate! I just picked it up and fucking ran as fast as possible. These little Pakistani dudes are running after me going, "Oh no! Fuck you!" It was hilarious. Their voices are so funny, even when they aren't going totally insane with anger. Anyway, I get it home. It's full of Stoli.'

I was at Bill's studio apartment on West 50th Street in about twenty minutes.

His pad was small. I sat on the edge of one of his mattresses. It felt good to be in someone's apartment besides my own. Bill walked into the kitchen.

'You like Five Alive in your vodka?' Bill asked me.

'No orange juice?'

'Five Alive *is* orange juice.'

'No it isn't. Five Alive is Five Alive. That's like calling Hi-C tomato juice.'

I heard Bill laughing in the kitchen, as if that was the most outrageous notion in the world.

'I'll take it straight,' I said.

He brought me a large, water-spotted glass, overflowing with vodka. As I took it, I glanced over and saw a shelf on Bill's wall. Action figures from the '70s lined the shelf in different poses.

'Holy shit. What's that?' I jumped up and walked toward it.

'That's my collection of toys. It's not large, not yet. But as soon as I get some real money . . .'

'This is a nice collection.' I zeroed in on a Fonzie doll from *Happy Days*. 'Hey, the Fonz.'

'When I was eight I had a little brown leather jacket and I put Vitalis on my head every day before I went to school,' Bill said.

'Didn't the other kids give you shit?'

'Hell no, dude. Everybody wanted to dress like the Fonz, but their parents wouldn't let them. Me, I came from a broken home, so I was allowed to do whatever I wanted. If my mom walked in on me sucking off a dog, she'd probably have said, "Hey, Bill, get that dog's cock out of your mouth and come in here and eat your Salisbury steak." '

Bill walked up beside me. We stared at the toys together.

'See, when you collect toys, you're supposed to have a *thing*, right?' Bill said. 'Like some guys collect postwar tin toys, and other guys get into Pez dispensers, and other guys just like Japanese stuff. My thing is like the TV toys. I'm starting out with the time when all the best TV shows were made, the 1970s. In fact, I'm getting close to having the entire collection of the great, never-to-be-matched ABC '77 Tuesday-night lineup. See: Fonz, Potsie, and there's Pinky Tuscadaro. There's Laverne, Shirley, Jack and Crissy. My favorite, though, is that Laura Ingalls Wilder. Mint condition. When I was a kid, I was in love with Melissa Gilbert. The first time I ever jerked off was to a picture of her in *People*.'

'*Little House on the Prairie* was on Mondays,' I said.

'Yeah. An exception.'

Bill's collection seemed to glow. I touched the rough clothing of the action figures. I was raised Catholic, but ABC-TV had been my real religion. These toys were holy relics. Tar, Gary Bauer, Nancy Zoomis and I would watch ABC every Tuesday night: *Happy Days*, *Laverne & Shirley*, and *Three's Company*.

Come and knock on our door
We've been waiting for you

I poked Jack Tripper's face, and I swore to God for a single moment I felt Gary Bauer's skin. A black magic was crawling over my flesh. Sinewski's apartment filled with the same dank, air-conditioned air the Bauers' house always had. Perry Como's voice wafted down from upstairs, where Mrs. Bauer was making a quilt. A welder reverberated in the garage, on the other side of the wall. Mr. Bauer was working on a car in there, a project for a friend. Tar squirmed around on the floor. He giggled as Nancy tickled him. Gary sang dirty words that he made up over the *Laverne & Shirley* theme. The credits ran; assembly-line high jinks. Tar, Gary, and Nancy were here with me, the three people I loved long before that love was plundered. My lower lip began to tremble. Jesus Christ! I'm about to fucking cry here!

I gulped down the vodka, trying to stuff the emotion back into myself. I stared at the floor. When I caught my breath, I spoke again.

'They're completely fucking beautiful,' I muttered.

'I get pretty moved when I look at them sometimes, too,' Bill said.

He drank from his glass. I drank from mine.

Bill had a Negro roommate who was also named Bill. One day black Bill left mysteriously and mysteriously took white Bill's stereo with him. The handsome, toy-collecting pill popper called me at my place in Harlem and asked me if I wanted a cheap place to stay. All I had was a mattress and a box of clothes, so it didn't take long moving in. I put my box beneath a folding table against the wall.

'You can have the folding table,' Bill said. 'It used to be

Bill's. Maybe he thought that he was trading my stereo for the table.'

'That's not a very good trade.'

'He was a nice guy. I don't know why he did it.'

The studio was small, but unlike my Harlem pad, it had a bathroom and a kitchen. The kitchen was only three feet by three feet and I didn't know how to work the oven, but it still seemed like a nice thing to have around, even if for nothing more than a status symbol. Like me, Bill only had a mattress. He had sold the frame one day for thirty bucks when he was broke and out of amphetamines.

'That's a sign of addiction,' he said. 'But oh well.'

I set my mattress next to the window. The window had bars and overlooked the garbage bin. Every afternoon, while I was trying to sleep, the garbage men would wake me up clanging around glass jars and other trash. Since I was a light sleeper I asked Bill if he would change places with me. This he did without hesitation. As Bill dragged his mattress across the floor, I was surprised to find myself moved. He carefully lined it up beneath the window while the garbage men crashed around outside. I reached out and poked him a little and made a face that was like a smile.

Barlow's Fun Antiques

Most every day Bill and I drank at Clancy's Tavern. Two doors down from the tavern was a place called Barlow's Fun Antiques. Bill would buy his action figures there. I had passed the shop a thousand times and never really looked inside or even noticed it.

'I'll take you there sometime to check it out,' Bill had said. 'I know the guy that works there. His name is Charlie Barlow. He named the store after his own last name.' Bill seemed excited that I might share his passion.

We stopped by Barlow's Fun Antiques one afternoon on our way home from Clancy's. I looked in the display window. There was a pyramid stack of toys from the '70s. A purple and green box grabbed me.

'Jesus,' I said. 'Scrunch 'Em, Grow 'Em Dinosaurs.'

Bill pressed his finger against the glass. 'I see it. What is it?'

'Christ. That was the greatest fucking toy ever. You remember it?'

'No. Oh, shit! Look! It's the *Little House on the Prairie* board game! Oh, fuck! I don't have any money.'

'Me neither. But I would like to buy that Scrunch 'Em, Grow 'Em Dinosaurs.'

Once, in a rare moment of eloquence, Bill called his hobby the Restoration of a Right World.

The interior of the toy store was exceedingly clean. It was a long, thin room with glass cabinets lined up along the walls. Toys filled every cabinet and every space around them.

'Jesus, it's like a little museum,' I said.

'A fucking Paul Michael Glaser figure!' Bill said. 'James, I want to get this Paul Michael Glaser. Time to move out of Tuesday nights and into whatever night *Starsky and Hutch* was on.'

Some of the toys were rusted. Others were broken or bashed. Most of them were old, and all of them were beautiful. A fat guy who looked like he was the king of the place was behind the counter. He had long brown hair tied back in a ponytail, a Fu Manchu mustache, and he wore a red T-shirt.

'Hey hey, there, Billy!' he said. The jolly type.

'Hi, Charlie. This is my friend James. He wanted to check out the place.'

'Welcome, James!'

I pointed my thumb back toward the front window.'

'How much is that Scrunch 'Em, Grow 'Em Dinosaurs?'

'That thing in the window? Sorry, pal, but I just sold it.'

'Shit. I would have bought it. That was my favorite toy as a kid. My brother's, too. I've never even seen it outside of the one that we had.'

'Yeah. I've never seen it either, besides the one in the window. Hell, if I woulda known more than one guy wanted it, maybe I would've started a bidding war!' The man had a deep Queens accent.

I leaned in toward the glass cabinet next to me. Robots. There were almost a hundred robots on five shelves. I felt

something for them, a spark. Maybe they were my thing,
like Bill's was TV toys, and someone else's was postwar tin
toys, and someone else's was Pez dispensers. A few of the
robots I had had when I was young. There was one in
particular I remembered.

'Hey, how much for this Rom Spaceknight?'

'They have Rom down there?' Bill said.

'Yeah. How much?'

'Well, let's see.' The fat man stroked his mustache. His
arms were covered with blue-ink tattoos. 'I'll give you that
for a hundred.'

'A hundred dollars?'

'He's in perfect working order.'

'A hundred dollars for a *toy*?'

'What's Rom in the robot section for, Charlie?' Bill said.
'He's supposed to be a man underneath all that.'

'Hey, cyborgs, robots. It's a thin line from one cabinet
to the other sometimes.'

'Ah, that's fucked,' Bill said. 'He ought to be in with the
superheroes.'

'Seriously,' I said. '*A hundred dollars?*'

The man laughed.

'Down in the Village they're charging one-fifty for him.
'Least that's what I hear. I ain't allowed to see for myself. I
walk in their store, they say, "*Charlie, get the fuck outta
here!*"' The man wheezed with laughter. 'They're jealous
because my store's much better than theirs.' He took a
handkerchief from his back pocket and wiped his brow.
The room was chilly.

'How much for Paul Michael Glaser?' Bill asked.

'Ah, eighty-five,' Charlie said.

'I want these robots,' I said.

'*Eighty-five?*' Bill said. 'Come on, Charlie. I don't even
have twenty-five.'

'What do you have that's a lot cheaper?' I said.

'What sort of price range you looking for?'

'A couple bucks,' I said.

'I got three dollars,' Bill said.

'Whoo-hoo ha-ha! Three dollars!'

Another cabinet had only GI Joes and Barbies. I looked in a large glass case filled with dolls at the end of the store.

'This is the coolest place I've ever been in,' I said.

'Whoo-ha!' Charlie said. He grabbed the shoulders of a stuffed Wizard of Oz Tin Man that was on the counter and shook him. 'Did you hear that, Tin Man? The coolest place ever!' Charlie looked at me. His face was swollen with pride.

'The Tin Man thanks you!'

Charlie looked a little tough with the Fu Manchu mustache, the tattoos, and all. But stare at him for a minute. The whole thing is a disguise, a permanent Halloween costume. There was a fat girlish boy in my class at Saint Ambrose who was caught playing with Star Wars figures in the eighth grade. In another state, in another school, in an earlier time, Charlie had been that kid.

Bill held up two little Godzillas, one in each hand. One was red and one was green. They were a couple of inches tall.

'Check these out,' he said.

'How much are they?'

'Five bucks.'

'We need them.'

Bill nodded. Charlie called us a couple of big spenders. He shook my hand before I left. Walking down the street toward the liquor store we each fondled the Godzillas in our pockets. It gave us a secret tie.

Rom/Mom

Rom Spaceknight was the most majestic action figure. In the commercial he stood on a hill in a child's backyard, the sun behind him. Beams of light came shining below his arms and between his legs. Once more Christ had come to earth. And this time he was plastic.

'But, Mom, pretty soon they'll all be bought!' I trailed her and her shopping cart through the toy aisle of Kmart.

She said no again and Tar began to weep.

'But, Mom, come on! Let's be fair!'

The battle wasn't long; our mother was a weak excuse for a foe.

Twelve long inches of polypropylene, forged to mimic metal. Rom's chest was plated and his eyes blipped red. His head was boxy, like a toaster set on its side. He didn't have a mouth. He didn't need one. He was too hard-core. His gun seemed like a vacuum cleaner extension except that it had more than one sound: *whirr, whee, chit chit chit, cambloo cambloo*, and *zwike*. Rom's hand was molded to fit the gun, so it looked like a fist. It was easy to imagine him smashing the fuck out of somebody's head, because he just didn't give a shit about anything or anybody.

Rom.

They had based a Marvel comic book on him and I read it. Here are some interesting facts about Rom:

- Once he had been a man.
- He came from a planet called Galador.
- Ugly beasts called Dire Wraiths invaded Galador. They looked like a cross between a bug and a toad, or even something worse. They were able to change their shape, become whatever they wanted. In this way they were able to infiltrate planets and fuck them up.
- I had a dream one night that my parents dropped me off at my grandparents, and they both ended up being Dire Wraiths, and they chased my dog and tried to turn her against me.
- Galador had a President-type character whom they called the Prime Director. When he learned about the Dire Wraiths he created an army of Space-knights.
- It would suck becoming a Spaceknight, because you would have to have the Spaceknight suit of armor grafted onto your skin. To save your planet you had to sacrifice your humanity.
- Rom was the first Spaceknight to volunteer. There-fore, his name, in Galadorian, means 'before all others' (strikingly, Mohammed, the Muslim pro-phet, is known as 'the first among many'—as far as I know there is no connection between him and Rom Spaceknight).
- Rom's gun was a complex machine with a number of applications. He could shine it on a suspect to reveal if it was a human being or a Dire Wraith in disguise. Or he could kill you. Or, if he discovered you were a Dire Wraith, he could send you to

Limbo. Limbo was just a black space with a bunch of meaningless, brightly colored objects floating around. The Dire Wraiths screamed when they went to Limbo. You would have screamed too. There's nothing to do in Limbo.

- Rom came to earth to protect it from the Dire Wraiths.
- Rom was in love with Landra, a female Space-knight. Like all Marvel comics superheroines, Landra, despite the fact she was wearing a metal suit, had big tits. She and Rom were doomed to be forever apart.

Lynea Chylnek had trained her entire life to be a mother. As a toddler she played with dolls. She changed their diapers. She bathed them with a hose. She taught them to crawl by tying a string to their waists and dragging them behind her. Lynea practiced her homemaking skills with her neighbors, playing house. She feather-dusted their cardboard home with regularity, and cooked meals of mud, clay, crabgrass, and daffodils. At Sacred Word High School Lynea took classes in child rearing, where she learned how to discipline a child through 'time out.' At Excelsior College, while majoring in psychology, she discovered *The Common Sense Book of Baby and Child Care* by Dr. Benjamin Spock. This was an instruction book on how to turn children into healthy adults. It taught her the importance of providing mental stimulation as well as hugging. She thanked God for allowing her to discover the works of the visionary Spock before it was too late. It was the final step in making her a perfect mother. Hug-equipped, fallopian tubes and ovaries in place, she was ready to produce the world's greatest children.

She married William Gunn, the Irish Catholic lawyer son of an Irish Catholic lawyer. Immediately thereafter, he impregnated his wife. Nine months later she gave birth to a male child. Eleven months later, another male was born.

William went out drinking with his friends. Meanwhile, Lynea had the freedom to put all her training into action. She placed the two children in stimulating environments. She bought them colorful toys to keep their minds alive. She took them to the park and the zoo and told them what a rhino was. She bought them a dog to give them an understanding of responsibility and love. She read out loud to them the books of a second visionary doctor, Seuss. She filled their playroom with enriching, classical music, despite the fact that she herself would rather listen to Three Dog Night. Lynea believed she was on her way to creating perfect children.

But these creatures, known as Jimmy and Tar, were a clear deviation from the plans. They set about destroying any objects within their path. They baptized themselves in mud and ink. They attacked other children. They tore apart bugs and Scotch-taped them to the porch window. They shunned enclosure and would roam freely when they were not watched. They saw any article as theirs to own and would steal it. They declared themselves the kings, of mother, father, earth, and court.

They did not come when called.

Neither being seemed to have any moral compass, except perhaps in regard to each other. And this bond between them was often employed in such a way to attack Lynea, to make her look foolish, or to fool her.

Lynea's training, as rigorous as it was, was not enough. She hired professionals, a group of hard-bitten experts who worked at a place known as Montessori Preschool. The creatures were imprisoned there for four hours a day, and the experts attempted to use modern technology and psychological maneuvering to transform these bad creatures into pleasant ones. But these professional controllers could not control these animals that were born, if not to be wild, at least to be little fuckers. The creatures bombarded one child they didn't like with colorful building blocks until he bled. They tricked another into drinking their urine. One day they stole the dress of a young girl and escaped from a window at floor level, disappearing for three hours. The Montessori professionals tried their damnedest but decided in the end that the creatures were corrupted past the point of saving. They refused them sanctuary.

Lynea lost all hope of having truly good children, and became obsessed with appearances. She dressed the two creatures in matching outfits—matching overalls and raincoats and swimsuits—until the older creature, at the age of five, stared at himself and his brother in matching yellow terry-cloth shirts and said, 'We look like fags.' Lynea joined the PTA. She became a homeroom mother. She and Mrs. Granger proved to the world that they were the two best moms in all the land by creating a Saint Ambrose Halloween Haunted House beyond compare. Had the strobe light near the Werewolf family's living room not set off a seizure in young Andy Cozine, it would have been perfect. Lynea filled the halls of Saint Ambrose with Easter and Presidents' Day. On Christmas, she dressed up as an elf. At Saint Ambrose, Lynea discovered that her fears were true: Other children were nicer, and better, and cleaner than her own. So to hell with the fruit of her own womb, she decided. She'd focus on the fruit of others.

Lynea created a special reading program. She traveled to Catholic schools all over Saint Louis with a dolphin puppet named Dokus who taught children how to read. All the children loved Dokus except her own, who dropped Dokus down the air-conditioning vent in their room and spit gum onto him. Lynea became the president of a charity devoted to Cardinal Glennon Children's hospital. She helped to ease the pain in the cancerous bodies of children, which was much easier than curing the cancerous souls of her own. And, eventually, through a constant movement on her part and a dedication to the world's youth, she was able to nearly forget her two creatures entirely. They were furniture, a sort of moving background for which she held neither fondness nor animosity.

Meanwhile, the two creatures played on, happy in their suburban Habitrail.

My father was perturbed that my mother hadn't cleaned the barbecue pit and it grew from there. Tar and I poked our heads from around the corner of the hi-fi and watched. My brother was holding Rom Spaceknight.

'I guess you're so fat that you can't fit your fat arm inside the barbecue pit to clean it yourself,' my mom said.

Tar made a squeaking sound in his throat. He knew what was coming, and so did I.

'So fat,' she said.

My dad's body trembled. He raised his arm, hesitated, and then raised it again.

Bam! My mom's head wobbled around like a doll with a spring for a neck, and she crumpled to the floor. She brought her hand to the side of her face. She began to cry in a way that seemed phony.

'*Fat man who hits women!*' she screamed.

My father dropped his face into his open palms and he began to weep.

Tar aimed Rom's gun at our father and he pushed the button on his back.

Cambloo cambloo.
He aimed the gun at my mother.
Cambloo cambloo.
My father lifted his face from his hands. My mother stopped crying. They looked around the room for the strange noise. Tar and I ducked back behind the hi-fi.
No one finds us here.

The Lovers

Bill and I would each receive a blue envelope every other week. Inside the envelope would be a check made out for five hundred and some dollars. Like all other members of the human race, we wanted more. So we pinned our hopes on Damia Wellington. She was our Thoroughbred; you could see it in her hungry eyes and her calves like footballs.

'Put all the bets on the pudgy girl to win!' we screamed. And Damia was off, wobbling and wiggling as she dashed to please her lover.

Bill and I would pick up prescriptions for patients in the hospital basement. It was one of our responsibilities. Sometimes we'd sample the prescription. Most of the drugs were unremarkable. Lithium did nothing for us. Erythromycin made us sick to our stomachs. Phenylpropanolamine at best took the edge off a drunk. But every so often we'd find a pill of note, like Ipinephrium, which robbed us of our motor skills and forced us to feign illnesses so as to get away from work. Normally, though, we'd continue on with our daily duties. We'd simply put the prescription back in the bag and pinch the staple closed again.

A new girl, a chubby one, was minding the pharmacy.

Her name was Damia Wellington. She wore too much lipstick, and it would leave streaks on her teeth. She had neon-green eyes that sought love, and breasts large and notably round. She had a cherubic face, eczema on her elbows, a fresh complexion, a Master's in Pharmacology, and Velamint breath. Like the other pharmacists, Damia was framed by an open window in the wall. Aisle after aisle of drugs were behind her.

'Hey, baby,' I would say to her. She would look at me for a moment, thinking. She had been working hard to get to know everyone's name.

'Hi . . . James,' Damia would say. 'Where's Bill?'

'You know that guy that's been molesting children in Central Park?'

'Uh-huh.'

'They finally caught up with him. Bill.'

'James!'

The linen crew's washers would be thundering down the hall.

This new girl had no problems with the English language. But around William Sinewski III the words had a rough go of it on her tongue. I supposed it was his brown puppy-dog eyes. I had to admit they could make you melt. But *his skin*, I thought. Doesn't anyone ever notice his skin?

One night Damia Wellington asked if she could sit with us in the hospital cafeteria, and we said yes, and then suddenly she was across from me every night. Her hands looked like an infant's, only larger. She'd touch Bill and pinch his shirt between her fingers. When he passed behind her on his way to filch some Evian water, he'd rub the back of her neck. Even early on, in the cafeteria, there seemed to be a reason in his ways.

*   *   *

I awoke and stumbled into the bathroom. I commenced pissing. The color was very yellow. I would have to be sure to flush quickly before Bill woke up and saw and gave me a lecture. I heard the faucet running, and I turned. Damia Wellington was brushing her teeth at the sink. She formed a blinder with her hand over the side of her eye.

'I'm not looking,' she said.

I stared at her, processed the information.

'You been here all night?'

'Well, I . . . no . . . like since maybe four,' she whispered.

'You guys sure were quiet.'

'It was a long ride to my apartment. We were at Clancy's. Bill said it would be okay if I slept here. I hope it's okay.'

'Where'd you sleep?'

'Well . . . I . . . uh . . .'

'Heh-heh-heh.'

Toothpaste foam dripped down Damia's chin.

'Don't be embarrassed,' I told her. 'Bill brings women back here all the time.'

She turned toward the sink.

'Anyway, thanks for being so quiet.' I shook away the excess urine. Damia glanced down at my penis and looked away, blushing hard.

'Caught you,' I said.

'What's this going on with Bill and the pharmacist?' Cora asked me. Her hair was parted in the middle and feathered back. She was Puerto Rican. We were in the waiting room waiting for a run.

'Which pharmacist?'

'The pudgy girl.'

'I don't know. What's going on with them?'

'I walked in on them in the linen closet. Bill, he is twirling her hair in his finger. Her face is turned away and I think she is crying. Bill is saying, "Baby, baby." Just like that, James, "Baby, baby." ' Cora took her finger and rubbed it around the rim of my ear.

'Baby, baby,' she said again. Cora was one of the ugliest people I had ever known. She was old and shriveled and bony, but still a nympho. My cock got hard.

Bill and I sat on the stoop behind the hospital and when no one was looking we'd sip vodka from a World War I flask. We were on a cigarette break. About three hours of every eight-hour day was a cigarette break. The sun was setting atop an ambulance. The ambulance was missing one wheel and all its tires. The hospital was in shambles. A pang of guilt would hit me when I realized my laziness contributed to the predicament. Then I'd write my attitude off as corporate culture, and the feeling would be gone.

'You sure Damia wants to do this?' I asked.

'I wracked my head for a way to buy more toys,' Bill said. 'This seems like the quickest path, right? I mean, if not for the toys I wouldn't do it. But I need to complete the lineup, right? I don't even have a Ralph Malph.' After much wavering on Damia's part, she had agreed to help us steal drugs to sell outside the hospital. It was Bill's idea, but I was the one with the know-how; I spent my year and a half at Columbia University dealing Hawaiian red bud for a couple of degenerates named Lou and Pennywhistle. The most difficult things to get, Lou had told me, were pharmaceuticals in large quantities.

'And she wants to do it?' I asked again.

'Not really.'

'Why then?'

'She says she loves me and she'll do it because of that. I told her about all my debts, and how –'

'Debts?'

'Well, you know, I wanted it to seem like something important. I mean, it is important, the toys. But I didn't think she'd understand that.'

Bill packed his cigarettes against the palm of his hand. I snickered.

'You love *her*, Bill?'

'She's a very nice girl.'

I laughed. Bill wasn't smiling in the least. He was making a statement by it. He had a lot of feeling for people, even when he was fucking them over.

Damia's smile was omnipresent until she became the third man in our team. She did it because Bill was a hunk, and she had never had a hunk for more than an evening before. Damia Wellington never liked me. To her I was the enemy, the dark side of Bill's personality, the rival for his affections.

But I honestly believed it wasn't me she disliked. It was him. Deep inside, she knew. Sinewski was only with her because he loved toys.

'*You* get in,' Bill said.

'I don't want to get in there. It's disgusting.'

'I'm the one that got us the pills *and* I'm the one that's supposed to get dirty?'

'I'm wearing a suit.'

'You're always wearing a suit, dude. You're going to use that excuse every week. Goddammit. What is it again, exactly, that you're doing to deserve half the money?'

'I'm the one with the connections, man. Without me, who are you going to get to buy that stuff?'

I guess that seemed reasonable to Bill, because he jumped into the trash bin. I leaned against the pharmacy's back door, so I'd know if someone started coming out. Bill pushed aside a couple soggy magazines, some chicken bones and candy wrappers. He smiled as he picked up the small boxes. There were eight of them, tightly bound, exactly where we had told Damia to put them. He tossed them to me. He jumped out of the trash bin.

The boxes rattled. We were laughing. We held them against our chests and ran down the alley. I thought of Rom and he thought of Ralph Malph. We were going to be rich in plastic.

Lou and Pennywhistle

Bill and I would meet them in Central Park, by the statue of Alice and the Mad Hatter and the Cheshire Cat. They were always late. Sometimes I would sit on the mushroom and Bill would sit on a park bench and sometimes Bill would sit on the mushroom and I would sit on a park bench. We'd hear them on the other side of the trees, around the curve of granite path. They were loud.

Lou was unshaven. He had long dark hair that hung in dirty clumps, and a hawk nose. Pennywhistle smelled and was the quieter of the two. He suffered from a hyperthyroid curse. His eyes bulged out and one of them wavered to the side. In the whites of one of his eyes a red line traveled from his iris to the inside corner. Despite all this, he told me he had twenty-twenty vision and didn't need to wear glasses. Lou and Pennywhistle claimed to be brothers, which was unlikely as Lou was white and Pennywhistle was black. Once, after drinking three zombies, Pennywhistle admitted that every once in a while Lou would go down on him. When I first met him three years before, Lou showed me a long slit of a scar on his stomach and one of the same shape on his back.

'You know where I got those, James?' he asked me.

'You fell on a big, pointy gate like the guy in *The Omen*?'

45

'Ha! Shit! No. This guy came up to me with two knives, sticking one in my back and one in my front,' Lou said. 'I like to tell that story so, when you're doing business with us, you know what kind of guys we are.'

'Guys who get stabbed?' I said.

'Damn straight,' Pennywhistle said.

Basically, they were gentle souls.

When Lou and Pennywhistle arrived I set the brown cardboard boxes on the edge of the mushroom.

'What'd you get this time, Jamesie?' Lou asked.

'Biphets mostly. Two canisters of Bennies. Two Luminals. And five canisters of rainbows, if you want them. Don't call me Jamesie.'

'Rainbows? Tuinal?' Lou asked.

'Uh-huh,' I said.

'Big effect?'

'I'm hardly walking,' Bill said.

'In mg's,' Lou said. 'I want to know how they affect normal people, not people who sprinkle them on cupcakes like sugar. Ha!'

'What?' Bill said.

'Nobody puts sugar on cupcakes,' I said. 'One-fifty mg's.'

'How much you want?' Lou said.

'Let's say one.'

'All right. That's cool.'

'Cool,' Pennywhistle said.

'Altogether, eight-fifty.'

'That's a twenty percent discount,' Bill said.

I glared at him.

'Ten, ten percent discount,' I said.

'Cool.'

'Cool. You take credit cards?' Lou asked, laughing. He made the same joke every week. He reached into the front pocket of his jeans and pulled out a roll of bills. He licked his thumb and forefinger, counted some off, and handed them to me. Pennywhistle stacked the cardboard boxes in Lou's arms. I started counting the money. Lou stared at me.

'Why do you always do that?'

'Just a minute,' I said, holding up a finger.

'No, really, man, why do you always do that?'

I stopped counting. 'Do what?'

'Count the money. I counted it off right here in front of you. I mean, I don't count the pills, why should you count that?' Lou rested his chin on the top box.

'I'm just making sure.'

'It hurts my feelings, man. Either you don't trust me or you think I'm stupid.'

'I trust you.'

'*Dude.*'

'Lou, it'd take you a million years to count the pills.'

'Oh, yeah? Well, maybe next time we'll sit here for a million years, then.'

'Right.'

'*Shit.* I'm going to put this stuff in the trunk. You guys want to go get a drink?'

I put my arms out to my sides. 'Does Humbert Humbert want to fuck a kid?'

Lou laughed and nodded his head for a few moments. A sparrow whistled in the trees overhead.

'So,' he said. 'Do you want to go?'

'Yeah.'

We put the boxes in the trunk of Pennywhistle's old beige Lincoln. Then we wandered up to the bar with the bamboo walls and giant African masks outside. We often chose this bar since Lou and Pennywhistle like to drink sweet tropical drinks out of coconut shells that sprouted pink and yellow plastic things.

*   *   *

Bill had reverted to childhood. Charlie Barlow's fat self was behind him like a sunset. My hands were trembling from the Bennies we had piled down after leaving Lou and Pennywhistle. Our pockets were packed with twenty-dollar bills. I was laughing. We were all laughing. Our laughter twisted and tangled together in a maze throughout the room. Bill ducked over. He had a demonic smile. He darted back and forth across the length of the store. His arms were full of toys. 'Look!' he cried, 'Scooby-Doo!' or, 'Look—an *I Dream of Jeannie* bubble pipe!'

I was plopping robots into a bag. One, and then another, and then another. My hand moved in front of them along the shelves. Certain ones would give off vibrations. Those were the ones that I took.

Charlie said: 'You ever seen one of them pits filled with the different-colored balls and the little kids jump around in them?'

We didn't answer him. Bill thrust a female action figure in my face.

'*Lindsay fucking Wagner!*' he screamed. '*The Bionic Woman!*' He stuck her under his arm and ran to the other end of the room.

' 'Cos that's what you guys remind me of now,' Charlie said. 'Them kids in them plastic balls—ha!' Charlie was our axis and we circled him. He stood in the center of the room, his fat self laughing. I passed Bill. He passed me. I snatched Rom and threw him into my bag. Amphetamine sweetness. God in plastic. Magic. Crime. Sweat. Laughing. Color, more color. Light was everywhere.

'That comes to nine hundred and twelve dollars,' Charlie said. He had a large, gummy smile. The cash register was the old tall kind that rang. Bill and I were breathing heavily.

'Huh?' I said.

'Nine hundred and twelve dollars,' Charlie said. Bill and I eyed each other.

'Nine hundred dollars,' I whispered to him.

'Oh,' Bill said. He cupped his chin in the heel of his palm and spread two fingers up over his face. He stretched down his cheeks with the tips of his fingers, exposing the muscle color below his eyes. 'Gee. Wow. That's expensive.'

I looked at Charlie.

'We have eight hundred cash,' I said.

'Cash?'

I nodded.

'I got a little money in my checking account,' Bill said behind me.

Charlie nodded. 'Tell you what. You give me the eight hundred and a check for fifty and I'll call it even.' Charlie winked. Bill was already writing the check.

The Flesh Bots

Though Tar and I both lived in Manhattan, we had
ended up on remarkably different paths. He joined
Alcoholics Anonymous after high school, in the wake
of our father's own sobriety. He graduated from Indiana
University in three years. After that, he did a bunch of
things I didn't have much interest in, and today, at
twenty-four, he was a VP of something or other for a
place having to do with animals, I think the Bronx Zoo.
He attributed all of this success to quitting mind-altering
chemicals and the serenity prayer and One Day at a
Time and other ideas I was blitzed with every time I
conversed with him or my old man. All of this was
good, I supposed. The only thing disturbing to me was
that Tar often had the light of idiocy in his eyes common
to fundamentalist Christians. At these times I would feel
as if there was a great wide river sloshing between us,
and I would become sad.

My brother had a live-in girlfriend, Amy. She was ash
blond and powdery fresh. She smiled too much. Born in
Iowa. I normally didn't take much notice of her. The
most interesting thing about Amy was that she had
appeared naked in a *Playboy* Girls of the Big Eight

pictorial. Bill had once offered me thirteen dollars if I would masturbate to the picture, but I didn't even want to look at it.

Damia Wellington threw a Valentine's Day party. I attended it in an attempt to get in her good favor. I brought Tar and Amy, whom I hadn't seen in three months.

Damia's building, in the West 70s, was more than forty stories high. Either Damia or someone in her family did needlepoint, because the apartment was covered in the stuff. I walked out onto the balcony and I looked out at the lights of New York City. It was so beautiful, I couldn't help myself, I began to cry. Tar snuck out through the sliding doorway behind me.

'What's wrong?' he asked.

'Nothing,' I said, and I knocked back my beer.

'Are you crying?'

'I'm prone to melancholy.'

'You're drinking again.'

'Yes.'

'I thought you quit.'

'I did quit. For eight days.'

My brother smiled in the fake way he always smiled when we discussed my alcohol intake.

'And what was wrong with the eight days?' he asked.

'The days were fine,' I said. 'But I myself was boring and horrible.'

'I think life is a lot less boring, to tell you the truth, Jimmy, now that I'm sober.'

'Right.'

'It's true.'

'Your life may be less boring for you. But for the rest of us, you were much more amusing when you were strangling people you hardly knew. But unlike you, Tar, I'm a selfless and sacrificing soul. Perhaps I'm miserable. But at least I'm entertaining.'

'Thank you for that.'

'It's only because I love you.'

'I'll remember that when you're dead.'

'You can make it part of your eulogy for me.'

'I didn't come here to fight with you.'

'That's interesting. Because that's why I invited you to this party, to fight. Also so you could badger me about my drinking.'

'Jimmy.'

'Tar.'

'Right. I'm sorry. I'll chill out. You know my thoughts on the subject. Right?'

'Mm.' I looked at him. He had grown sideburns. I had an impulse to throw him over the balcony.

'Yeah, well, I'm going to get another Coke,' Tar said. 'It's chilly out here.'

'Right,' I said.

'See you inside.' He headed back into the party.

I gazed out on the city again. The lights were still beautiful. My brother hadn't ruined them.

When I walked back inside Tar and Amy were sitting on the couch. They snuggled, giggling. I caught them looking at me and laughing. They were laughing at me because they thought I was an alcoholic.

Tar and Amy helped to carry me up the stairs to my apartment. I was drunk and happy as hell.

'Lift your leg,' Amy said.

'Amy,' I said, as they prodded me up the stairwell. 'Let me tell you how it was.'

'How was it, Jimmy?' she said.

'A theory Gary had describes it best. Remember his theory, Tar?'

'Gary had a lot of theories. Come on. Walk. I'm not going to just carry you.'

'Gary believed that the four of us—me and Tar and him and Nancy—we were the only bodies containing souls on the planet. Everyone else was like a sort of flesh robot, all right? They were programmed to make faces and say words and do various actions to appear as if they had souls, when in fact they did not have souls. You could look into their eyes. But there was no guy looking out.'

'Yeah,' Tar said. 'I remember. Left us a few moral loopholes. Life was like a video game.'

'He really believed that?' Amy asked.

'He thought it was possible, that's all,' I said. Tar and Amy guided me to my apartment.

'How did he know there were souls inside of you and Tar, then?' Amy said.

'He devised a test. You see, Amy, flesh robots aren't able to move their pupils quickly to the left five times, then to the right once, then say 'Ordbökon,' and then press their noses like a button. If they did that, they would explode. Go ahead, Amy, do it.'

'I'm not going to do that.'

'AHA!'

Tar pulled my Banana Splits key chain from my pocket and unlocked the door. As the door swung open, they saw our collection lined up along the walls.

'Oh my God,' Amy said.

The top four shelves held Bill's TV toys: the Tuesday-night folks, *Romper Room* and *Welcome Back, Kotter*, *Charlie's Angels* and *What's Happening?*, a Mr. Ed doll, and perhaps the largest collection of *Little House on the*

Prairie toys in the world. My four shelves were almost all robots: Captain Future Superhero, Changing Prince, Deep Sea Robot, Dux Astroman, Interplanetary Spaceman, Chief Smokey, Electric Robot, Winky, Zoomer, Mr. Hustler, New Astronaut Robot Brown, C3PO, Rotate-O-Matic, Space Commando, Astro Boy, Robby, Maximillian, and others. More gewgaws and trinkets lay on the other horizontal surfaces in the room.

'I didn't believe there would be so many,' Amy whispered.

My brother's eyes flooded with awe, and that was a sign of the power of our collection.

'Where'd you get the money?' Tar said.

'What?'

'That must be a couple thousand dollars' worth of antiques.'

I didn't tell him it was closer to seventeen or eighteen thousand dollars' worth.

'Where'd you get the money?' he said again.

'Tar, how can you think of money when you see them? LOOK at them!'

'I saw them. But you don't make enough money to afford— What are you doing? Jimmy, it's one thing after the oth— What are you—? You're selling pot again.'

'No.'

'What, then?'

'Nothing. But I'm starting to see something very obvious, Tar.'

'What?'

'Because one of these things that these toys represent to me is a person's SOUL.'

'What?'

'You heard me. Your soul is left out of you, and now you yourself have become a flesh robot.'

'What?!'

'Tar,' Amy said. 'He's drunk. Let's go.'

'I grew out of toys, Jimmy. I grew out of GI Joe, and Batman and Robin. Because when a person *grows up*, they don't play with toys. They play in their careers, they play in an intimate relationship—'

'Shut up.'

'You shut up!'

'Tar,' Amy said.

'Get out of here!' I said.

'I wanted to get out of here a long time ago, but I had to carry your drunk ass up the stairs. And you know what else, Jimmy?! The kicker is I lent you three hundred bucks six months ago! Where's that?!'

'I LEFT IT IN MY ASS!'

Tar was still easy to anger. He spoke through clenched teeth.

'*I lent you three hundred dollars for rent, and you don't pay me back?*'

'Right!'

'*You use MY money on children's toys.*'

'Exactly!'

'*And then, on top of it all, you say you left my money IN YOUR ASS!?*'

'That's where I happened to leave it.'

'*That's the WORST THING anyone's EVER said to me.*'

'Tar,' Amy said firmly. 'Let's go. Now.'

Tar raised his hands in surrender. He twirled on his heel and flung himself out the door. Amy looked at me.

'Get some sleep, Jimmy,' she said, and she left behind him, closing the door.

'See?' I heard Tar say on the other side of the door. 'I told you. This is how he is.'

I stared at the door. I raised my arms high up toward the ceiling in triumph. The robots gazed at me with their mechanical seeing devices. The action figures stared with their unmoving eyes. They all looked at me, with awe, as the giant I was. They would always remember this moment. James Gunn chased the infidels from our camp! The story would pass down through generations as part of their oral history.

Old Scratch

Charlie patted Bill's shoulder.

'Hey, pal, you're looking down today. What's going on?'

'Nothing,' Bill said. He ducked out from under Charlie's arm and toward one of the glass cabinets. 'You got any new TV stuff in?'

'I got that *Land of the Lost* set you was asking about.'

'Oh, yeah?'

I was looking at the robots. An old man in sunglasses was standing next to me. He was staring in at the mechanical banks. He spoke out the side of his mouth.

'You like these old things?' The old man was leaning on a cane with the head of a swan.

'I collect robots,' I said.

'Ah, an innocent pursuer of beauty,' he said. 'Sucked in by the collection racket.'

I turned away from the old man and looked again at the shelf. There was a $250 Astro Boy that looked mighty tasty. The old man tapped me on the shoulder.

'What?' I said.

The old man pointed a crooked finger at Charlie, who was talking with Bill.

'He, back there, that's an evil man.'

'Charlie? Charlie's not evil. Just goofy.'

'Oh, evil he is. A man who destroys history by super-imposing a price tag over it. A man who lives off the blood of collectors such as yourself. That's the problem with the collection racket, son.' The old man was getting worked up. A bubble of spit inflated near the corner of his mouth. 'They substitute the true value of things, their beauty and memories, with a quantitative measure.' The old man flattened his tie on his chest. He turned back to stare at the banks. His sagging neck was quivering. He stared at one bank in particular. It was a chicken and a nest. You'd set the coin in the nest and the chicken would sit on it, depositing the coin into the hollow of the base. After a few moments, the old man turned back to me. He nodded.

'Good day,' he said.

'You're a very interesting old man,' I said.

He nodded again. He walked out the door. It slammed shut behind him. As he walked down the sidewalk past the front window, he pulled on a knit cap.

'Hey, Charlie,' I shouted up to the other end of the store. 'What was with that guy?'

'Old fart kept offering me twenty bucks for a three-hundred-dollar bank,' Charlie said. 'Can you believe it? Said it was the same one his father had given him on his fifth birthday and he'd been looking for it for years. Said he lost both it and his father in a fire. He was following me around the store waving a twenty-dollar bill over his head. I thought he was gonna punch me.'

I told Bill what the old man had said. We were in our beds lying on the brink of sleep. Through the window came the sounds of people just beginning their day.

'It all fits,' Bill said.

'What does?'

'Charlie is Satan.'

I laughed.

'It's true,' Bill said. 'He's like the Pied Piper leading us to Hell with a trail of old toys. Charlie's stealing our souls. Want to go forward? Can't. Gotta stay in the past. It's because of Charlie.' Bill turned over on his side, facing the wall. 'He's totally stealing our souls.'

Bill pulled the comforter up over his neck and soon he was snoring.

I stared at the ceiling. Nostalgia, I thought. We're trapped in it. Was this lust for toys my way of refusing to accept the present? I had dropped out of school. My brother was ashamed of me. My old friends were gone. I was going nowhere. A loser.

I didn't want to think about it anymore so I staggered into the bathroom and masturbated.

Rubber

The truth is at first I thought my grandmother was crazy like everyone else did. And then she called us her two little warriors. I could see that. Now that made sense.

My mother's father, my grandfather, was a drunkard too. He had met his future wife in a traveling show entitled *The Last of Vaudeville*, where he was billed as the human pool table. There is a brown-and-white picture of my grandmother on a wooden stage. A backdrop is painted behind her. She is pulling her leg up against her, proud of the leg for the camera.

And so my grandmother had several small rubber beanies. I later found hot-water bottles in her bathroom cabinet with circles cut out of them. Around the bottom of the caps were elastic bands that snapped beneath the chin. She snapped one on each of us, my brother and me.

She had already snapped one on herself. Her bouffant hairdo was depressed in the center, making a volcano shape.

'Your hair is messy, Grandma,' Tar said.

'The price you pay,' she said.

She set us on her lap. I was five, beginning to feel too old for all of this. I shifted around.

'In the sky over the sky,' she said. 'In space there are satellites. And they are robbing us of everything that makes us human.'

She showed us the magazines that proved it. The magazines had pictures of horrible creatures in them, and diagrams, and small personal ads in the back from lonely men who wanted to be married. No one understood these men. They had a hard time with their lives. It is difficult to live with knowledge.

'An interplanetary farming community, and these dark ones exchange delicacies. That is what they're trying to create. To make us cattle.

'I could see it in you, boys. I could see it in you since the days you were born. You were born warriors, to see what is real and destroy what is wrong. It's too late for me. I found out too late. But now, you see, the satellites have stolen away most of the truth from me. It is only through willpower alone that I can see any of it at all.

'Your mother, she sees nothing. I show her the magazines, and she flips through them with dead eyes, as if there were blank pages inside. That is what they want her to see. They are waiting to erase every ounce of thought from every single one of us. They make others think that those who know the truth are crazy. Listen to your grandma. Does she sound crazy? I am completely in control of my faculties. They are watching us, and waiting. They can see through our heads. As soon as every single person across the world's head is like a pecan shell without a nut, they will strike. We become cows, and they will process us in many ways, and our biggest plus will be flavor, because they think that human flesh is delicious.'

I looked out the window and onto the driveway. My parents' car was no longer there. They were probably halfway to Chicago by now.

*　　*　　*

My grandmother's doll collection was in a glass case next to her. There were kewpie dolls, black mammy dolls, porcelain dolls, dolls of all types and sizes. An enormous, gawking Shirley Temple was horrifying. Against my parents' orders, I had watched a *Night Gallery* episode that starred a similar doll.

'Whenever your head is up straight you must have on the caps. You may take them off when you go to sleep, but wait until you are all the way lying down and set it next to you on your bed stand. In the morning, don't sit up in bed until you put it on. That way your brains will remain fresh and new, seeing things as they truly are. Your sight will be a thousand times wider than most. Where others' worlds end, yours will begin. Tar and James . . .'

My grandmother began to weep.

'You will know terror. You will know the deepest parts. You will look straight into the eyes of the dark heartless things and never again be the same. But this will make you stronger. My warriors. It is a difficult thing to say, but you are better than other people. It is that simple.'

Socks, my grandmother's cat, slithered around my leg. He had a little cap on his head as well.

'Thank God for rubber,' said Grandma.

Grandma was clutching each of our heads. Her skirt had ridden up over her girdle. Nonsense words were coming out of her head. She was speaking in tongues, and she was rocking. Her eyes were rolled into the back of her head.

Tar was screaming and he wouldn't stop. At first I cried as well, but then was filled with something new.

They are the cows. They will be the cows. We will process them and use them for flavor, and even if they taste disgusting we will eat them. My brother and I will tear them apart and gnaw on their bones. A taste of their own medicine.

Even before she flipped out, she was a different type of grandmother. When she stayed with us, she would do the old soft shoe for us every night before we went to sleep. She told us about the lovers she had had before Grandpa. She said our mother had always been ashamed of her, and that our mother was a bit too straitlaced. 'But she has to be that way,' Grandma said, 'with a crazy family all around her.' Grandma would kiss each of us good-night and ask which Grandma we loved more.

Her.

My grandmother was right. Eventually, my brother and I did look straight into the eyes of the dark heartless things. And death touched us so hard as to almost kill us. And she was right that we have never been the same. Tar is not the same in that he shudders every time he thinks of childhood. And I have not been the same either. I looked into their black eyes and I never looked away.

Tar rolled a little truck around some blocks in the grass.

'Vrrr,' he said. A rubber beanie was on his head, as one was on mine. Gary Bauer was with us. He was wearing a Ziploc bag on his head since we didn't have any more of the beanies.

'Plastic bags are rubber,' I had told him.

'Plastic bags are plastic,' he had said.

But it was the best we could do on short notice.

Earlier, my mother had set us on the bed and had a talk with us. She told us that our grandmother, since Grandpa had died, had started to believe the writings of lunatics (of course Tar and I knew where our mother had gotten *those* ideas). My mother said that this was a new situation for her, our wearing beanies for three days since she and our father had returned home ('What are those things on the kids' heads, Lynea?' my father had said. 'My mother told them that aliens would control their minds if they didn't have them on,' Mom said. 'Oh,' said Dad, and returned to reading his newspaper), and she didn't know how to handle it.

Mr. and Mrs. Bauer, however, were used to Gary doing things like wearing Ziploc bags on his head for days at a time.

Gary had grabbed a hold of a plastic jeep. He was making it fly.

I was getting ready to knock the jeep out of Gary's hand when I saw Nancy Zoomis coming over the hill into our backyard. Her hands were in her pockets. Her shoelaces were undone, flipping around as she walked. She had a serious expression.

'Hi, Nancy!' Gary said. He raised his arm and waved at her. Nancy glanced at him, then she stopped in front of me and stared down. Tar looked up briefly, then went back down to the trucks.

'I talked to your mom, Jimmy,' she said.

'I talk to her every day,' I said.

'Yeah. Big whoop,' Gary said.

'She said there ain't no such thing as aliens,' Nancy said.

'She never uses the word *ain't*.'

'You should take off those dumb hats.'

Tar looked up at her. He placed one hand over his head.

'No,' he whispered.

'There aren't any mind-making rays!'

'Mind-controlling, Nancy!' I said. 'They go through your skull!'

'Malarkey!'

'That's why you don't believe it, Nancy! Because you don't have one on!'

'Malarkey!'

'That's true,' Tar whispered.

Gary shot upright. He pointed at her.

'My dad says you're a flirt, Nancy Zoomis!' he yelled.

'Those hats are dumb! They look stupid and make people laugh at you! Kelly drew a picture!'

'He did too!' Gary said. 'He said you're a flirt!'

'Take it off, Gary!'

'Take off your hair,' he said. 'This is my hair!'

Nancy twirled around to face Tar and stood there over him. She bunched her fists at her sides. Tar grabbed each side of his beanie with the tips of his fingers.

'Take it off, Tar,' she muttered.

Tar shook his head a little.

'Take off that gay hat!'

'He's not gonna take it off!' I yelled. I stood up beside Gary. 'Why would he take off something that's his protection?!'

Nancy ignored me and focused in on Tar.

'You have to take it off! You have to take it off! Your mom wants you to take it off! You're being a brat!'

Tar began to weep. He pulled the beanie tighter onto his head. Nancy's mouth was knotted. She kept flicking one of her fists to her side.

'Get away from him!' I yelled.

'Flirt!'

'Now!' Nancy cried. She reached down and grabbed Tar's beanie. Tar clutched at it wildly but couldn't keep hold. Nancy ran with it clenched in her fist. Nancy was the fastest girl in our kindergarten class, quite a bit faster than Gary or me.

Tar froze with panic. He opened his mouth all the way and hollered. I yelped.

'His hat!' Gary yelled. Tar threw his hands over the top of his head to block the aliens' rays from entering his brain. He spun his head to look at me, wailing, his face soaked with tears, his eyes filled with terror.

'*Nooooo!*' I hollered. I darted off after Nancy, forcing my legs to keep up with her. Gary ran beside me and quickly lost pace. Tar followed too. He desperately slid his hands around the top of his head trying to protect as much area as he could. Nancy darted by the side of my house and out into the street. Her long, thin legs kept at a brisk speed. She barely missed colliding with the Delgesses' mailbox. She crossed over their lawn and ran onto her own. She jumped onto her porch and lunged for the doorknob. In that millisecond I caught up. I grabbed her from behind. I wrapped my arms beneath her shoulders and pulled her backward.

'*Give me back my brother's hat!*' I screamed.

'*Nooo! Nooo!*' Nancy shrieked. She was crying. I pulled her back off the porch. I felt her tears on my forearms.

Nancy and I toppled onto the lawn. Tar hopped in by our side. He grappled for the beanie with one hand while keeping the other moving over his head. Gary bent down and tried to grab Nancy's wrists. She slipped them from his grip repeatedly. She flailed her body wildly. I forced her down into the grass. I sat on top of her. Her eyes were squeezed tight. She whipped her head from side to side. She flapped her arms and legs without aim, bruising us and knocking us off balance. Finally Gary got a good grip on Nancy's wrist. He held it tight in both hands and tightened her elbow between his knees. Gary bit down on Nancy's fingers. Nancy screamed again, so loudly it sounded as if a cheese grater was scraping flesh from the back of her throat. I tore the beanie from her hand. She glared up at me.

'*I hate you, Jimmy Gunn. I hate you.*'

I turned quickly toward Tar. He lowered his hands by his sides as he stood with his shoulders slumped, waiting. His body shuddered with his sobs. I jammed the cap on top of his head, pushing it down hard, blocking the rays from his skull.

Tar rolled a little truck around some blocks in the grass. The blocks were many different colors.

'Vrrr,' he said.

Gary was tying each one of Stretch Armstrong's arms to a stick in the dirt. Gary looked good in his new beanie, which our grandmother had sent us in the mail after Tar called her.

'Jimmy,' Nancy said. I looked up at her. She looked frightened. The elastic string had broken beneath her chin. She held one end in each hand.

'It just snapped, I don't know why,' she said. 'Can you fix it?'

Nancy had both Gary and I beat in athletics. Gary was all over us in rudimentary math skills. But my eye-hand coordination was not to be surpassed. I was the only one of us who knew how to tie.

I took the ends of the elastic strings between my fingers. My knuckles brushed against Nancy's neck. After a couple attempts I succeeded in tying the strings together. The tips of my fingers stuck for a moment between the elastic and her chin.

'It's done,' I said.

'Maybe your grandma can send us some new ones,' Nancy said. A rainbow went across the top of her beanie. She had painted it with an acrylic painting kit, which her mother had given her for her birthday.

'She'll send as many as we want,' Tar said, without looking up from his truck.

It Has to Do with His Hands

The Fred Flintstone night-light was on. Tar was sleeping. Because of his asthma, he had a slight purring noise while he slept. To this day I sleep better with women who smoke, since they often have a similar purring.

I was drifting off to sleep when I heard a tapping sound. I turned onto my side. Through the parted shades was the moon. I heard the tapping sound again. It was coming from the window.

'Tar,' I whispered. His blankets were curled beneath his chin. A string of drool connected him to his pillow.

'Tar,' I said louder. My brother opened his eyes and looked at me.

He said, 'There's a monkey in the kitchen.'

'Wake up.'

He blinked. He stared at me for a minute.

'Tar.'

'In my dream we had a pet monkey.'

'That's not important now. Listen.'

The tapping sound happened again.

'Do you hear that?'

Tar nodded.

'Go see what it is,' I said.

'Why don't you go see?'

'Because if it's a monster and it bites your head off then I'd have some sort of warning.'

Tar pursed his lips.

'If you make me cry, I'm telling Mom,' he said.

'All right, I'll look,' I told him. 'I just didn't want to have to get out of bed.'

I pushed the covers away from my body and sat up. The tapping happened again.

'The monkey was like our little brother,' Tar said. 'He had one of those things you put in your mouth for going scuba'ing.'

I walked to the window. I pushed aside the shade. Below, next to the huge oak tree in our backyard, were Gary and Nancy. They looked ruffled, in clothes that didn't match. Gary was jumping up and down like the maniac he was. Next to him was a large suitcase. Nancy was holding a gym bag, beckoning me down with her arm.

'It's Gary and Nancy,' I told Tar. He came up beside me. He placed his hands on the window frame.

'They want us to go down there,' Tar said.

'I know.'

'If Mom and Dad hear we're in deep shit.'

'Fuck 'em.'

We tiptoed downstairs so our parents wouldn't hear.

'We're running away,' Nancy said. Her tangled hair was back in a band. 'And you guys get to come with us.'

The four of us stood on the porch to our house.

'For what reason?' Tar asked.

Nancy shrugged.

'Gary is,' she said.

'Why are you running away, Gary?' Tar asked.

'Because I hate my mom.'

'Why do you hate your mom?'

'For a lot of good reasons.'

'Gary's mom hid all the soap in the house,' Nancy said. 'She said if he wanted to wash his hands he would have to do it in front of her.'

Gary turned toward her. His face and neck were red. His arms were stiff at his sides.

'*That was a secret, Nancy!*'

'If we're a good family there aren't any secrets.'

'Are you guys going to get married, Nancy?' Tar asked.

'That's dumb, Tar,' I said. 'They're too little to get married. It's illegal.' I wiped my nose. A lot of stuff came out onto my arm. 'You're running away because your mother hid the soap?'

Gary crossed his arms. 'Among *other* things,' he said.

'Are you guys coming or not?' Nancy asked. 'We're only asking you. We're not asking Steve or Corey or Brendan or Kelly or Robert. Only you.'

'Our dog is dead,' Tar said. He bit his lips so he wouldn't cry at the thought.

'She is,' I said. My brother and I were thinking alike. 'If she wasn't dead we would have to stay here. But since she died I guess we can go with you.'

Tar was seven and the rest of us were eight. Tar and I wrote a note to our parents:

Dear Mom and Dad,
    Your waking up and drinking your coffee now. There is probably a look of surprise on your face that says James and Tar are not in their beds I wonder where they are. Do not worry. Something we do sometimes is hide out in the bushes but don't look out there because if you do in true life we'll be somewhere else like maybe New York City where they make Marvel comics and so

we might get a job. We have ran away. But also it is just like a moving like when Nancy's dad was transpited to Cleveland because since theres four of us, this is a family. So in this way you are now like the grand-parents who are far away and maybe we'll drive a plane back at Christmas. $$$$$$. If Shawnee was still alive we of course would not have gone because I was like Shawnee's Dad and Tar was like Shawnee's Mom but now I am like the Dad and Nancy is like the Mom and Tar and Gary are like our kids or maybe some other way besides that. Good luck,

James Tar

P.S. We took alot of money from the place where Dad hides it beneath that statue of that woman in the den. We'll send you some it might be from the money Marvel comics gives us for a couple of very good superheros Gary made up. In case we get caught or throwed in jail remember that this is all Gary Bauer's idea. It has to do with his hands. Goodbye.

My father had twenty-seven hundred dollars beneath the porcelain statuette in his den. Sometimes, when we bothered him working, he had flashed the money for us. He had let us touch it. Now I had it in my pocket and I could touch it for a long, long time.

Nancy had stolen ninety-one dollars from her mother. Gary had got six that he had saved in his bank. His was mostly in quarters.

We left the counting up to Gary. He did it in the bushes behind our house. For a minute, a hundred-dollar bill blew away, but we got it back.

After counting our treasure we had to decide how we were going to get to New York.

'There are three ways,' Nancy said. 'A bus, a car, or a plane.' She closed one eye. 'Four ways, I mean. Trains.'

'Five ways,' Tar added. 'A helicopter.'

'Six ways,' Gary added. 'A P-51 escort bomber like were on the boats that my dad was on when he was in the Navy.'

'That's a type of plane,' Nancy said.

'A very fast plane, though!' Gary said. 'A separate category!'

'A hot-air balloon would be a fun way,' Tar said. 'But unrealistic.'

It was late at night, but I wasn't tired. I leaned back against a bush. A cobweb got stuck in my hair. Nancy picked it off my head.

'Let's take a taxi cab to the airport,' I said.

Which we did. In a deep voice, I called the Yellow Cab Company. I told him we'd be at the bottom of Troll Court. That way the cab wouldn't wake my parents.

The driver's round face turned back over the edge of the seat.

'Hello! My name is George! Welcome, little ones, to my Yellow Cab!'

He had a thick accent and white hair. His nose was swollen and pink.

'Can we put our suitcases in the trunk?' Nancy asked.

'Ah, yes! We will put the suitcases in the trunk!' George jumped out of the front seat. He was a large, chubby man. He danced around to the back of the car and opened the trunk. He helped Nancy put in her gym bag. I put in Tar's and mine. Gary was grunting, trying to pick his large suitcase up that high.

'Why's your suitcase so heavy?' I asked him.

'Soap,' Nancy said.

'Shut up, Nancy!' Gary said.

'He's got a lot of soap in there,' Nancy told me. 'He found where his mother hid it.'

'I can't lift it,' Gary whined.

'You can get that free at hotels,' Tar said. 'And towels.'

'And you can keep the hotel room key and go back and steal new people's money,' I told Nancy. 'Tar and I made a plan once.'

'Let me help you with that, strong little one,' George said. 'Ooooh! Heavy! Ha ha! Here, let's put it here.' George closed the trunk.

Nancy and Tar hopped into the backseat. George was turning his head, looking around the street.

'Where are all your mommies and your daddies?'

'They're asleep,' I said. 'My dad was the one who called on the phone. He gave me the money.'

'Oh, eh . . . yes? Your father?' he said.

I nodded. Gary's body was stiff. His eyes were wide, looking at me.

'Well, okay. Welcome to my Yellow Cab!' George said again, spreading his arms out in front of him. Then he got back into the driver's seat. Gary and I squished into the backseat with Nancy and Tar.

'I don't want to be on the hump!' Nancy said.

George looked in the rearview mirror.

'We are going to the airport, yes?'

'Yes, sir,' I said.

The streets were deserted. The lights at most the gas stations were off. My heart was racing. My shoulder was tight against Nancy's.

'So where are you going to at the airport, little ones?'

'We're meeting our grandparents at the airport,' Nancy said.

'All by yourselves?' he said. His worried eyes were framed by the rearview mirror.

'Our parents didn't want to come,' I said. 'They said we could come by ourselves.'

'I can't wait to see Grandma and Grandpa,' Tar said.

'Ha-ha!' George said. 'I have a grandbaby, but she is very far away. All of you are brothers and a sister?'

'Yes,' I said. 'Nancy's oldest. And then me, and then Gary, and then Tar.'

All of us nodded. This was in fact the actual order of births, though Nancy was only four months older than me and I was only a month older than Gary. I looked down at Gary, who no longer seemed frightened. He was looking serenely out the window. The cab passed the Great Western restaurant, where I had never been inside but where a large fiberglass horse stood on the roof.

'What's wrong with his voice?' Nancy said to me.

'Shhh!' Tar said. 'He's retarded!'

Gary smiled. 'Where are you from?' he asked the cab driver.

'I am from Czechoslovakia. Do you know where that is?' George asked.

'Underneath Germany and Poland,' Gary said. 'On top of Austria and Hungary. Are you a Communist?'

'Oh, no!' George said.

Gary put his hands up to his sides.

'Hey, my dad says it isn't so bad. He says that priests are Communists—and nuns.'

'Especially nuns,' Tar said, just making conversation.

'Priests?' George said. 'No, they are not communists. Communists want to take over everything.'

'So do priests,' Gary said. 'They want everyone to be Catholic. That's their job.'

At the airport George hopped out of the car and helped

us with our bags. I realized then it had been wrong for Nancy to say we were meeting our grandparents, since we had all our luggage, but George didn't seem to notice. He whistled as he set our things on the sidewalk in front of TWA. The ride costs twenty-seven dollars, he said to me. Gary counted off thirty dollars from our roll.

'A tip,' Tar whispered to him.

Gary added another thirty.

Clocks lined the wall next to the baggage claim. The biggest one said two o'clock. Few people were left in the airport. Most of the ticket counters were closed. The United Airlines counter was still open. A pretty young black woman was doing paperwork there. We sat on one of the steel benches. A fellow with a cart of luggage passed by and smiled at us.

'The cab was dirty,' Gary said. 'It got on my elbows and on my clothes.'

Nancy was staring straight ahead. The areas below her eyes were pink. They would always get that way when she got tired. Tar had his finger in his mouth.

'Quit sucking on your finger, Tar,' I said.

'I'm not sucking on it. I'm biting it.'

'How much is a plane ticket?' Nancy asked.

'About fifteen dollars,' Gary said.

'Are they going to let us buy the ticket even though we're kids?' she asked.

Gary said he had an idea that he thought of two years ago. He explained it to us.

The pretty young black woman leaned over the counter. She smiled sweetly.

'Well, hello there. How are the two of you tonight?' she said.

I cleared my throat. Nancy took one of the baggage tags from the box on the counter and pretended to read it.

'Our mom and dad are parking the car,' I said.

'Oh, they are?'

'They said for us to go in and buy the tickets.'

'They were in a fight,' Nancy said.

'Mom called Dad a dirty word,' I told the black woman.

'They said if we didn't get the tickets we'd be in real big trouble,' Nancy said.

'Dad will hit me in the stomach,' I said. 'And her too.'

'It doesn't bruise in the stomach,' Nancy said.

The woman's face melted into horror and compassion.

'We want four tickets to New York City, please,' I said.

It took a long time to find Gate 44. Tar was hungry and wanted some eggs. But the tickets had been a lot more than fifteen bucks. We only had eighty-seven dollars left.

Pots with trees and flowers lined the hall. Nancy took a blue flower and put it in her hair.

'Does that look good?' she asked me.

'I guess.'

Tar wanted one in his hair too. Nancy put one there for him.

The pretty black woman had told us that the plane wouldn't be leaving until five-thirty. We would have to wait three hours. Near Gate 44 were some hard bucket seats. We sat in them. We waited. One by one we drifted off to sleep.

'Jimmy!' Gary was shaking my shoulder. I blinked at him. He made a squealing sound and pointed down the hall. Our parents, Gary's parents, and Nancy's mother were walking quickly down the hall. Their clothes weren't tucked in. Mr. Bauer was wearing a pajama shirt. Ms. Zoomis's hair was in curlers.

Nancy woke up and saw them. She started crying. She jumped up from her seat and ran down the hall. Ms. Zoomis took off after her. The old cow could run fast.

'We're busted,' I said.

Tar awoke. He waved sleepily at our parents.

Gary flung himself over the bucket seats. He tried to hide behind them. You could see him easily through the cracks.

'Jimmy!' my father cried. He jogged toward us.

'Hi, Dad.'

'What the hell are you doing?'

'Waiting for our five-thirty connection.'

My mother picked up Tar and pulled him against her. She was crying.

'Why did you want to run away?' she asked him.

'I got a ticket.' Tar held the ticket up for her to see.

My father started crying. His body slumped into a pitiful sunken shape.

'Why did you want to leave us?' he mumbled.

I shrugged.

My mother looked around at the airport workers, who were watching.

'Everyone here must think we're horrible parents,' she whispered to my father.

Mr. and Mrs. Bauer were crouched in front of the seats where Gary was hiding. He was holding the two chair backings like jail bars, sobbing.

'Come on out, Gary,' Mrs. Bauer said. 'It's all right, honey. You can have your soap back. I shouldn't have taken it from you.'

'Come on out of there, son,' Mr. Bauer said. 'Hell, we been all over this place looking for you. Your mommy and daddy love you, son. Come on out.'

*　　*　　*

Ms. Zoomis had a hard face on. She was staring straight ahead. She had ahold of Nancy's ear, and was using it as a handle to pull her down the hall.

'Ow!' Nancy screeched. 'Let go!'

'I am *not* letting go, young lady. You're coming home this instant and I'm going to pull your ear the whole way!'

'Shit! It'll come off!'

'No cartoons for you for eight weeks!'

'Eight weeks?' Nancy sobbed.

'Eight.'

'One week!'

'Eight weeks, young lady, eight weeks!'

'Two!'

'Eight.'

'Next time we'll be in New York before you find us!' Nancy cried.

'Oh no, you won't! Next time you'll be locked in a cardboard box in the basement at home! I'll feed you canned vegetables through a hole in the top!'

Nancy caught my eye as she passed me. She cupped one hand over the other so her mother couldn't see. I could. She was giving her mother the finger.

In the car. Tar was curled up next to me in the backseat, fast asleep. My mother was turned around, her chin on the headrest.

'What compelled you to do such a thing?' she asked me.

I shrugged.

'Gary wanted to,' I said.

'Goddammit, Jimmy,' my father snorted. 'If Gary wanted you to jump off a bridge would you do that too?'

I thought for a moment.

'It depends on how high the bridge was and how deep the water,' I said.

Amphibians Cracked

During recess I had to sit in the classroom. I had been put on detention for spitting a goober in a sandwich Joe Moscowitz ate. If I hadn't told him he would have never known.

I took a seat near one of the windows where I could see the other kids on the Saint Ambrose playground. Gary came and stood outside the window. He tapped on it with his fingers. I opened it up.

'What am I supposed to do?' he said.

'Go play.'

'Play what?'

'Go look for turtles in the woods.'

'We're not allowed to go in the woods.'

'So? I'm in here for three days. Big punishment. I get to draw cartoons for three days. And there's not even a monitor. Look. Watch, Gary.' I said loudly: '*Fuck*.'

'Ha-ha! All right. I'll go to the woods. I'll try to get caught.' Gary stuck his hand through the window so I could give him five. Then he did a funny walk backward toward the woods, shaking his hands up by his head for my amusement.

I opened up my crayon box, took out a sheet of paper, and was ready to get to work, when Greta Holthausen came marching in through the door. She had a pale blue vein that traveled down her temple and curled beside her eye. She was frowning and her lips were turned down. I froze. Greta was strange—she ate her pencil erasers and didn't talk to anyone and only played by herself. I loved her. I had told Gary that someday Greta and I would be married, and when we were married I would fuck the shit out of her every night.

'What did you do?' I asked her.

'Nothing,' she said. She stomped toward the back of the classroom and took a seat. She took out a piece of paper and some crayons of her own.

'As if peas are so sacred,' she mumbled to herself.

I sat and drew and occasionally snuck a glance back at Greta.

'I need a green crayon!' she shouted, not really to me.

'I have one.' I took one from my box and walked back to where she was sitting. Without looking her in the eye, I held the green crayon out in front of her. Greta snatched it out of my hand. I walked back and sat down.

'Jimmy,' she whispered. It was the first time she had ever said my name. It made my spine sweat.

I turned around, looked at her.

'All I was doing was sticking some peas below the table. I hate peas!'

I laughed.

'*I* spit in Joe—'

'I know,' she said, and continued drawing.

Gary came running up to the window. He was holding a turtle out in front of him. It had yellow squares on its back.

'Jimmy! Look!'

'Cool.'

'Take it, quick! Put it in my desk! I like its coloration!'

'Okay.'

Gary maneuvered the turtle through the open window and I took it. Greta came and stood beside me.

'Can I see?' she asked.

'Sure.'

Greta touched the turtle, withdrew her hand quickly, and laughed.

'*Ow!*' It was Gary's scream, coming from outside. Greta and I looked at the window. Gary was holding his face, and grappling for his glasses on the pavement. The side of his face was red and a soccer ball was rolling in front of him. Stan Boeppling, a sixth-grader, picked it up. Although he was only two years older than us, he was a foot taller and twice as broad. With all his force, he threw the soccer ball at Gary again. It knocked him over. Stan and two of his friends, Alan Ebbing and Jeff Lipton, were laughing. Stan's body was almost completely covered in freckles.

'Yesterday they tried to pull off my skirt,' Greta said. 'Then they spit on me. I cried.'

'*Hey!*' I yelled out the window. '*Leave him alone!*'

Alan Ebbing covered his brow, keeping the sun out of his eyes, and looked in my direction.

'Who is it?' Stan said.

'That Gunn,' Alan said.

'Hey, Gunn,' Stan said. 'Watch this!'

Gary was standing up. Stan brought his fist down onto the top of Gary's head. Then he quickly did it again. Gary collapsed and began to cry. The boys were laughing.

'I hate them,' Greta said.

I looked around the field for Tar or Nancy, to try and get them to help. They were nowhere to be seen.

A small nun came out onto the field carrying a large brass bell. She rang it, signaling the end of recess.

'Good job, Bauer,' Stan said, and he slapped Gary on the back as hard as he could.

'Yeah, good job,' said Jeff and Alan, and then they slapped him too.

'Good job.'

'Good job.'

'Good job.'

The boys left and walked in toward the school. Gary pushed himself up off the ground. He wiped off his glasses with his shirt, then put them back on. He looked at me through the window, then started to make his way inside as well. Greta stared at me. I hid my face from her.

After school Stan Boeppling sat on a railroad tie with his friends. Behind him was a large flagpole with an American flag at the top. Nancy and I were sitting across from them, on the edge of the school porch. Saint Ambrose had two bus runs. Everyone left was waiting for the second run. Gary and Tar had gone off to the woods to look for more turtles. Nancy cradled Gary's turtle in her lap like a baby.

'I don't know why he left me with this thing,' Nancy said. 'He must be more hard up for a dog than I thought. This is like a big bug. He says he's going to teach it tricks. Retard.'

I stood.

'Where're we going?' she said.

'I don't know.' I walked toward the flagpole. Nancy rose to follow me. I stopped in front of the older kids. My hands were in my pockets and I was trembling. They looked up at me. Stan had a little smile. An especially large brown freckle was half on and half off his lip.

'What's wrong with you, Gunn?'

'I had a question.' My voice wavered. Boeppling eyed Jeff Lipton, the little smile still there.

'What's your question, Gunn? I'm the man of a thousand answers.'

'I was wondering . . . why you . . . liked . . . to . . . suck
. . . cock.'

A muffled shriek came out of Nancy, who was standing
next to me holding the turtle. Stan snorted, shocked. He
dropped his head.

'*What?*'

'I was wondering that.'

'Get the fuck out of here, you little faggot.'

I looked at Jeff Lipton and Laura Krieger. They were
both laughing at me. I smiled at them. I turned and walked
back toward the porch.

'Boy,' Nancy said. 'That was stupid.'

'Kick his ass,' I heard Jeff say to Stan.

'Little faggot,' Stan said.

They were sitting on the railroad ties. Sometimes they
would glance at me. I was staring at them.

'You better quit looking over there,' Nancy said.

I eyed her. 'Shut up.'

'You shut up, H.R. Puffinfag.'

I looked back at the older kids beside the flagpole. I
stood.

'Hey!' Nancy said.

I walked toward the flagpole.

'Uh-oh, here he comes again,' Jeff said loudly.

'Get the fuck out of here,' Stan said.

'I had another question.'

'Get the fuck out.'

'I had—'

'Get the fuck out.'

'Another question.'

'I mean it, Gunn, now.'

'God, you're a freak,' Laura Krieger said to me.

'I was wondering if you—'

'Fuck off.'

'I was wondering if you liked the taste of spit.'

'Spit, yum. Now get the fuck out of here.'

'You said yum.'

'Gunn, you better fucking not—'

'You said yum.'

I hawked phlegm from deep in my chest. I had just gotten over a cold. Stan moved back a bit. I spit the phlegm at his face. It landed across his mouth in a lightning-bolt shape.

'Ewgh!' Stan said. He jumped up from the railroad tie. I stepped back. Laura Krieger was laughing. Stan slapped his face with both hands like Curly from the Three Stooges, wiping off my spit.

'You're dead, fucker!' he yelled. 'You're dead!'

'Tough man,' I said.

His fist rose and came down hard into my chest. I crumpled to the grass. Nancy shrieked. Stan Boeppling came down on top of me. He punched me in a lot of different places, very fast and very hard. My lip opened and bled. Nancy ran toward Stan.

'Let go!' She clocked him on the head with the turtle. Stan slammed his elbow back into her neck. Jeff Lipton pulled her off, twisting her arm up behind her back. Stan grabbed my head with both hands. He pushed my head into the grass, scraping up dirt with my teeth. I was crying. He turned my head over. He held it in both hands.

'How do YOU like the taste of spit, huh, Gunn?'

I tried to push him away but he was kneeling on my arms. I wrenched my head back and forth but he opened my mouth by squeezing my chin with both hands. He hawked phlegm. He spit into my mouth. I felt the thick chunk drip down the back of my throat. He hawked again. He spit again. He kept spitting. His mouth was a relentless faucet.

What started off thick turned into straight saliva. And I felt something down below as well. His cock was hard. I couldn't cry because my throat was filled. I gagged. I coughed. I was drowning and going to die. His cock pushed up harder against me. Stan Boeppling's spit dripped down the sides of my mouth. He punched me one final time, in the face. Blood from my nose was on his fist.

I knelt on the grass, propping myself with my elbows. I coughed the spit out of my mouth. I was crying. Stan Boeppling was walking away from me. Laura stared down at me with no expression. Jeff Lipton was laughing. I wiped my face and stood up. I moved toward the school doors. Tears and blood blurred my vision. Nancy came up to me, spitting.

'*They spit in my fucking mouth!*' she said. She walked toward the porch. She looked around frantically. 'Oh, shit.' She looked at the turtle on the ground. Its shell was cracked open and it was bloody and dead. 'I killed it,' she whispered, and she began to cry. 'Gary's going to kill me.' She looked at me. 'Are you okay?'

'Give me a pencil.'

'Why?'

'Just give me a pencil.'

'Why do you want a—'

'Give me a pencil!'

Nancy knelt on the porch. She opened her yellow plastic pencil box. She handed me a number two pencil. I snatched the pencil and threw open Saint Ambrose's front doors. The air-conditioning was freezing. I marched down the hall. I passed the upper-grade classrooms. I passed the bulletin boards. Orange mayflowers were pasted on the walls. I turned swiftly into the fourth-grade classroom. Sister Gregory was at her desk grading papers.

'Jimmy . . . ? What happened?'

I gripped the pencil out in front of me, pointing up straight.

'I need to sharpen this pencil!'

'You're bleeding, son. Come here.'

I turned toward the pencil sharpener on the wall. I stuck the pencil in and began turning the handle quickly. Sister Gregory walked toward me and placed her hand on my shoulder.

'Jimmy, sit down.'

I pulled the pencil out of the sharpener. I felt the tip. It wasn't very sharp.

'Let's have the nurse look at you.'

I put the pencil back in and turned the handle some more.

'Jimmy.'

I pulled it back out. Now it was sharp. I yanked myself away from the nun's hand. I walked briskly into the hall, leaving Sister Gregory behind. As I flung open the front doors I heard her saying my name behind me. Nancy was sitting on the front step. No one was around the flagpole.

'Where is he?' I said to Nancy.

'You're not allowed to go near him!' Nancy yelled. 'I say!'

I left Nancy behind me and walked up around the building. Some girls were playing hopscotch. There was a space between the convent and the school where the older students sometimes hid and smoked cigarettes. I entered the area. Stan and Jeff were sitting at a picnic table there. The picnic table just barely fit in the space. Their faces were partially hidden in shadow. Stan quickly hid his cigarette below the table. Then he saw it was me.

'Jesus,' Jeff said. He was amazed that I had come back.

'Come here, fuckwad,' Stan said. He pointed behind

him with his thumb. 'You like the taste of brick?' He cackled.

My lips clamped together to stifle my sobs. I squeezed behind the seat of the picnic table. I moved rapidly toward him with my back against the school. Stan flicked his cigarette toward me, but missed. I crawled up on the seat. I crawled on my knees toward him. I began to sob in heaves.

'Man, you're a glutton.' He brought his fist up from under the table.

With both hands I raised the sharpened pencil. I aimed for the dark cashew-shaped hole of his ear. I slammed it toward the hole, but Stan swung his arm up and knocked mine aside. With his other hand, he punched me and I fell back onto the bench and down from the bench to the pavement, beneath the table. I landed on my side and flipped onto my back.

'Fuck!' I heard Stan say. 'He tried to kill me!'

Stan's leg was directly next to me. I still had the pencil. I looked at it. The tip wasn't broken.

I drew my arm back and jammed the pencil with all the strength I could muster into the side of Stan's calf. It penetrated deep. Stan wrenched his leg away from me. The pencil snapped in half, half of it in my hand, the other half imbedded in his leg.

'*OWWWW!*' Stan screamed. He jumped up onto the bench. I looked over and saw Jeff's legs quickly disappear from beneath the table, as if he thought I had a whole bunch of very sharp pencils with me.

Stan hopped around on one leg on the bench, crying. He reached down and tried to get the pencil out of his flesh. He couldn't. Blood was spurting out of his leg. His uniform pants were soaked red.

I heard people running my way. I tilted my head back, looked behind me. Sister Gregory was jolting toward me, her black gown flipping up around her thin legs. Nancy was next to her, crying. Gary and Tar were running behind them. They were each precariously clutching five or six turtles against their chests. They had found them in the woods.

Sister Gregory's wrinkled old face ducked down below the table. Her gray eyes stared straight at me. She looked angry.

'Ask *him* what he did to *me*,' I whispered.

Her arm snapped out, grabbing me beneath my shoulder. She dragged me out from beneath the table. Another nun arrived. She told Stan to sit down and everything would be all right. Sister Gregory picked me up at the biceps and held me there in the air, marching toward the school.

'Jimmy Gunn!' she said.

'*Let him go!*' Tar screamed. He later told me he thought she was taking me to reform school. He hit her with the only thing he had: the turtles. He hurled the creatures at her like bombs. There was a *clunk!* as one struck the side of her head. She turned and saw another one coming. Gary looked over at my brother and then back at me. He began throwing turtles at her as well. The old nun dropped me, trying to cover her face. Amphibians cracked and splattered around her.

My father tightened his grip on my underarm, his thumb digging between the muscles. He jogged down the stairs into the basement. I was in my underwear. I tripped down behind him, slipped. The carpet on the stairs burned the back of my leg. My father threw me up against the wall. This was the room where we would talk when I got in trouble.

'*You know how much money this is going to cost me? Do you have ANY IDEA?*'

I hung my head to avoid his gaze.

'*That boy's going to be on crutches for a month!*'

I looked over at a stuffed clown lying on the couch.

'Good,' I mumbled.

'*WHAT?*' My father grabbed my hair. '*WHAT DID YOU SAY?*'

'Nothing.'

'*WHAT . . . DID . . . YOU . . . SAY?*'

'*It's good!*' I spit out. I began to cry. My father brought his arm across my face. I slammed back against the wall and fell.

'*It's good!*' I cried.

'How could you say—!' My father kicked me in the torso. I crawled away on the floor.

'IT'S GOOD! IT'S GOOD! IT'S GOOD! IT'S GOOD!' I was sobbing, the kind that came from the lungs. My father followed by my side, he bent down toward my face, his elbows on his knees.

'*You cripple a boy and you say it's good?!*'

'*EXTREMELY GOOD!*' I screeched.

My father whined through his angry closed mouth. He kicked me in short, quick strokes. I hid my head behind my mother's sewing table, but no more of me could fit behind there. My father's heel came down on the base of my spine. I plopped down, splayed out flat. Tar was sitting on the stairs. His face was between the rails. He was screaming.

'*Stop it!*' he cried. '*Dad! Stop it! DON'T!*'

My father slowed and stopped. He stood over me, staring down. He started to cry, then bit his lips and pulled it back in.

'There's something wrong with you,' he whispered. 'That's something that psychopaths think. Psychopaths think that it's all right to cripple people.'

I wouldn't look at him. He has nothing to do with me, I thought. He's the type that spits on smaller kids and throws soccer balls at their heads.

My father turned away. As his footsteps disappeared upstairs I closed my eyes. I turned there with my back against the wall. Tar came down and knelt next to me. He reached out and touched my shoulder. He was sobbing.

I was having a vision. We were in a lifeboat on the ocean. Me and Tar and Gary and Nancy. The sun was bright. It glittered in rivulets on the water's surface. Nancy was whittling something from a block of wood. Tar and I were playing Othello, the travel version so that the black and white circles wouldn't spill off the board as the boat rocked. And Gary was singing softly, his voice a fluid soprano. 'Come and knock on our door. We've been waiting for you.' The lifeboat floated toward an island, an island more beautiful than any we had ever seen, with monkeys and pandas and lemurs, leaf-eaters all.

And the continents behind us were blackened. Everyone there was dead. They were all horribly charred.

They put me on suspension for two weeks. When I came back there was a crumpled drawing stuffed in my desk. I pulled it out and looked at it.

It was signed G.H.

The Pigeon

I had met a woman in a bar the night before. Her name was Madeleine. She was a divorcée with enormous breasts. Maybe she was forty-four or forty-six. I didn't like her very much, and she was no beauty, but she had taken my hand in hers and licked it. This gave me a hard-on, the kind you can't help and feel queasy about. She was showing off to her other old friends that she could excite a young guy. It was sick. She invited me to her flat afterward. There was beer there. My decision-making process was in bad shape at the time.

'Bill, I'm going home with the broad in the glitter dress.'

'I think you should reconsider that,' Bill said.

'Or maybe YOU should reconsider it, Bill,' I said.

The hag pulled me away and toward the door. My pal made a disgusted face.

Madeleine was sucking me off. There was a bottle of beer on the nightstand by my side. I'd reach over and gulp some of it. The blow job wasn't provoking any reaction in me.

'Are you a fag?' she asked.

'Occasionally. Like tonight.' I didn't know what this meant, but at the time I thought it was pretty funny. I started giggling. The poor old lady got angry.

'Let's try something else,' she said. She got on her back and hiked up her dress. She pulled down her panties. She wanted me to eat her pussy.

'I don't remember reading about that in the schedule of events.'

'Come on!' she yelled. I looked down and she had her hand between her legs, diddling herself.

'From now on I'm going sober. It happened to my brother and my father. Now it's my turn, I guess. There are some things I don't want to see.'

'Faggot!' Madeleine shouted. She turned on her side. Her back was to me. She masturbated to orgasm. Then she fell asleep, and I felt relieved. I passed out for a couple of hours.

When I woke the daylight was coming in through the window. There was a clock that told me it was six A.M. Madeleine snored.

I went through her drawers searching for something to steal. The old bitch had practically raped me! I said to myself. A string of pearls was beneath some brightly colored sweaters. I put them in my pocket. A headache was inching its way up my neck.

A bottle of Cutty Sark was in her kitchen cabinet. I found a clean glass and sat down at the kitchen table. I drank a quarter of the bottle. I thought about a lot of things, like how other people had things to think about, and things to do, and driving passions and interests, and how I didn't. There were only the toys, which, really, were foolish. I cried a little bit. I screwed the cap back on the Cutty Sark and put it away. My headache was gone.

On my way out I thought about how the string of pearls might have been a gift from Madeleine's father before he died. Goddammit! I thought. Now I couldn't go through with it. I threw them on top of the cabinet, so she wouldn't find them for a long time and think they were missing. That was punishment enough. Then I left.

I walked down to Central Park to find some answers. The sky was a magnificent blue, the color of the 1973 Zerak the Destroyer robot. It was warm for March.

I sat on a park bench and I watched the birds. I enjoyed them, a bunch of little creatures, running around, happy, eating things. Inspired by the birds, I began to imagine an ideal human life, a kind of worriless ornithic living. I was feeling better until I remembered I had to be at work in an hour and a half. This made me remember how dark existence actually was. I had told Cora I would fill in for her on the day shift. A bird would have never done that.

I walked out of Central Park and up onto the sidewalk. There, sitting on a Volvo's hood, was a small, beautiful girl with brown hair, almost black, that hung over her face. The girl nibbled on the nail of her pinkie finger. She was reading a book. Her legs—which I'll describe as willowy—stretched down the hood of the Volvo. A crease in her navy slacks dissected each leg lengthwise. But most strikingly: A pale blue vein traveled down her temple and curled beside her eye; she looked amazingly like Greta Holthausen, my first crush. This girl was younger than Greta would be today, and her hair was dark instead of blond. But still.

The girl turned a page. The book was old and faded. This girl was probably the type to say she liked old books because they had a smell, a history, a flavor to them. Fuck that philosophy, I thought. I'd rather have new books, books that haven't had all the juices wrung out of them by idiots.

Oh, I was drunk.

I headed down the sidewalk. I placed the girl in the corner of my eye as I passed her. I commanded myself: Think of something clever to say. But my skull was an empty cavern with only the dull echoes of Take Five bouncing around inside.

The girl pushed her hair from her face. Her black eyes seemed to be all pupils. Purple-red lipstick sheathed her boxy lips. It was the only makeup she wore. She so resembled my memory of Greta Holthausen that her face was now replacing the memory in my mind. The word *witchery*, it was on her like morning.

I avoided stepping in some gum.

The girl's pupils were flipping up and then returning to the book. *Party Going*, by Henry Green. At first I thought she was looking at me. Then I followed her gaze to a red car parked in front of the Volvo. A bouncing grayness was near the car's rear Firestone.

A pigeon, white with gray swirls, was between the curb and the tire. It had a bloody wing with an inch scraped away to reveal bone. A few feathers stuck up at awkward angles. One of the pigeon's legs was a loose, stringy thing. The pigeon did a sad dance, jerking itself around the tire. It seemed to be trying to push its wing back into place. Maybe it had been hit by a car. Or maybe it had fallen asleep and dropped out of a tree, although I wondered if that was possible. I stopped and watched it. The pigeon triggered many emotions in me, the ones you'd guess. My face didn't register them.

I looked at the girl and she looked back at me. Of our two faces hers was the more adequate sensor. It intoned bewilderment.

'There's something wrong with that bird,' she said.

'This pigeon,' I said, 'is not happy.'

'I think it's dying.'

'That would constitute something wrong.'

'I don't know what to do.'

'Lots of people would think you should kill it.' I fumbled with a piece of lint inside my pocket. I was trying to think of a way to use this pigeon as a thruway to the girl.

She kept her place in the book with her finger as she slid down the side of the Volvo. Her pants were pleated, pushed out by small but firm hips. She came to my side and folded her arms as she looked down at the bird. She had the fresh smell of a child. I tasted Cutty in my mouth and tried not to breathe in her face.

'I had to kill a frog once,' I said. 'But that was a reptile.'

The girl nodded as she stared at the bird. She pursed her lips and twisted them to the side. A bus passed in front of us. I could smell the burnt fuel.

'What should we do?' she asked.

I shrugged. 'You can have the responsibility of deciding since you saw it first. But if you want me to do the killing, I'll kill it for you.'

She winced but didn't look at me.

'Although I don't enjoy destroying creatures,' I said. 'Not pigeons at least. I admire them. They're able to get fat without much effort, mooching off the charity of others. There's a man in Harlem has a pigeon circus.'

The girl was fixing herself a cigarette. An Hermès scarf was draped over her shoulder. Greta Holthausen would never have had one of those; her parents were poor and she lived in a house that had wooden planks for a garage.

'Do you think he wants to die?' she asked.

'He'd probably just roll out into the street if he did. Mercy killing, I guess, is under the presumption that we know better than they do.'

'Do you think a vet could fix him?'

I shrugged.

She flicked her fingers in the direction of the Volvo.

'I have a box in there.'

The window was open. Hot air swallowed my face and neck. The Volvo had the milky windshield of a heavy smoker, but besides that it was clean. The pigeon's wing slapped against the inside of the cardboard box, which I held on my lap. This beat countered the rhythm of the radio.

The girl looked at the bird. Her face froze halfway between polite smile and grimace. Her irises were as dark as the pigeon's. She hadn't said, but I knew she asked me along because the dying bird frightened her. So far she had been stony and cool and had mostly ignored me.

I looked at the bird. Its body inflated and deflated with desperate, panicked breath. It made me feel sad and sick. Then I looked at the girl. She made me feel desire. I was touching more parts of myself at once than ever before.

We passed a McDonald's.

'I just thought of something,' I said. 'A dog or a cat would have come along and eaten this guy.'

The girl looked in her rearview mirror as she switched lanes.

'I thought of that,' she said. She stretched her back and her small breasts momentarily became prominent. 'I couldn't leave him there. But I couldn't smash his head either.'

I thought, but didn't say, I could have done either. It was only a bird, and a bird from one of the planet's scummier species to boot. But, still, it felt good to be doing a good deed that I personally didn't have to shell out money for. The Yellow Pages' veterinarians page, which I had torn from a booth outside the museum, crinkled beneath my leg.

The girl glanced at me.

'I'm Evelyn.'

'I'm James. Saw you reading Henry Green.'

'You're a reader?'

'Signs, postcards, television credits.'

'I'm reading it, Green, for school. But I like it. I'd read it anyway.'

'Good for you.'

'Your accent isn't New York.'

'Saint Louis. I've been here five years.'

At 232 West 22nd Street Evelyn slowed. She looked up at the address and then at me, and I said, 'Yeah, this is the right place, this is it.' I looked at my watch. I was supposed to be at the hospital in two minutes. Screw it, I thought.

'So it's not a pet?' the vet asked again. He wore Theodore Roosevelt glasses. In fact, he looked a little bit like Teddy Roosevelt all around, a Teddy Roosevelt whose ass I could kick. A poster with pictures of all the different types of cats was on the wall behind his head.

'No,' I said.

'But we like him,' Evelyn said. 'He's not afraid of us. He let James pick him up.'

The vet squinted, leaned on the counter, removed his glasses, and rubbed his naked eyes. A steel rolling table was beside me. I scanned it for something to swipe while he was distracted. There wasn't anything I could dispose of—a glass jar filled with cotton balls, a box of plastic gloves, a box of red thermometer tips, some bandages, a tiny photo of an ugly woman. I slipped the picture of the ugly woman in my back pocket. For the hell of it.

'Well, I'm going to have to suggest that you euthanize,' the vet said.

I shook my head in disappointment.

'You're asking us to step into an ethical black hole,' I said.

'I broke my arm as a child,' Evelyn said. 'No one wanted to euthanize me.'

'And, honestly, doc, that's just the tip of the iceberg,' I told him, not really knowing what I meant but feeling like a maverick nevertheless. The girl's black eyes focused hard on me.

So the veterinarian fixed the bird. He rubbed some ointment on the wound and, on my suggestion, added a couple of stitches there as well. He dressed the broken wing in a sling of cloth. He braced the leg with two tongue depressors and wrapped it in tape. When the job was finished, the vet handed us a bottle of medicine and said to place it on the wound twice a day to check any infection. He passed us some extra slings. Evelyn charged the seventy-five bucks to her MasterCard. The vet nodded good-bye as we left. The weather wasn't quite as hot as it had been. We got into Evelyn's Volvo and moved up Broadway toward my apartment in Harlem.

The pigeon wheezed twice, loudly, and died.

I dug the hole with my hands. Evelyn packed the excess dirt into a tight pile on the side of the hole. Insects droned on around us. Birds did many kinds of tweets. Over the trees surrounding us, skyscrapers sprouted, alighting the dark ceiling of sky.

'Is it safe to be in the park this late?' Evelyn asked. Her voice was soft with a husky corner.

'I have a pocketknife. With that I can protect us. If someone challenges me to a knife fight it will be just like *West Side Story*.'

'The Jets,' she whispered. The knees of her navy slacks were dusty with the dirt.

'Flip her in there, Ev.'

'Should we touch her?'

I bent over and lifted the bird from the box. The body was a little stiff. I set her in the hole. As Evelyn pushed the dirt into the grave, her hand grazed the hairs on my wrist. A speck of dirt sat on the pigeon's open black eye. And then the dirt came down and covered her completely. I stamped the earth down with my palms.

'Perhaps you should say a few words,' Evelyn said.

'A few words?'

'I think it would be a good idea, to say something. Since we were her last friends.'

'All right.' I cleared my throat. I looked up at the sky. I raised my cupped hands to my sides, imagining I looked like Saint Francis. This made me feel saintly, which made me want to cry because of all the bad things I had done in life.

'God, take care of this pigeon,' I said. 'Even though we took her to a vet who didn't like her and we thought she was a male pigeon, she still didn't bite me and give me a disease. Thank you.'

'That was beautiful. Should I make a little cross with sticks?'

'You believe in that stuff?'

'No. I could draw a yin-and-yang symbol in the dirt.'

'The only religion that's worse than one that started most wars in history is one that hasn't started any wars at all. Let's just set a rock on top so a cat won't dig her up.'

Which we did.

'Wait.' I pulled the framed photo of the woman out of my back pocket. 'Since this woman's husband had a great part in the murder, the pigeon gets this memento.'

I propped the photograph atop the rock. Evelyn squealed and she laughed and I laughed too. We were both laughing.

We backed up the hill beside the grave: a circle of dirt with a rock at the center and an ugly woman's photograph on top of that. We watched it. A jet passed overhead, wings lined with red lights. I wondered if the grass would stain my slacks. Evelyn lit a cigarette and, after a moment, I did as well. A blessing of cool air swept down upon us, washing away the harsh heat of the day. It was the time of day when, as a child, Tar, Nancy, Gary, and I would capture lightning bugs for our bug farms. The sounds around me seemed sharper. Every time Evelyn shifted I heard: fabric rubbing fabric, nicotine escaping from her lungs, her buttocks against the grass, blades bending then springing free again. The smoke from our mouths intermingled and disappeared.

'Not too many boys would do this,' she said.

'Boys, heh. I'm a "boy." '

'You're a good guy, to do this.'

I shrugged and I took a drag.

'Maybe I have a confession,' I said. 'If you weren't so stunning I probably wouldn't have come along.'

Evelyn folded her knees up to her chest and hid her mouth behind them. She stared forward, where a fountain was mostly hidden by trees.

'Maybe I didn't care about the pigeon as much as I pretended either,' Evelyn said.

The Meteor

'Where were you last week, Jamesie?' Lou asked.

'James was with his new girly-friend,' Bill said. 'He's spent every day this week with her. And she's nineteen.'

'Nineteen, whoa,' said Lou. 'Tell me about her.' He took the box of Christmas Trees from me. I noticed that Lou was missing part of his right pinkie finger. It was bandaged up.

'No,' I said. 'What happened to your finger?'

'These guys,' Lou said. 'Everyone takes life so seriously.'

'I'll tell you about her,' Bill said. 'She wears suede jackets with a lot of tassels, crimps her hair, and has an extra pussy on the back of her head.'

'AN EXTRA PUSSY ON THE BACK OF HER HEAD!?' Pennywhistle said, almost falling off the Alice in Wonderland mushroom.

'He's kidding,' I said.

'Oh,' Pennywhistle said. 'Man, if I saw a bitch with a vagina on the back of her head. I'd be like, "That's some weird fucking shit." I'd be like, "When did I fall on fucking Mars?" '

'He and the new chick are going away together this weekend,' Bill said.

'Really?' Lou said.

'I like her,' I said.

Lou and Pennywhistle and Bill looked at one another and began to laugh.

'Whoa,' Pennywhistle said. He darted around the mushroom statue, looking cautiously up into the sky.

'What are you doing, freak?' I said.

'Looking for the fucking meteor,' Pennywhistle said. 'You LIKE somebody. That's a definite sign of the coming fucking 'pocalypse.'

I smiled.

'He's liked people before,' Bill said.

'Like who?' Lou said.

'Me.'

'I don't like you,' I said. 'It's just easier getting toys with two people.'

'No, come on, dude, be serious. Admit that you like me.'

'I am serious. To me you're just there.'

Lou and Pennywhistle started laughing.

'No, seriously, James.'

'What am I supposed to do? Lie? I hate you.'

'Come on!'

Lou and Pennywhistle laughed harder and Bill got angrier and angrier.

'No, really, Bill. It's not that there's anything wrong with you. It's just that you don't have much of a personality.'

'He likes me,' Bill said to Lou. 'I know he does.'

A Bomb Between Us

One week Evelyn's aunt and uncle went vacationing to one of the many foreign countries. Normally, they lived on Long Island, and we invaded their home during their absence. Above the mantel was a rococo engraving that I despised.

Evelyn had gone to the store to buy swordfish. The liquor cabinet was dainty with four thin legs and lattice doors that flaunted its contents. I fixed myself an old-fashioned, in honor of Evelyn's uncle, who was the conservative type. After downing three more, I brushed my teeth. I brushed my tongue. I brushed my throat until it made me gag and the smell of whiskey was gone.

After the swordfish dinner, Evelyn pinched my whiskers with her long fingernails.

'Why don't you ever shave?' she asked. She was sitting on my lap. Her knees were draped over the arm of the couch.

'I did three days ago,' I told her.

'I shaved brand-new for you. Feel.' Evelyn put my hand on the inside of her knee, below her sundress, and I felt the smooth skin there. Other women had pulled this same trick, but it still gave me wood. My penis sprung up Evelyn's crack. She giggled, gloating, and kicked her legs a little.

Evelyn grabbed my pinkie in one hand and my thumb in the other.

'There's a place I want to show you, where I went a lot as a child,' she said.

'Is it far?'

'Down the street.'

'Let's go.'

'We can drive.'

My mouth played in the furrows between Evelyn's ribs. Her chest was like a boy's except for nipples pointing up straight. Her right nipple surfed the skin between my index finger and thumb. My legs were squashed against the car door, bent up awkwardly behind me. My calves and feet framed Evelyn's vision of the pond. That was where she and her brother would play Billy Goats Gruff when they were little on trips to visit her aunt and uncle.

'It's like being teenagers again,' Evelyn said.

'You're only nineteen.'

'Like in high school, then.'

A triangle of moonlight cut a pie slice in her face. The lower lids of her eyes protruded just a bit, mimicking happiness.

My elbow knocked open an ashtray on the back of the front seat. Evelyn's cold hands slid down the back of my pants. My belt was open and it jangled. She brought her hands up and unbuttoned my shirt. She traced her fingernail down the curve of my slight pectoral muscle.

'Tattoos. How many?'

'Two. I also have a tattoo of a penis on my penis, only larger. This one is cool, though. You like him?'

The lizard had fire-red eyes and an emotionless expression. He twisted around himself in a circle. Evelyn placed her lips on my chest and poked out just the tip of her tongue and ran it the length of the lizard's tail.

'I don't like tattoos,' she said.

I ran my fingers down the bumps of her spine, over her slab of hip, under her sundress, up her inner thigh. I cupped her crotch in the palm of my hand. The damp and secret heat beneath the cotton made my heart beat faster. She pushed the veiled hole against my hand. She lifted her leg, cramming her ankle beneath the headrest. I stretched the panties aside with my thumb. My finger wandered up the fleshy tent, into the moist, onto her clit. Evelyn opened her mouth. She made a face. It reminded me of the pleasure-pain expression women in Japanese pornography had. I kissed her hard to knock this image away. Evelyn's tongue wiggled inside my mouth. Her hand was around my cock.

'Inside,' she muttered.

She twisted my cock sideways. It wasn't pleasant. She sucked on my shoulder. The vinyl seat squeaked in our sweat as our bodies shifted. Evelyn squeezed, a mighty kung fu grip, and the helmet of my penis ballooned with blood. My breath quickened.

I said her name.

And then I said, 'I'd break my own sternum with a blackjack for you. I'd do anything.'

'James, James,' Evelyn panted; my new favorite song, a chart topper on the planet of my brain.

For a moment, we were still. The tip of my cock rested between the folds of her pussy. Warm.

'Let's keep it there forever,' I whispered. 'Just almost, but not quite. Everything up until now has been unique, right? But sex is essentially the same, essentially the same from cunt to cock to cock to cunt. All relationships are equalized after it. Let's stay like this, Evelyn. Let's refuse to be like the rest of the world.'

Evelyn pointed her chin toward me, smiled, and shook her head. Three drops of sweat lined her upper lip. She gripped my shaft. She thrust the sphere of her hips up, and she plunged me down deep inside her.

Our bodies smacked for some moments. Evelyn's eyes sprung tears. She was falling in love, you see.

'Don't do that,' I whispered.

'I'm happy.'

'Dependable isn't one of my primary character traits.'

Evelyn grabbed my head in both her hands. She placed my skull next to her own, pulling it close, and ground our heads together. It was a bit painful, and frustrating; no matter what effort she exerted the two orbs were not going to merge.

Let's not lie to ourselves, I thought. Let's not make connections where there aren't any. I kissed Evelyn's cheek.

I grabbed onto her buttocks as if they were everything I had ever lost. My penis bounced on the drum of her womb. And the guilt came attacking, as it did so often when my defenses were down.

I remembered the screaming, and the juices from the open skull sluicing down my hand.

The mass of memories twisted in their tunnel behind me. I gripped even more tightly to Evelyn's ass so I wouldn't be dragged back into it. The faces of the women I had fucked swirled behind me, each one gazing at me with disappointment and disgust. How they all hated me. Shut up! I thought.

I thrust twice and emptied myself into Evelyn Mako. For a minute there was no me. I was nothing.

Evelyn pulled my head even closer. She started to squeal.

Goddamn, I thought. I looked out the car window.

Gnats clustered around a street lamp. Evelyn kissed my collarbone. She buried her face in my neck. I petted her soft dark hair.

Love's so strange when you take it apart.

Her hair was in her eyes. Her eyes were shaped like almonds. Her heart was beating, beating, beating a million times.

'I have never fucked like that,' she said. 'I have never, I didn't know I could sense anyone so much. Do you feel it? I know you do.' Evelyn lay on the backseat and I lay on Evelyn. Her hip nestled in the sweaty hollow of mine. She touched her fingers to my brow. 'A bomb between us,' she said.

I slid from her body. I propped my ass on the edge of the seat. I had to hunch; the ceiling of the Volvo was low. The moonlight shone in the sweat on Evelyn Mako's tummy, a concave swoop and turn of light. I thought, So this is what the word *swoon* means, what she is doing to me now. It's tricky, she's got a way with it.

Her dark eyes waited for my voice. I turned toward the car window and wiped the steam away with my fingers, clearing a circle there for us. Outside there was a pond; there were tennis courts, a basketball hoop, a statue of a boy with the arm broken off, tulips lining a boscage, houses, and stars. It was dark. Some of the windows in some of the houses were lit. After all this time, I had fallen back into the suburbs.

'Yes,' I said. 'I feel that way too.' A Marlboro Red dangled from my mouth. I tilted my head to the side, caught a glimpse of myself in the rearview mirror. Evelyn didn't know about the four old-fashioneds. But I could see them in my face, pale with eyes withered and pink. I struck a match. I cupped my hands over the flame.

Evelyn wiped her vagina with my handkerchief.

'I'll wash this for you,' she said.

'Forget it. Toss it out. Jiz stains.'

Evelyn touched my back with damp fingers. I peered through the clear circle. A line of ducks waddled into the pond. A brown mamma duck led—one, two, three, four, five—five ducklings into the water.

'Little ducks,' I said. The smoke rose from my cigarette, the white contrasting the car's blue interior.

Evelyn's arm slipped around my neck. Her calves slid up over my stomach, her ankles crossing at my belly button. Her nipple grazed my shoulder blade. Her wet spot was at the base of my spine. Evelyn, a warm blanket on my back.

'I love you,' she whispered.

'That is similar to my feelings,' I told her.

She scraped her nose on the nape of my neck. She scraped her nose on the tip of my spine. Her mouth came down where her nose had last been, sending tremors up my back.

'James,' Evelyn said. I felt her mouth become a smile against my neck. Then she leaned sideways over the front seat, stretching her arm toward some tissues on the dash. I placed my hand on her thigh. I held her there, firmly.

'Stay where you are,' I whispered. 'I like you there. It's like having my heart wrapped around my body.'

'That would mean you don't have a heart inside yourself!'

Grass slanted in the wind outside. I had counted the ducklings wrong. There were six, not five of them. They floated on the pond in curling patterns.

A Little Cream

'Oh, Damia, you are an idiot,' I said. I dropped my head against my fists. 'Oh no, oh no. You could have confided your troubles to anyone in the world and you chose Phil Sandine?' I looked at Bill. 'Oh, God, we're fucked. We are super fucked.'

Damia was on the couch in her apartment. Her makeup was smeared from tears. Her lower lip buckled in. Bill was sitting beside her. He held her under his arm.

'I'm sorry,' she cried. 'He said if I ever had problems . . . I could come to him . . . he said he could be trusted.'

'*Goddammit!*' I hit the wall beside me a few times. When I noticed the plaster was caving in, I did it one more time and then stopped.

'I just was feeling a little bad about things . . . I was feeling down . . . there's no one to talk to about this.'

'What is Bill? Bill is no one?! *Are you calling Bill no one?!*' Damia sobbed.

I spoke calmly: 'You could have just said if you didn't want to do it, Damia. Bill, James, I don't want to do this— that's all you would have had to say.'

Bill gave me an incredulous look. Then he turned and looked at Damia. His facial expression completely changed.

'You know what would happen to us, babe?' he said

softly. 'Me and James might go to jail for a whole lot of years.'

'Uh-uh. Wrong. Not jail, prison. Jail is fun compared to that.' I paced back and forth in front of the couch. 'You and me are going to be fucked in the ass by some huge white power motherfucker, and his huge cock is going to be sticking AIDS in my ass, and you know what I'm going to be thinking? I'm going to be thinking, this is *Damia* sticking *her cock* in *my ass* throwing *her* AIDS into me!' I stopped and looked down at her. 'Damia, there's no way that that fucking Sandine is going to be able to bring this to the cops like he says without bringing you into it too. Do you know that? Do you know you're the first cause?'

'The first . . . cause?' Damia said.

'You've fucking unloaded forty thousand dollars' worth of pharmaceuticals out onto the street this year. You would have thought you would have picked up a book and read about your craft somewhere along the way. Since you're too vacuous to do that, let me tell you. The law has a very well planned out hierarchy to do with drug dealers. On the bottom rung are the lowly pushers, such as our good friends, Lou and Pennywhistle. They're a good catch for the cops, but the system will gladly trade two of them for two of their suppliers, intermediary suppliers as they may be. That's me and Bill. But the real Holy Grail, the person who the fucking cops will jump up and down and do a high-five for is the first cause, the place where all the drugs originate. Damia, you fucking stupid imbecile, that's you!'

Damia's mouth, silent at first, opened wider and wider. Her eyes spilled thick tears and then came the wail. I grabbed my jacket and walked toward the door.

Phil Sandine crossed the hospital parking lot, took his keys from his pocket, and began to unlock his Chevy Capris. I scraped my cigarette out on the brick wall and headed toward him.

'Come on,' I said.

'That the motherfucker?' Pennywhistle asked.

'Yes.'

'He probably never owned a toy in his life.'

'Unlikely.'

Phil Sandine was a bodybuilding pharmacist who worked with Damia. He had curly hair, short on the sides and long in back. He looked like a model for romance-novel covers. Pennywhistle crept up behind him and stuck the barrel of the .34 in his neck. I leaned against the car beside him, and breathed in deeply.

'That door open yet?' Penny said to him.

Sandine's face began to quiver. He turned pale. He nodded.

'Okay, let's get in,' I said.

Sandine got in the driver's seat and Pennywhistle got in the rear. I walked around and got in on the passenger side. When I did, Sandine turned and looked at me in a pitiful way. Perspiration had broken out along his forehead. His sculpted Roman face seemed about to cry. I felt sorry for him. So I punched him in the face as hard as I could. His head snapped to the side. I had caught his chin in a strange way and it hurt my hand.

'What are you doing, man?!' Pennywhistle said.

'I just got angry.' I cradled my fist in my palm.

Sandine turned to face me and he was blubbering. A splotch of blood widened on his lower lip.

'I'm sorry! I swear I won't tell anybody! I swear!'

'Fuck, you got a hard face.' I kneaded my knuckles; they were going to be bruised. 'Why the fuck are you doing this, Sandine?'

Pennywhistle shoved the gun into the back of his head.

Sandine lifted his hands up by his sides. He wept like a child.

'*Yeah, man, why are you doing this?*' Pennywhistle shouted. '*I ought to kill you for even thinking about it. You hear that, punk? If you think about saying anything to anyone, I mean even your fucking Aunt Mathilda, I'm taking you down! You don't know who you're fucking with, honky. Me and my Negro friends have a fucking army. This thing is too fucking big for you.*'

'Shut up, Pennywhistle,' I said.

Penny's mouth dropped open in awe.

'What?!'

'I said shut up. I don't want to do this.'

'That's exactly what you told me to say!'

'Well, I changed my mind.'

'Oh, fuck, man. First you come in and fucking smack him. Then you tell me to shut up. You know how long it took to memorize that shit?'

Sandine's hands were trembling at the sides of his head. I looked at him out of the corner of my eye.

'I'm sorry for punching you,' I mumbled.

'What do you want me to do?' he said.

'Put your hands down. Somebody's going to come by and see that, they're going to think it's peculiar.'

Sandine slowly lowered his hands. Pennywhistle slumped back into the seat.

'This is totally fucking unprofessional,' Pennywhistle said. 'You give me a script, man, tell me what to say. I'm talking two hours of memorization, man. I am pissed.'

'I'm gonna punch *you* in a second,' I said.

'Me? You're gonna punch *me*?' Pennywhistle started laughing. 'Oh, that's rich!'

I looked at Sandine, who had acquired a strange,

nervous smile. Here was my test. I was going to live honestly. How Evelyn would want it. I took the jump.

'Listen,' I said to him. 'We were gonna come in here and scare the shit out of you, tell you you were gonna get killed if you spoke to the cops about what you know. We had this little play to put on that was gonna make me look innocent, which I'm not. I don't want to do some stupid scam to you. I guess you didn't really do anything that wrong. I don't mind humiliating someone who deserves it, but now I'm going against my own moral code to save my ass. Sorry I hit you.'

'That's all right,' Sandine said.

'Ha!' Pennywhistle said.

I pointed to myself.

'I am not a bad guy. I try not to physically hurt people who don't deserve it. I believe in free trade, and I think that if someone wants to buy drugs they should be able to. I do not feel bad about stealing from the big guys, in this case, Saint Dominic's, owned by the Catholic Church, who tells starving countries they will go to Hell if they use birth control. That makes me angry so I do not feel guilty stealing from them. Granted, this may all be a rationalization.' I looked down into my lap. 'This girl—Evelyn, her name's Evelyn—has got me all wound up. She's even got me stopped drinking. Eight days now.' I looked at Sandine. 'You ever been in love?'

'You got to be fucking kidding me, James,' Pennywhistle said. 'Fucking *two hours* of memorization and now it's the fucking *Love Connection.*'

'Yeah,' Sandine said. 'I've been in love.'

'Yeah? What was she like?'

'She was . . . blond. She worked in human resources, here at the hospital.'

'Good body? She pump the iron?'

Sandine nodded.

'What was her name?'

'Michelle.'

'"Michelle" comes from "Michael," which means "Who is like the Lord?" in Hebrew. Did you know that?'

'No.'

'So every time you're saying her name you're asking a question.' I ran my finger along a silver line on the dashboard.

'You're not asking a question, moron,' Pennywhistle said, his arms crossed tightly against his chest. 'They mean "who is like the Lord," as in the prepositional phrase, "who is like the Lord." Michelle, who is like the Lord.'

'How do you know that?' I asked.

'My born name was Michael,' Pennywhistle muttered. 'Moron.'

'Oh,' I said. 'Anyway, I guess Evelyn's making me soft. Because I understand where you're coming from. You think we're blackmailing Damia into this thing. I can't lie to you and say I wouldn't be bummed out if she stopped. But it wouldn't be the end of the world. I can always figure out some other way to make a living.'

'You might feel better if you did,' Sandine said.

Pennywhistle poked Sandine in the back of his head with his finger.

'Don't you go teaming up with him now, shithead,' he said.

I looked from Sandine to Penny and an idea came to me.

'Hey, Phil. You ever consider scraping a little cream off the top?'

'A little cream?'

'You got sections that Damia doesn't?'

Sandine nodded.

'It'd be a lot of money. You just take a little from there every other week or so, get it to me.'

'Oh, man, I don't think so.'

'You don't have to do it for long, just a few times so my partners become satisfied you're not going to rat on them. You get cash straight up. You stop anytime you want. Be good to yourself, Phil. Get yourself a new car. This Capris ain't gonna cut it with the ladies anymore.'

I looked at him, raised my eyebrows, and pretended to be turning a steering wheel. I didn't know what the hell I was doing. I had thought I was being honest at first, but now it seemed like maybe this was the place my instincts had been working to get me all along.

Sandine was nodding slowly, starting to smile. Now we're in a whole new ballgame, I thought. Enough with the cheap robots. Now I could play with the big boys.

'This is the weirdest fucking approach I ever fucking seen in my whole fucking life,' Pennywhistle said.

Something Big and Magnetic

Raindrops struck Charlie's window. Metal backings propped up the action figures in the window display. Behind them stood us.

'Charlie. This is Evelyn. Wanted to see the shop.'

'Hi,' Evelyn said. She was wearing the plaid skirt I had bought for her; it looked a lot like the uniform Greta Holthausen wore at Saint Ambrose.

'Well, hello there, young lady.' Charlie stuck out a swollen paw. A white and yellow sore was between his thumb and finger. She put her tiny hand in his. Charlie shook it vigorously, her thin arm whipping up and down.

A kid was at the back of the store, looking at the display of Shogun Warriors. He was pounding his fist in a baseball glove.

'I love those fucking Japs, man, I love those fucking Japs!' he said, over and over.

Evelyn walked slowly around the front of the store, taking it all in. She put her purse on the counter. I walked to one of the glass cases. On two shelves were rocket ships and flying saucers and other rusty, celestial gems.

'Hey, Evelyn.' I motioned toward the case with my hand. 'Come here and see this.'

Evelyn came up to my side. She propped her hair behind

one of her ears. The ear was a little saucer.

'These here, these are some of the tin toys I can't afford yet,' I told her.

'You *woulda* been able to afford them, James,' Charlie said, 'had you used one of my payment plans instead of coming in here and buying them chintzy hundred-dollar robots every other day.'

Evelyn gazed at the space mobiles. One of the flying saucers had three wire stems coming out of it. At the end of each stem was an astronaut with a bubble helmet.

'Oh, wow,' she said. 'They're excellent.'

'Twenties through the fifties,' I told her.

Charlie rolled up next to us. A frayed pocket dangled from the back of his jeans. Charlie pointed to a rocket ship. A man poked his head out of the top, pointing a gun.

'That one there's a Marx Buck Rogers,' he said. 'It winds up. Works.'

'How much does something like that cost?' Evelyn said.

'Aw, hell, I'll give you a deal on that one. Five grand.'

'Holy cow!' Evelyn said. She rolled her head around as if she was dizzy.

'Ha-ha. Ain't kid's stuff.'

I was leaning in toward the case.

'Charlie's one of those evil guys who destroys history by superimposing a price tag over everything,' I said. 'That's the problem with the collection racket. They substitute the true value of things, their beauty, their memories, with a quantitative measure.'

I stared into the glass case. Buck Rogers's face was serious. He frowned. He had red lips. His cheeks were pink.

'Charlie's a Dire Wraith,' I said.

'Ha-ha,' Charlie said. 'What's a Dire Wraith? I think I have one of them in the back.' He waddled next to us as we walked to the other end of the shop.

'You know, James, I'm surprised to see you in here with a pretty girl.'

'Why's that?'

'I don't know. You and Bill coming in here together all the time I always figured you were a couple of homosexuals.'

'You're a charming man, Charlie.'

'Well, you got to be to keep a place in business these days. You wish that the quality of the place would be all that you needed, but that just ain't the truth. You gotta have a personality behind it is what I always say.'

Evelyn stopped next to one of the many glass cases. She placed her finger on the corner.

'These,' she whispered.

'Them is mechanical banks,' Charlie said. He pointed to one. The bank had so much paint chipped away that it was almost black. There was a pitcher and a batter and a catcher. They were on a playing field. 'That there is the Darktown Battery,' he said. 'You put a penny in the pitcher. You pull back his arm. *Whappo*, he throws it toward the batter. Batter swings. Misses! He turns his head to see where it went.' Charlie whipped back his own head to demonstrate. 'The penny's disappeared into the catcher's chest!' Charlie looked at Evelyn. Evelyn stared at the Darktown Battery. Wonderment played at her lips.

'Fuck computers,' Charlie said.

On my way across the room, I spotted a tiny yellow figure of a woman on the action-figure shelf.

'Shit,' I said. 'It's Ellen.'

'Who?' Evelyn said.

'Ellen. My neighbor Nancy had her as a kid. How much, Charlie?'

'Mmmm . . . twenty-one.'

'You're a fucking extortionist, man.'

'Ha-ha! That ain't true. I'm not even limber enough to touch my toes.'

'Not a CONtortionist, bitch, a— Just set her aside for me.'

'Okay. But her real name ain't Ellen. She was a camera-woman in the Fisher-Price TV van.'

'I know.'

I walked over to the robots, five shelves of robots.

'This is the place,' I said to Evelyn. 'Come here.'

'Hell, Eva don't want to see no damn robots,' Charlie said. He tramped to the back of the store. 'She probably wants to see some dolls. You want to see some dolls, honey? I got lots of dolls.'

'Leave her alone, you fat pusher,' I said.

'Ha-ha-ha-ha-ha,' Charlie said, loud and forced. His smile quickly dissipated. He walked to the back of the store and squeezed behind the counter. He wrote something in his book. Evelyn came to my side.

'You're mean to him,' she said.

'He's Satan.'

'He's jolly. He's a friendly man.'

'You've been had. He's the Lord of Darkness.'

Evelyn sucked in the corner of her mouth.

'He's no Lord of Darkness,' she said.

'Look at my robots, babe.'

At the top were Hap Hazard, Space Explorer, Noguchi, Tomura, Topolino, Mr. Atom, Irwin: Man from Mars, Laser 008, some Shogun Warriors, Flashy Jim, Robbie, Mr. Mercury, a Space Dog Tin, Moon Explorer, Interplanetary Explorer, Mister Atomic, and a wondrous Daiya. Below that were Mirror Man, Mighty 8, Hi Bounce, Billy Blastoff, Diamond Planet Robot, Changeman Robot, Chief Robot Man, Lantern Robot, Door Robot, Dino Robot, Thunder Robot, Atom Robot, Jupiter

Robot, Powder Robot, Tuliphead Robot, Nando, an Attacking Martian, another Thunder Robot, Musical Drummer, Tetsujin 28, and more on down the line to the tiny wind-ups, Shoguns, and Astro Boys on the bottom shelf. Evelyn's eyes were filled with a new light. She had the look. It didn't have anything to do with brains or taste or character. It had to do with how you saw history, the history of the world around you and the history of yourself. It had to do with a longing for innocence. Bill had the look. I guess I probably did. Now here was Evelyn. It was all over her.

Evelyn stopped halfway down the block from the toy store. She put her hand over her lips.

'Oh, shoot. I forgot my purse.'

A light rain was coming down. We were both hunched over, trying to stay dry without umbrellas.

'Let's go back and get it,' I said.

'I'll go get it. You wait here.'

'I'm fine, Evelyn. I can go.'

'No. Wait here.' Evelyn pivoted on her heel and turned. She kept her head down. Her fists moved back and forth at her sides as she moved toward the store. Her green dress clung to her legs in dark, wet strips. She almost ran into a tall woman. She looked up at her. 'Sorry!' she said. And she swung around her into Barlow's.

I followed slowly. I passed a liquor store on the way. I walked inside. I looked at all the bottles on the walls, smelled the dusty smell.

'I help you?' an old Chinese man at the counter said.

'No. No.'

I walked out.

I had been twelve days without a drink. I had been feeling good.

I looked in through Barlow's front window. Over the action-figure display I could see Evelyn and Charlie at the counter. Just as I thought, the purse was an excuse. She was buying something for me. Charlie placed an item in a small bag. He took her money. He said something. Evelyn smiled politely. Charlie said something else. This time Evelyn laughed.

It was when she laughed. Something big and magnetic pierced my gut. I grabbed my stomach. You could see Evelyn's mouth, open, teeth cutting loose like wild cattle. The big and magnetic thing went shuddering through me. People walking behind me might have thought I was having a seizure. The feeling bounded up my chest, flowing through the cavity behind my breastplate. I bent over, clutching myself. For a minute I thought something fucked up was going to happen, like the times I had heard of when the spirit leaves the body and floats up overhead looking down upon the world. But instead the shuddering radiated from the inside of my body to my skin and settled on me in a warm, wet way. It felt horrible and pleasant at the same time. It was something doomed. It was something holy.

I was responsible for her.

Tears spilled from the corners of my eyes. I covered my face with my hands and I couldn't help it, I began to sob in heaves. The sound of traffic and the solidity of the world reemerged around me.

After my tears subsided, Evelyn came out the front door.

'Hi,' she said. She held up her purse to show me she had it.

I nodded. I wiped my face. She looked at me.

'Are you all right?' she said.

'The rain. I hate the fucking rain. It's all polluted. It's in my eyes!'

*   *   *

Nobody was at the entrance of the C line on 22nd Street. The rain came down harder. Evelyn's hair was plastered to her face and neck. Little beads of water clung beneath her eyes.

'Your suit,' she said.

'It's seen worse. Vomit, for instance.'

Evelyn grabbed the sleeve of my jacket. She walked backward, pulling me away from the subway entrance.

'I have to go to work,' I told her.

'Come here.' She pulled me across the sidewalk, past a Doberman, a kid, a cop, an old lady with a walker. She pulled me beneath a bus stop. The rain was plinking on the roof. It sounded like a musical instrument from another planet.

'I'm already late,' I said. 'I'm an hour and a half late.'

'There's a surprise. Something I got for you.' She pushed her wet hair behind her ear. She wriggled her hand inside her purse, trying to locate it. 'Here. It's a Thanksgiving gift.'

'When's Thanksgiving?'

'Tomorrow, goof. That's why I'm going to Philadelphia tonight.'

Evelyn pulled out the little bag I had seen her get earlier. I didn't know what was inside of it. I reached into the bag. I felt plastic, warm from being in her purse. I pulled it out. It was Ellen, looking cute in her little yellow jumpsuit. I remembered the little figure, years before, the back of her skull cracked open, the gray of her brains beneath. And here she was again, good as new.

'Evelyn,' I whispered. Again, I felt the big and magnetic thing shuddering inside me. The tears came. I tried to push down the force within myself, but was unable.

'James?'

'Something weird is happening.' I began to cry and

couldn't stop. I was holding Ellen in front of me with one hand. I doubled over and staggered a couple steps forward. This must be something that happens when you quit drinking, I thought.

'What is it? Are you all right?' Evelyn sounded panicked.

I grabbed her hand. She let it lie in mine. I pulled it against my face. The skin over her knuckles was soft. I held her fingers against my mouth and wept into them.

'Evelyn,' I said, but it came out more like 'Ev-la' because my mouth was mushed.

Evelyn, looking worried, brought her hand to the side of my face. A crowd of people had gathered around the bus stop to watch. I pulled her against me. Her head fell against my chest. She squeezed me with her spindly arms. I cupped her chin in my hand, and lifted her face toward mine.

I set my lips on hers. They set there for a moment, the softest scraping in the world. Neither one of us moved. And then Evelyn began to kiss me. My tears stopped. My tongue was out; the tip of Evelyn's tongue touched it there, like two dogs meeting in the park. Her saliva was a minor deity.

I removed my face from hers.

'I love you, too,' I said. 'At your uncle's you said it to me, I never said it back. I never said it to anyone before when I wasn't drunk or naked.'

Evelyn giggled.

'Okay!' she said. She held out her hand, thumbs up. I smiled.

'I guess you got to go to class,' I said.

'And you have to go to work.'

'Yeah.'

'I'll see you when I get back, okay?' she said.

I sat down on the bench beneath the bus stop. I watched Evelyn go, until she was a dot, and then she was nothing. I'm never going to drink or do drugs or be unfaithful again.

'Happy Thanksgiving,' I whispered.

'Happy Thanksgiving,' came a deep voice behind me.

I jumped a bit in surprise. I turned around. There was a blind black man sitting there with a white cane, and *he had no eyes in his eye sockets*! They were just two gaping black holes with useless little eyelids hanging down, flapping back and forth. A little yelp escaped between my lips. I stared at him. He was smiling.

'I wasn't talking to you,' I said.

'That's all right, son. Happy Thanksgiving to you, anyway.'

'Yeah. Happy . . . you know . . . Jesus! What happened to your eyeballs?'

'A knife.'

'Fuck!'

How the Motorcycle Rider
Found Gratitude

The new wave of Fisher-Price characters had arms and legs. They were the same size as Star Wars people, but were released a couple years earlier. We focused our attention on four of them, who we called the Action Pack.

- **CHUBS!** Their leader. He was usually manned by Gary. Chubs wore red pants, a white shirt, and a blue tie. As his name insinuates, he was chubby. He also had gray hair and was visibly older than the other characters. Gary claimed that Chubs gained super strength when he became enraged. This was a good idea. But, as Gary did with many things, he took it to an extreme, and Chubs became almost invincible, disintegrating enemies with the force of his breath. We made him tone it down.

- **ELLEN!** Nancy's character wore a yellow pantsuit. She had a movie camera. The movie camera could of course make movies. But it could also freeze enemies in the statue position. This was important not only in winning battles, but also in making our enemies look ridiculous. For instance, you could strip them naked (the clothes couldn't really be

removed from the action figures, but with imagi-
nations in high gear, we would actually see this)
and stick marbles inside penises and butts. Most of
Ellen's time, though, was spent in torrid love
affairs with the other action figures.

- **OSCAR JR.!** Tar's character had a red beard and
  mustache. We called him either Oscar or Junior.
  He knew kung fu.
- **LARRY!** I controlled Larry. He wore a space suit.
  Over his head was a bubble, which he had to wear
  because he had a disease like John Travolta did in
  The Boy in the Plastic Bubble. Larry had little
  immunity to germs, and even a flu bug could kill
  him within days. Therefore, the bubble and the
  oxygen tank. Although witty, Larry wasn't athletic
  at all. He wasn't good at shooting. His driving was
  terrible. He was famously weak. But what he did
  have was a ray gun that could control the mind of
  anyone he shot.

Lord Tyco stood atop the hill, his robes twisting in the
wind. Tyco was a Satanist, a sadist, a sexual deviant, and
bald. His followers marched beside him on both sides.
Their zombie eyes stared at nothing, seeing nothing,
feeling less. They were there not by their own will, but
through the dark force of Tyco's mind control.

I knelt behind the air-conditioning unit. Nancy, Gary,
and Tar sidled the railroad ties beside me. Nancy was
panicked.

'They're coming down!' she said. She wore a faded T-
shirt that said FOXY LADY in glittery cursive.

At our knees stood the Action Pack. Chubs, Larry,
Ellen, and Oscar Jr. gazed up at the descending army: a
Godzilla, two giant GI Joes, the superhero Bulletman, a

giant Cher, at least ten humans, and more than thirty of the smaller Fisher-Price characters without arms or legs (robots). The massive Baby Alive loomed in the rear on hands and knees, growling.

Chubs fingered his cuff, as was his habit.

'Christ on a cross,' he whispered. 'I haven't seen anything this big since Troll dolls overtook Jersey. There's too damn many of them.'

'Christ on a cross,' said Oscar Jr.

The Pack had fought Lord Tyco before, and had barely walked away. But now there were twice as many of them. Dots of perspiration beaded on Oscar Jr.'s face. Ellen cupped her elbows in her hands and trembled. Larry's breath appeared and disappeared on the inside of his bubble helmet.

Tyco signaled for the army to halt. Guns and weapon belts jingled as they did.

'You down there!' Tyco shouted. 'Chubs!'

Chubs nodded.

'Behold my subjects!' Tyco sneered. 'Witness their magnitude, their enormous and huge power! With my dark underlings, there is no hope for you, Chubs, nor your loathsome Action Pack! Any attempt at retreat would be futile. We run faster, and some of us fly.' Tyco had a slight lisp. He curled his evil fingers beneath his chin. 'Not me, but some of the others. Like Bulletman and Cher.

'But I'll tell you boys something,' he said. 'We can strike a bargain. Hand over the girl, deliver us the one known as Ellen, and the rest of you may go as you please.'

Larry touched Chubs on the shoulder.

'What's that asshole saying?' Larry said. 'I can hardly hear through this damn bubble.'

'He wants Ellen.' Chubs's eyes were weary and red. His face was pale and haggard. He had seen too much death in his day, and Ellen was the closest thing he had to a daughter. Chubs couldn't have his own children, because the lightning bolt that had given him super strength had made him infertile.

'Ellen! Whoo! Big surprise!' Oscar Jr. said.

Lord Tyco had wanted to possess Ellen from the beginning. She was one of the few female action figures around. And most the others were either ugly or had chipped faces. Ellen's face was as smooth and pristine as the day it came out of the box.

Tyco was a sex fiend known on occasion to make it with stuffed animals.

Ellen tried to hold back the tears. But her face was an insufficient dam for the waves of sadness striking behind it, and she began to weep.

'I'll go with him,' she said. 'There's no choice. Even though he's evil and will fuck me whether I want to or not. To save you, I have to go now.'

'No!' Larry said. 'Ellen, stay with us!'

'Stay with Gus? Who's Gus?'

'No. *Stay with US.*'

'Oh. Sometimes it's hard to hear you in that bubble.'

She cried some more and said, 'But look at how many of them there are! If I don't go we'll all die anyway. There's no choice.'

'She has a point,' Chubs said. 'It's only logical.'

'Friendship isn't logical,' said Oscar Jr.

'Hm. That's a good point,' said Chubs. 'I guess you're right.'

Chubs turned. He faced Lord Tyco's dark battalion.

'Hey Tyco!' he yelled. 'I got an answer for you. Go fuck yourself!'

Tyco's eyes alit with the fires of Hell. Our defiance made him happy, giving him an excuse for his lust for blood. The Satanists came marching forward. Larry scanned them for the most powerful Satanist to shoot with his ray gun. (Lord Tyco himself was impervious to the ray gun; we never knew why.) It's got to be Baby Alive, Larry thought. He aimed . . . but the giant Bulletman came streaming down over the hill, flying toward him. He grabbed Larry's arm and threw him; Larry pinwheeled through the air. His neck bent as he slammed against the air-conditioning unit. He fell unconscious.

Lord Tyco's troops howled like demons as they attacked. Oscar Jr. dodged Baby Alive's massive pulpy arm, but was then besieged by twenty-seven of the tiny Fisher-Price characters. Cher grabbed Chubs in a headlock. Chubs threw her over his back. He jumped toward her, but she threw her foot into his gut. Ellen killed two of the humans. One of the GI Joe dolls crept up behind her.

I heard a clacking noise and a whimper. I looked to my side. Oscar Jr. lay face down in the grass before Tar's knees. The smaller, armless, legless Fisher-Price people were piled around him. Tar had a guy in each hand. He jammed one down on Oscar's back, then up, then down again, one after the other. Tar's nose was running. Tears rolled into his mouth. He sobbed, pulled in his lower lip. Tar looked up at me, the jolt of fear in his eyes.

'They killed him,' he cried. 'They killed him. Oscar Jr.'s dead.'

'Larry's unconscious,' I told him.

Chubs gritted his teeth. He picked Cher up over his head. He threw her back against two of the humans, knocking them down like bowling pins. Nancy shrieked. Tar and I turned. The GI Joe doll had pulled Ellen's movie camera from her grip, breaking her fingers in the process. He smashed the camera across her cheekbone, knocking her to the ground. Ellen futilely tried to protect herself, covering her head with her arms, and scurrying forward on her knees in the grass. But Joe brought the camera down onto the back of her head, once, and then again.

'*Ullllgh*,' Ellen said. Her skull cracked open. The gray of her brains dripped over the side. Bone and flesh were splattered around her. Her eyes washed over in death. GI Joe threw the camera over the Delgesses' fence. He ran toward Chubs, ready to murder again. It was too late. Bulletman had removed Chubs's head. He held it above him and wiggled his knees back and forth like a football player after making a touchdown.

'Jimmy,' Gary said. 'Tar's crying.'

'Oscar Jr. died,' I said.

'Didn't Tar do it?'

'No. Those little robots did it.'

'Oh. Chubs is dead too.'

'I saw. Sorry.'

'Maybe my dad will take me to get a new guy. Do you think he will, Jimmy?'

'I didn't know everyone was going to die,' I said. I knelt in the center of the dying battle, death and blood and cracked plastic all around me.

Larry slowly opened his eyes. His body was broken. He was paralyzed. He could only move one hand. He pressed it flat against the air-conditioning unit.

'God help me,' he whispered.

'Larry's waking up,' Gary said.

'I heard him,' I said.

'God please . . .' His voice was parched. 'My gun . . .'

His gun lay across the lawn. He was too weak to move toward it. Everything had so quickly fallen apart around him. He began to weep. I knelt by his side. Gary and Nancy came toward us, kneeling at his feet. Tar wandered toward us. Behind him the Satanists were celebrating, whistling and hooting. Two of them were playing catch with Chubs's head. Lord Tyco stared down the hill, where Ellen's body was face down.

'God, please,' Larry whispered. He was on the brink of unconsciousness. The tears pooled in his bubble helmet. 'My neck's broken. My spinal cord's severed. My spinal cord's severed, my friends are dead . . . Satanists are overtaking the earth.'

Lord Tyco sauntered down toward Ellen's dead body. He was grinning. He began undoing his pants. Larry spotted Tyco from the corner of his eye.

'No!' he wailed. 'You can't let my life end like this! *God, listen to me!*'

Gary, Tar, and I watched as the little man squirmed helplessly in the grass. We looked at each other, wondering what to do. Tar stared at me. He stood up. He bent down and picked up the gun. Tenderly he set the gun in Larry's palm.

'There,' Tar said. Tears of joy flowed from Larry's eyes. 'Thank you, God,' he whispered.

Lord Tyco yanked Ellen's pants down over her blue body. He hadn't unbuckled her belt, and her pants scraped away the skin on her hips. Tyco spread her legs. Tyco held his engorged cock in his hand, and worked it into Ellen's vagina.

Larry aimed his gun at a motorcycle rider on the hill. We didn't know him yet, but his name was Dan Occansion. The green ray jolted from Larry's gun up the hill, over the grass, and into Occansion's body.

Larry whispered: 'Kill Lord Tyco.'

Occansion revved up his motorcycle. Lord Tyco was ramming his hard-on up into Ellen's dead body, laughing hysterically. The motorcycle came speeding down the hill. It hit a ramp of mud. Tyco turned, and saw the motorcycle flying through the air in front of him.

'Eh?' he said.

The evil man barely had time to shake his head. 'No,' he started to say, denying the truth in front of him.

Splack. The front wheel hit Tyco's face. It knocked his head off his body, but not completely. Tyco's head dangled by a flap of skin and a few nerves behind him. Tyco stood up unsteadily. For a few dying moments he saw the world upside down behind him. He opened his mouth to scream. But no sound emerged; his vocal cords had been severed. A fountain of blood spouted up from his neck. He stretched his arms out to his sides, struggling to achieve balance, but this was impossible. His lifeless body fell back flat in the grass. And Tyco's soul went immediately to Hell.

Dan Occansion stopped his motorcycle beside Larry. He kicked his kickstand down with a flourish and got off. He knelt down next to the man who had released him from Tyco's Satanic mind spell. Thank you, Occansion wanted to say. But Larry's corpse had already entered into rigor mortis.

Gold Star for Robot Boy

Evelyn Mako's hands were so small I imagined I could fit her whole fist in my mouth. This was one of the things, along with Evelyn's dark eyes, that I considered while she was in Philadelphia for five days. God had attached a string of responsibility between her soul and my own. This was as real as science. I felt invulnerable. I felt idiotic and wonderful. It was love, and, as these things go, I was about to fuck it up.

The day before Evelyn returned I called my brother.

'Hey,' I said.

'What's up?' Tar said.

'I'm sorry about that day I wanted to push you over the balcony,' I told him.

'You wanted to push me over what balcony?'

'That's right, I didn't tell you. That day at Damia's I had an impulse to pick you up and throw you over the balcony. So, sorry for that.'

He paused a moment.

'That's okay,' he told me. 'I forgive you. Mom wants to know if you're going home for Christmas.'

'Maybe. And maybe I'll bring a certain lady friend.'

'Really?' Tar said. He chuckled.

We talked for a while longer. We discussed sex with our

respective girlfriends. I told him when I had entered Evelyn's vagina for the first time it had been as if there was a whirlpool of all the other women I had fucked behind me, and they were shaking their fists and screaming at me.

'Hm,' Tar said. He had never had that experience.

Tar told me he had recently had anal sex with Amy. It was his first ass fuck. I was surprised that Tar and Amy hadn't done this in their two years together. It was like owning a museum and never entering the room with the Picassos. Tar thought anal sex was too much hassle. Amy was embarrassed about it. Tar promised her he would keep it secret, and he was only telling me. He made me swear not to tell anyone, and I did.

Tar read me part of a poorly written story in the *New York Post* about a child dying of leukemia. We giggled over that for a while, and after a few minutes we got off the phone with a hasty good-bye. It was the best conversation we had had in four years.

I took a trip to Men's Wearhouse to buy a new suit. I paid eight hundred dollars for a Hugo Boss three-piece. It was the first new suit I had worn since I was a child. I checked out myself in the Men's Wearhouse mirror. I imagined that many women would want to fuck me, looking as slick as I did. I had thought old vintage suits were cooler, but maybe I was wrong. Now that I had money I was only going to buy new suits.

I went to the dentist. Twenty-five years and still cavity-free! I had my teeth whitened. I stole a book with photographs of mouth diseases.

I went home and rested. When Bill came home, we played Risk. Instead of flags, each country had a national mouth disease. Australia had macroglossia, France had periodontitis, and Kamchatka had Ludwig's angina. I looked at the clock. In exactly eighteen hours Evelyn would be back, and I'd be picking her up for our date.

New suit, clean teeth, and sober for eighteen days. I showed up at Evelyn's apartment in a stolen Dodge Lou had lent me. Evelyn wore a red dress, above the knee and pleated. We headed for dinner at Genet's, one of New York's most expensive restaurants. We parked valet. A man stepping out of a Mercedes gave me a look. He was wondering what a guy in a beat-up Dodge was doing at this expensive restaurant. But I hardly cared.

The interior of the restaurant was elegant, dark and candlelit, with black glass dividers so that every table had privacy.

'Evelyn, order anything you want.'

Her eyes smiled. They were dark and they shone at the same time. I told her I loved her. She said she loved me too. I told her I loved her more than I thought I could love someone. She said this was true of her as well. I said, 'You could be a burn victim, your face covered in pustules and scars, and still I'd love you.'

She blushed.

A Belgian waiter handed me the wine list. I didn't know anything about wines, so I asked for a bottle named for a bird that cost more than a hundred dollars.

'Don't do that. You don't need to do that,' Evelyn said. But I did it anyway.

At first I wasn't going to drink the wine with Evelyn, but, Jesus, it was more than a hundred dollars. It tasted luscious, and it went down like a kiss. It felt romantic to be drinking now, and safe. I made a toast to grace.

We conversed about her Thanksgiving. Evelyn's father was a softy. She had issues with her mother. I drank most of the bottle of wine, and then ordered a second. Evelyn made a comment about the velocity of my drinking.

'It's okay, it's okay,' I said to her. I told her I was just excited about her being back and I would slow down.

She told me about her brother who was having problems in his last year of high school. I told her about my brother who just had anal sex with his girlfriend. She was surprised to see that I was almost done with the second bottle.

'Hey, come on,' I said. 'This is a celebration here! You're back, everyone's happy! Chill out.'

After all, I had eighteen days to make up for. Nothing was as good as drinking after you hadn't had a drink for a while. I was slipping back into my skin.

I paid the check, and excused myself to urinate. On the way to the restroom my thigh tapped a middle-aged gentleman's table. The tap was so light that a regular person wouldn't have even noticed it. But the gentleman's wife couldn't keep her comments to herself, and she muttered something about me sobering up.

'What?' I said. 'You have something to say to me?'

'Excuse me?' the middle-aged gentleman said.

'She said something to me about sobering up. Maybe she ought to do us all a favor and sober up her face. No one over here's been able to finish their soup because she's so disgusting.'

The gentleman stared at me.

'You gave me a look when you pulled up in your Mercedes,' I told him. 'Because my Dodge isn't good enough for you.'

'I don't drive a Mercedes.'

'Well, it's a guy like you.'

'We're trying to eat dessert here. Please just move along.'

Evelyn came to my side. She was holding her purse in front of her like a squirrel holds a nut.

'Hey,' she said.

'Evelyn,' I said. 'Evelyn, I've got a problem with this guy right here. He wants to make me the brunt of all of his problems.'

'I didn't say anything to him,' he said.

The Belgian waiter approached us.

'Yes, sir,' he said. 'Can I be of some assistance here?'

'I want this guy out of here,' I told him. 'I just bought about five hundred dollars' worth of your various foods, and then I was going to the bathroom, and this man and his fat, ugly wife—'

'She's not my wife,' he explained to the waiter.

'Put out their legs and tried to trip me.'

'We did not!'

'Because I drive a Dodge, but'—I looked at the middle-aged gentleman—'let me tell you something, sir. You don't know who you're messing with. I have a friend who's a black guy who would love nothing more than to shoot you in your neck if I told him how you tried to trip me! His name is Pennywhistle, but his real name is Michael!'

The other diners were all staring at me. Evelyn shared their awe.

'*I* was the one he tried to trip!' I said to Evelyn.

'Let's go,' she pleaded.

'No,' I said. 'I'm going to do something ridiculous!' I grabbed the end of the middle-aged gentleman's table. 'I'm going to flip over this table and make a scene!'

'Sir, please!' the waiter said. 'I'm going to have to ask you to—'

'James, let's go.'

'You don't think I'll do it!' I said to Evelyn. 'BUT I CAN! I CAN DO IT! I'VE DONE WEIRDER!' I made a little thrust forward, as if I was going to toss the table. The woman at the table yipped. Everyone stepped back from the table. Now they knew who held the power. You can't fight a man who doesn't give a fuck.

I looked at Evelyn. She was starting to cry. Her eyes darted back and forth. She couldn't figure out what to do next. My throat clutched up on me. I let go of the table.

'See,' I said to her, sadly. 'You don't know me at all. This is the kind of stuff I do. Sometimes even stranger. And I don't even know why.'

'Call the police,' one waiter said to another. Evelyn started pushing me away.

'James, let's go.'

I pointed at the older gentleman.

'This guy is lucky. This guy is very lucky.' I stumbled through the restaurant. I bumped into a tray stand on the way, and I slapped it angrily to the floor. Evelyn followed me, her head down like a geisha.

Evelyn stood with a stony face as we waited for the valet to bring us the car. She didn't say a word. I took the keys from the valet. Evelyn held out her palm.

'What?' I said.

'Give me the keys. You're not driving.'

'All right,' I said. I handed them to her. 'You think I'm going to put up an argument, but I'm not. You can drive. I don't care. It's fine by me. I don't even like driving. I'd rather have someone drive me, which is like having a chauffeur.'

Evelyn drove. She didn't say anything. After a while, I heard sniffling. I stared at her. She was crying.

'I don't know where that came from,' she said. 'Throwing over the table. Yelling. Calling that woman fat. They didn't do anything.'

'That's who I am,' I whispered. 'This is what I do.'

Evelyn cried harder.

She told me that she would drop me off with the car, and she would take the subway home. I asked her what about me going home with her and having sex with her in her bed. Evelyn said that she didn't want to sleep with me at this time. This made me angry. I noticed a Club on the floor mat and I picked it up and smashed open the passenger side window. The glass shattered into thousands of little pebbles. Evelyn screamed. The car swerved, squealing.

'WHAT ARE YOU DOING?!' she yelled.

I had little pieces of glass stuck to my face.

'This is safety glass,' I said. 'It doesn't hurt at all.'

'YOU'RE ACTING LIKE A MANIAC!' she said.

'You don't know anything about me! You don't know anything about my life!'

'What are you talking about? Why are you doing this? I couldn't wait to see you!'

'You don't care about me! You don't know who I am, you're so fucking stuck in your own stupid little princess fucking world! Fucking Long Island fucking rococo engravings! Why do you people continue to think you know what it's like to be me!?'

'James, I'm going to drop you off. I'll talk to you tomorrow. When you're sober.'

There was silence for a little while. We drove. The lights and colors of the city blurred around me. I had the feeling I was watching myself. I was reading lines that meant nothing to me, that meant nothing to anyone at all. But they were the lines, and I had to say them. The words flashed across the front of my brain like a TelePrompTer. If I stopped reading them I'd fall back into something dark and wrong that I didn't want to think about. I don't live my life, I thought. Life lives me.

'No,' I said.

'What?'

'I've been meaning to tell you. I don't want to see you anymore.'

'What are you—'

'And it's not because I'm drunk, goddammit! It's not because I'm drunk. I just had to drink to summon up the courage, Evelyn. I find you to be the kind of thing that I don't ever want to talk to.'

Evelyn's mouth was open slightly, the black hole between her lips in the shape of a butterfly's cocoon or a snow pea. She was stunned.

'I'm sorry, but that's the way it is,' I said, and I shrugged my shoulders.

Evelyn didn't cry or speak for the rest of the ride. She dropped me off on the sidewalk in front of my building. I got out of the door.

'I'll park your car down the street,' she said.

I kicked the side of the car three times as hard as I could.

'I don't want to speak to you again!' Evelyn shouted.

She pulled away from the curb. I stood on the corner. I watched her go. What I had just done started to sink in. These things are never easy, and you take them to your grave.

Mr. Experience

The Bauers' Winnebago was parked in one of many lots. Beside each lot was a white wooden column with hand-painted red numbers, and a metal column with electrical outlets. The campground was blanketed with unmowed grass, a spattering of trees, and a wood along the edges. I sat in the gravel and leaned against the side of the Winnebago. I waited for Gary to get finished in the bathroom. I folded my hands between my knees. I looked at the sky, which I thought was stunning. Chain links of white clouds inched over solid baby blue.

Urinating always took Gary a long time, because of his nerve problems. Adding at least five minutes to his bathroom time was his fondness of washing hands. I was used to waiting. I scooped up a handful of gravel from the lot. I separated the gravel into three piles: the gray pile, the brown pile, and the light brown pile. I threw the brown rocks at the column with the electrical outlet. I pretended the column was a Nazi. A deep scar ran down his face and neck.

Gary's father swung open the door of the mobile home. He was a bear of a man, muscles swollen from a lifetime of roofing. He came down the metal stairs, rocking the mobile home against my back as he did.

'Hi there, Jimmy.'

'I'm trying to hit the pole with these rocks,' I said.

'Very challenging.' Mr. Bauer's head was bald. It shined in the sun. There was a thin ring of gray hair around it. My mother said he had the most beautiful blue eyes she had ever seen. His movements were graceful. He had fought the Nazis in the Navy, and I thought that he must have acquired his peaceful nature through combating evil. Gary was proud of the fact that his father had fought the Nazis. It was something he held over me, since my father hadn't been lucky enough to have even been born.

'Did you kill any of them?' I had once asked Mr. Bauer. He was sitting in an orange-and-brown chair.

'No,' he said. 'I was on a boat, Jimmy. We didn't see too many people getting killed, not up close at least.'

'Too bad. It'd be cool to see a Nazi blowing up up close.'

Mr. Bauer had laughed. He called me a sadist. I smiled. I thought that was like calling me a cheeky rascal.

Now Mr. Bauer stretched some cord extensions from the Winnebago to the electrical outlets.

'Where's Gary?' Mr. Bauer asked me.

'I see his big head through the window, coming out of the bathroom.'

Gary jumped out of the mobile home and onto the first step, then the second, then down to the ground. He was wearing a bow tie. 'Bow ties,' he had once said, 'are debonair.' Gary's parents had tried to dissuade him from wearing the tie, but he had seen Cary Grant wear one in a movie. Cary Grant was his hero. There was a short phase in the fourth grade where he insisted his name was Cary Bauer. Gary promised his parents he would stop talking like Cary Grant all the time if they let him wear the bow tie. They said okay without being happy about it. I didn't like it either. But it was less embarrassing than being with someone who talked like Cary Grant.

'I'm done going to the bathroom,' Gary announced.

He and I moved to the corner of the Winnebago, out of his father's earshot. Mr. Bauer was hooking up a vacuum cleaner-like tube from the mobile home to a hole in the ground.

'See that tube?'

'Hell, yes,' I said.

'That's where all the shit goes.'

'Ha-ha,' we both yelped.

'Let's put a bucket under there tonight and collect some and throw it on somebody's head,' I said.

'Ha-ha,' we yelped.

I have had a good sense of humor as long as I can remember.

A sign half covered the sun at the front of the campground. The sign was dark, making it difficult to read FRIENDLY VILLAGE. The sunlight sparkled on the metal parts of the tens of mobile homes around us. The boxy kind. The rounded kind. The kind that connect to the back of a car. And the truck kind. The Bauer family owned the boxy kind, the best of all types. They belonged to a camping adventures club. Often they took me on their camping adventures with them. Gary and I slept in a loft bed squished in over the driver's seat. This was like sleeping over, only it took a whole weekend. Also, if Gary and I got into a fistfight the Bauers couldn't just send me home. The worst thing about the camping adventures is that they would barbecue the hamburgers well done. My mother made them rare. The best thing was that Gary and I could meet chicks from all over the state. Sometimes we would talk to them. Since we had turned twelve, the desire to talk to girls was strong. But where we wanted the talking to lead, even though the facts of sex were known, was amorphous.

Now Gary and I sat in the gravel throwing rocks at the post. Mr. Bauer crouched next to the shit tube. He unwrapped a Tootsie Pop and put it in his mouth. He stared at the road ahead of us.

'Your sister's hanging out with that little slut girl again, that Pinkerton girl,' Mr. Bauer said.

'Ha-ha,' Gary and I said. Gary's head fell back.

'Slut!' he rasped. It was a word we knew from *Penthouse*. *Penthouse* had outlined sex for me. It was a map. The first issue Gary and I found belonged to his father. It was below a mat in the bathroom cabinet. I was very surprised to find out that women had hair on their vaginas; I had only seen Nancy Zoomis's and some of the other girls' in the neighborhood. When I heard my parents breathing heavy late at night I imagined *Penthouse Forum* behind their door. Had Mrs. Delgesse from next door come over for a cup of sugar and ended up in a ménage à trois? Was my mother covered in honey? Were there handcuffs? Dildos? Camcorders? Ben wa balls? I covered my ears. I shut my eyes. In my formative years, television was my mother. But *Penthouse* was an aunt who often took me to the zoo.

'Gary, watch your mouth,' his father said.

'Dad the famous hypocrite,' Gary said.

The girls walked along the main path. Gary's sister Laura was fifteen. She was bony and awkward. I often wondered what she looked like naked. That little slut the Pinkerton girl's hair was red and frizzy. She was tall, her hips were wide, her shirt was yellow terry cloth, and her breasts were enormous. She swiveled one hand as she talked. Gary, his father, and I watched the girls pass. The Pinkerton girl stuck her breasts out, doing an imitation of somebody. Laura was laughing hysterically. They passed in front of a swimming pool, kids splashing behind them.

An old man sunbathing across from us lifted the brim of his baseball cap to look at the girls. They giggled onward.

'Let's go to the lake and capture some frogs,' Gary said. 'Whoever gets the biggest one is winner.'

'Be careful, boys,' Mr. Bauer said.

Later, near the pond, two dragonflies landed on my arm. They were attached.

'They're fucking!' Gary said.

'Ha-ha,' we both said. We smashed them.

I caught a frog under some brush on the edge of the water. It was enormous. I needed both hands to lift it. This frog was missing a leg.

Laura said, 'James, this is Angie. Angie, this is James.' This was something an adult would say. Laura lately had been pretending to be an adult.

The slut was sitting on the picnic table. Her tight jeans dug trenches in her wide hips. She had many freckles. A cigarette was between her fingers, pointing upward.

'Hey,' she said. Each of her breasts was the size of the frog missing the leg.

'Hey.' My hands were in my pockets. I was moping. No chicks my age were on the camping adventure. Laura lit a cigarette for herself, which was a surprise. Gary and I had never seen this before.

'You better not tell Mom and Dad,' Laura warned.

Gary shrugged. 'Who knows?' he said. 'I might go crazy, lose control of my mouth, something might slip out.'

'Keep your trap shut,' Laura said. 'You too, James. You better not say anything.'

'Let me have one of those smokes,' I said.

'How old are you, kid?' Angie said.

'Old enough, kid.'

'You've never smoked before.'

I pointed at her.

'Two words: fuck and you,' I said. 'I have often smoked.'

She sneered a little.

'Fuck you,' she said.

'Hey, fuck you,' I said.

Et cetera.

Finally she passed me the cigarettes. I had stood my ground. As I sucked in on the cigarette my face turned red. But I didn't cough. Still the girls laughed at me.

Mr. and Mrs. Bauer had gone to a square dance in a barn on the edge of the campsite. They wore white cowboy hats. Laura and Gary and Angie and I sat around the kitchen table in the mobile home. It was like a booth in a restaurant with hard plastic seats. The window next to us was open and the night air swept in around us through the screen. Each of us held a beer. Boys had bought it for Angie.

'I have friends in high places,' she said.

'That must mean your friends are high,' Gary said.

Beer tasted almost as bad as licorice. But the point was to swallow as much as possible.

'You never drank beer before,' Angie sneered.

'I drank more beer than your whole family put together,' I said, which was a lie. I had seldom drunk beer. But for years I had pillaged the liquor in my parents' cabinet when they would go out for the night. Intoxication and I became acquainted at the age of nine and were slowly growing closer.

I would catch Angie's muddy green eyes staring at me. Her nose was wide. She had a mole on her neck.

The four of us blew smoke out the screen window. Some blew back in. Gary became afraid that his parents would smell it so he went to the bathroom and washed his hands

five times. When he came back his bow tie dangled, half
unclipped.

A green bug was loping up the outside of the screen
window. I slapped my hand against the screen and it flew
away with wings of a surprising size.

A black ashtray was in the center of the table. In gold it
depicted a man fishing. Angie Pinkerton tapped her cigarette ash in with great fluidity. I mimicked the way she did
it, but added a masculine edge. Laura was pale from the
beer and nicotine. Gary kept looking outside to see if his
parents were coming back. Angie told a story about how
some guy named Bran Eckert felt her up. Even though
Brian Eckert was nineteen, he kept grasping at her underarm instead of her tit like he was supposed to.

'Nobody'd want to feel you up,' I said.

'I'm not going to slap you upside the head, because I
used to be a little shit just like you,' Angie said.

'Ha— "Slap you upside the head"—nigger talk!' I said.

'My friend Sheila's black and she doesn't talk anything
like that. She talks white.'

'Excuse me,' I said. I looked at Gary. 'Nigger talk.'

Gary had his hand over his mouth and was laughing
every time I used the word *nigger*.

'Jimmy, if you say that word again I'm going to tell your
mom,' Laura said.

'That'd be a bad idea on your part,' I said, 'because if
you did I'd take a garden spade to your cat's neck.'

Everyone looked at me for a moment.

'No, you wouldn't,' Gary whispered.

'Probably not,' I said. 'But why doesn't Laura test me
out by telling my parents I said "nigger"?'

'HA!' Gary said. He looked at his sister. 'Go ahead,
Laura! Test him out! Tell his parents he said "nigger"!'

Gary and I laughed, reveling in our momentary power over the older girls.

Angie shook her head in disgust.

'You are the most obnoxious little kid in the whole world,' she said.

'Not as obnoxious as me!' Gary said. He stuck his butt out to the side and made a farting sound.

We started to play truth or dare.

I dared Gary to stick a Starburst candy up his ass for two minutes, and then eat it. Which he did.

Gary asked me, truth, how many girls I fucked. I said twenty-seven. Gary found this hilarious, but the girls disputed its fact.

'You wouldn't know how to fuck anybody,' Angie said.

I slammed my beer can on the table.

'I do too! That's how come the twenty-seven chicks are lining up around the block!'

Angie brought her drunk head in close to me.

'How do you do it, then?'

'By sticking the dick in the pussy! And rubbing the clit!'

Angie dropped back in her seat.

'Shit, you've never gotten laid before,' she said.

'Twenty-fucking-seven,' I said. But in truth I had never even masturbated.

Laura dared Angie to put a lit cigarette in her mouth, which Angie did. It was obviously a trick she already knew how to do, and I argued that a TRICK is not a DARE.

'You're really annoying, you know that?' Angie said to me.

'Maybe I want to be,' I said.

'Maybe I want to be too,' Gary said. We high-fived.

'My parents say Jimmy's ego is huge,' Laura said.

'They do not!' Gary said.

'They do, you know they do, Gary.'

Angie dared Laura to show everyone her pussy, which she refused to do. So she showed us part of her butt instead.

I made Gary admit to the humiliating fact that he had had sex with eighty-nine women.

Gary dared Angie to make out with me.

'Gross!' I said. 'That's like making out with one of those rotten, sunken-in Halloween jack-o'-lanterns someone leaves out on their porch until November.'

'Shut up!'

'You shut up!'

Angie's head came at me with an open mouth and a tongue protruding from it. I had to react in some way. I chose to stay still. The mouth clinked against my mouth. The tongue drove between my teeth. Once inside, it slammed back and forth as if it was trying to crash through the flesh of my cheeks. I probed the tongue a little with mine. It was my first French kiss. We finished.

'You suck at that,' I said.

'Shut up.'

Shortly after that, Angie whispered something in Laura's ear. Laura and Gary said they needed to go outside to check on something. I went to the bathroom and pissed for what seemed like three hours.

That year I had spent a great amount of time inspecting my penis, for recently my penis had become my father's. It had gotten much larger. It had grown a shade darker. Little hairs were beginning to sprout out of it. On my father this penis looked normal, but on me it seemed a bit mutated, since the rest of me was so small. I walked back and forth in front of the mirror holding it in front of me like a little pet.

*   *   *

When I came out of the bathroom I discovered Laura and Gary had locked the front door. I turned toward Angie. She was leaning back against the table. The beer cans had been knocked aside.

'Go ahead, Mr. Experience,' she said. 'Go ahead, do it.' She was sneering. Her eyelids were at half-mast. She pushed up her hips. The outline of her vagina was obvious against her jeans. It had bulk. This took me aback. A vagina is something there, like a penis. It's not something absent. Up the middle went a groove.

'Now you can do everything you say you do, Jimmy!' Laura yelled through the door.

'Yeah!' Gary the turncoat yelled. He was giggling.

'Let me out!' I screamed. I looked over and saw Gary's dark hair bouncing up and down in the window frame as he jumped, trying to peek inside. Then I looked back at Angie Pinkerton. Drunkenness had stranded me here.

'All talk, no action,' she mumbled.

'I'm action, but you're ugly!' I said.

'Faggot!' she said.

I turned back toward the door. 'If you don't let me out of here I'm going to break down the door! I'll tell your parents you locked me in here and I got claustrophobia!'

The door quickly started unlocking.

I stepped drunkenly out onto the mobile home step.

'What'd you do in there, Jimmy?' Gary said.

I threw my arms triumphantly into the air.

'I fucked her!' I said.

Angie yelled behind me: 'You did not! You did not!'

'He did too!' Gary said. 'Jimmy fucked her!'

Gary and I threw our arms into the air. We whooped; we hollered; we hugged, rejoicing in my conquest.

Keystone Bacchanalia

Bill and I needed to get away from the noises of the city. I didn't want to see buildings or street signs or park monuments that reminded me of Evelyn. We also needed to dry out. Our health had gotten bad. I had been on a binge since I had mysteriously broken up with Evelyn. She wouldn't return my calls. I couldn't stop coughing and Bill couldn't lift a cup of coffee without shaking and making it splash. We told Saint Dominic's we were taking five days off and headed for Bill's father's and stepmother's place on Long Island. We left our pills and alcohol in the apartment. On Long Island we'd be able to clean our brains of all the gunk and get our bodies back up to par.

By the time we got off the bus Bill was sweating and scratching under his arms.

'I can't stand it,' he said.

'It's psychological,' I told him.

He didn't think much of this opinion.

We arrived at his folks' place. I met Bill's stepmother, who had large breasts. Bill excused himself to the other room and he rang up an old acquaintance. The old acquaintance got him a half-ounce of crystal meth. The drug was in powder form. Bill used a straw cut in half to snort it.

'You're on your own, man,' I said. 'I came here to clean up.'

I walked around and looked at some interesting things in the house, family pictures on the wall, a picture of Bill with a baby elephant, cooking utensils, et cetera. Then I came back and snorted a line. I kept the straw in my nose, tilted my head back, and watched the ceiling fan spin on low.

'Fuck,' I muttered.

'There's no way of getting away from the noises of the city when the noises of the city are in your head,' Bill said.

We went to a dance club named Hawaiian Retreat. There we met two girls named Karen and Gerry, who were students at Long Island Community College. Karen was the prettier of the two, with long brown hair, a concave belly, and lips that appeared to be injected with collagen but were in fact real. Gerry had dyed red hair and bright green eyes. Her head looked like Christmas. They were twenty years old, aggressive, and tripping on acid.

The four of us walked out to the parking lot. Bill and I couldn't remember where we parked his stepmother's Honda Civic.

'Shit!' I said. 'Dammit.'

We decided it could wait until morning. The girls drove us in an Impala back to the house of Karen's brother. Karen was watching her brother's dog while he was out of town. The dog had run away, but she wasn't worried.

'Oh God, no,' she said (she had a raspy voice). 'Dogs have such a good sense of direction, you wouldn't fucking believe. On TV I saw what was essentially a dog, you know, and his family moved and left him in the abandoned house. *The dog followed their trail across the country*. Six months later they opened the door and—

boom!—there's the fucking dog. Besides a missing leg and no fur, he was in perfect shape. Wagging his tail. Hello, family. I don't know how he lived or ate. Maybe he ate squirrels and chipmunks, crippled birds.'

'Why would a dog want to be with the people that deserted him in the first place?' Bill said.

'For the same reason you collect toys,' I said.

'Holy shit, I can see through my fucking hand!' Gerry said. She was the one driving.

At the mildly extravagant home of Karen's brother, we all four squeezed onto a couch. I reached in Bill's pocket and pulled out the bindle of crystal.

'Oog!' Bill said. I had accidentally tickled him.

A glass table was in front of the couch. On the table was a collection of Baccarat crystal figures: dogs, a koala, a mother holding a child, some tulips, an elephant, a bear and fish, a fish by itself, grapes, a water tower, an ashtray, a kitten, a porpoise jumping over surf, a—*Oh my God, what's that?* I thought. *It was a Baccarat figure of a child cut in half lying next to a chain saw.*

'Karen, what *is that*?!'

'Two baby little piggies and a chicken.'

'Oh.'

We pushed aside the Baccarat figures and snorted crystal on the glass table.

I made out with Karen a little bit. Her aggression was refreshing. She grabbed my cock through the front of my pants.

'You're so fucking beautiful,' she said. 'Your suit. Your fucking suit.'

She rolled her hand down my back and pressed her finger down hard where my asshole was.

'Whoo!' I said.

'You like that, huh? You want me to fuck your asshole?'

'Uh, what exactly do you mean?'

'I saw you in the club. I love your fucking eyes. You've got the most beautiful eyes.'

I turned my head away from her face and began coughing phlegm into my hand. I looked at it, then wiped it on the side of the couch. Karen grazed her knuckles on the side of my face.

'You're like an angel,' she said.

Karen and I messed around a while longer. Her hand was in my pants, jerking me off. I had pulled her pants down a bit and was probing her with two fingers.

'You want me to be your little slut!?' she said, gripping my fingers inside her vagina and then releasing them. This was a pretty amazing trick and I was getting damn turned on. Then I started coughing again. This time it wouldn't stop. I ran into the bathroom and vomited a great amount of green and yellow phlegm spotted with specks of my own blood. I flushed it.

When I came back, Bill had snuck himself in there for the better one. He was rolling around on the floor with Karen. The bastard!

I sat down on the couch next to Gerry, who was weeping.

'What's the matter?' I said.

She pointed to Bill on the floor.

'I love him,' she said. 'He looks like Brad Pitt.'

I smoked a cigarette, and then Gerry and I began making out. I kept forgetting whom I was kissing. Evelyn? Karen? I would have to open my eyes to see who it was, and this was disappointing. Some kid named Gerry. We didn't know what Gerry was short for. Our tongues were a tube attached from mouth to mouth. We flapped around on the couch. She wore a latex dress, and it was pushed up around her waist. I will never know goodness again.

Bill was lying on his back on the ground. His pants and boxer shorts were down around his ankles. He had hilarious white legs sprinkled with black hair. Karen's shirt was off. Her breasts were only tiny sunken nipples. She was leaning over Bill's semi-erect cock. She flipped it back and forth, onto his stomach, then down on his thigh. Bill had quite a huge schlong. Then Karen pretended that Bill's dick was a joystick to a video game. She shifted it back and forth, making crashing and laser sounds.

Bill looked over at me. He shrugged and smiled.

'Whatever,' he said. His nose was bloody. Streams ran down from both his nostrils. Drops spotted the carpet around his head. He set his hand on a half-full bottle of Jack Daniel's beside him.

'I'm not even drunk,' he said.

'Where's your bottle of vodka?'

'I drank it. I'm not even drunk.'

'You drank a bottle of vodka and all that whiskey too?'

'And I'm not even drunk.'

Bill poked Karen's cheek with his finger. Karen looked up and saw all the blood on his face. She started laughing.

'Holy shit!' she said. 'Check this out! Holy fucking shit!'

She turned to me while laughing, pointing at Bill's face with one hand while holding his cock with the other. I pointed at her.

'Heh-heh,' I said. Coughed. 'Pretty funny.'

'It's like Night of the fucking Bloody Beasts on your face there, Bill,' she said. She shook her head, unable to get over it. Then she leaned down farther and took his cock into her mouth. Bobbing followed.

I turned back toward Gerry. She was bored with me and was lying on her stomach on the couch. I got to playing with the tip of my vodka bottle between her legs, along the crotch of her panties. Gerry started thrusting her hips back against it. She was murmuring the Dr Pepper theme song. Eventually, I pulled aside the panties and stuck a finger inside her pussy. She liked that, so I took my finger out and stuck the stem of the bottle in.

'Uhl,' she whispered.

I pushed it in deeper.

Gerry screamed. She grappled upward, away from me, pulling herself to standing on the couch. The vodka bottle stayed in her. It dangled there between her legs.

'*Wow*,' I said.

'You fuck fucker!' she yelled.

'What?'

'You stuck a bottle up my twat!'

'A sex toy,' I said.

Gerry yanked out the bottle. She whacked it across my head. I buckled backward and threw my arms over my skull for protection. She sprung off the couch and hit me again. The bottle cracked but it didn't break.

'Pervert!' she screamed.

I was curled up in a ball on the floor. She walked into the other room with the bottle and went to sleep. I touched the wound. It wasn't bleeding. I could see through glass doors out into the backyard, where there was a swimming pool. My hard-on propped my pants out in front of me. I decided I could go out beside the swimming pool and jerk off.

Bill and Karen were now fucking. His white ass pumped into her. His face was red. It clenched. Drops of Bill's blood were on Karen's face. She was spitting out obscenities about things to do to her. She saw me as I wandered by.

'Where are you going, dude?' she said.

'Out.'

The one-quarter-full bottle of Jack was on the floor beside them. I went to grab it and fell down next to it. I lay down on my side. I pulled the bottle into my lap, against my erection. Bill was sweating and gritting his teeth as he fucked Karen. He appeared to be in pain, which served the prick right, considering he backstabbed me by stealing her. He opened his eyes. His face looked bitter and sad.

'I'm so screwed up,' he said.

Karen was looking straight over at me.

'Your eyes are really fucking beautiful, man,' she said. 'They're like something out of outer space. Damn, they're fucking blue.' She reached out from under Bill's propped arm and grabbed the eyelashes over my right eye in her fingers. She pulled on it a little, so that my eyelid pulled away from the eyeball below.

'What are you doing?' I said.

'Come here,' she said.

Karen pulled my face toward her. She craned her neck to kiss me. She wiggled her tongue between my lips and into my mouth. I kissed her in return. We lay there kissing for a few moments while Bill fucked her.

'James,' Bill whispered.

I removed my mouth from Karen's and looked up at him.

'You're kind of freaking me out,' he said. 'Stop that.'

'Oh, shit. Sorry, Bill. I'm not thinking. Damn. Shit. Heh-heh. I must be a fag.'

'No, no. It's just weird.'

'Yeah.'

'I've always been sort of conservative, you know, in sex.'

'Well, you know, you got to try different things sometimes, Bill. Right, Karen?'

'Fuck me like a slut,' she said.

'I'm all for that,' Bill muttered. 'But the two-on-one
thing, it's— Dude, you're making me lose my concentra-
tion. I can't have a conversation now.'

Karen was pinching my lower lip, a bit too hard. It hurt.
She gazed into my eyes as she thrust her hips up against
Bill.

'Fuck me,' she said.

Even though my head was on its side I poured some of
the whiskey into my mouth. Most spilled out onto the
carpet. I saw the splotch widen on the carpet, soaking it,
until it covered the area around Bill's knee. Bill's knee was
bleeding also, from the rug burn. He thrust himself back
and forth. Karen ran her finger over the top of my lower
set of teeth. She moaned.

Bill's penis came flapping out of Karen's body. It was
only partly erect. Bill nervously scrambled for it with his
hand. He stuffed it back up into the girl's body. He turned
toward me. He shook his head.

'I keep trying and trying and trying,' he said. He looked
like he was about to cry. 'But I can't.' He started pushing
again. Karen raised her eyebrows and looked at me.

'Did he put it back inside?' she asked me.

'Yeah,' I said.

'Shit. I can hardly tell. Let's go! Err!'

She began slamming her pelvis up against him again,
but continued looking at me. She swung her hand down
suddenly, grabbing my crotch. My cock was still hard.
Karen pulled on it through my slacks. She tried to un-
buckle my belt with one hand, but couldn't do it because
of the hallucinogens and being fucked and it was a hard
belt to undo. I undid it for her. She wrapped her hand

around my cock and started jerking me off. She looked up at Bill, who had his eyes closed, and then over at me again.

'Come on me,' she said. 'Come on. Fuck my hand. Come on.'

I closed my eyes. My jiz shot out with impressive force. Bill squealed. I opened my eyes. My come was splattered across his thigh.

'Oh, fuck! Oh, Jesus Christ!' he screamed. 'How'd that happen?!'

'Heh-heh-heh,' I said. I squished the tip of the whiskey bottle against my eye. 'Sorry, Bill.'

Karen began laughing. She and I laughed together at Bill, which was pretty good revenge on him for backstabbing me.

'Get it off of me!' he said.

'With what?' I said.

'Calm down, Bill,' Karen said. She lifted her mouth to his and bit his lower lip. She bit it again. Then they began kissing and fucking harder. I looked down at my shriveled wet dick.

Lit a cigarette.

Got up and walked outside to the swimming pool.

I stood on the diving board. The toes of my Rockport shoes jutted out over the edge. Moonlight squiggles shone in the meager surf and the skeletal remains of leaves floated by. A piece of bark passed beneath me, or perhaps it was a dog turd and it resembled a piece of bark.

A voice inside me whispered, 'Lean.'

So I did. I lifted my right leg straight behind me so that the top of my body leaned in toward the water, like one of those top-hatted birds that dips its face in a martini glass. I raised my arms. I shifted the Jack Daniel's bottle for balance.

The cool wind stung my pores. The pool lights ran waves of shadow over my body. I was the tiger with moving stripes! I leaned even closer toward the water. My water spirit gazed back up at me. I leaned in closer still, to kiss myself. I didn't fall. I wouldn't fall. Narcissus didn't have my legs.

The next day Bill and I were very, very, very sick. I swore to God I would never have a drink or do drugs again. Karen drove us back to the Hawaiian Retreat parking lot and we found the Honda Civic. Neither one of us kissed her good-bye. We dropped the Honda Civic off at Bill's dad and stepmother's house with a note. Then we took the first bus back to Manhattan.

'I can't believe you came on my leg,' Bill said.

This started me laughing. And then he started laughing. And pretty soon we were doubled over in hysterics and everyone on the bus was looking at us. Then I began to vomit up blood.

'Sorry,' I said. 'What's that smell?'

'I took a little shit in my pants,' Bill said. He began to cry. 'I'm losing control of my bowels.'

'Jesus!' I said. I moved to one of the backseats of the bus. Then I started to feel guilty. After all, I had come on his leg. So I moved back up next to him.

'Thanks,' he said.

'Let's think of something interesting to talk about,' I said.

We didn't speak again until we got to Manhattan.

What You Hid

'Evelyn, this is James.'

Long pause. I could hear her breathing.

'Remember me?' I said, pathetically.

'Ha.'

'I'm sorry, Evelyn. I shouldn't drink around you—'

'You're drunk now.'

'That's a coincidence.'

'What do you want?'

'I'm sorry,' I said.

Pause.

'What do you want?'

'What are you doing for Christmas, Evelyn?'

'I'm going home, of course, to Philadelphia with my parents. I'm thinking about hanging up now.'

'No! Wait! Listen, my mother got ahold of my number. She's been calling me and trying to get me to go home to Saint Louis. She's employed Tar in this FUCKING CRU-SADE.'

'Why are you so upset?'

'These bastards all want me dead.'

'I don't ever want to speak to you again, James. I told you that. There's something about you that needs serious mental help. I don't know what it was that happened to you.'

'I know. But wait. Evelyn. Evelyn, what kind of stuff do you do with your family over Christmas?'

'Eat food, church.'

'You eat food?'

'Yes.'

'What types of food?'

'Christmas types of food.'

'Where do you go to church?'

'Why do you care?

'Making conversation.'

'Noon mass at Saint Gabriel's. I'm going now.'

'I haven't been with my family for Christmas since I was eighteen. And what my family does is they fight. Some triangular fucking arrangement. Tar and me against my old man. Or me and him against Tar. And something priceless always gets broken.'

'What time is it?'

'This year, though, I'm the outsider, Evelyn, so I know what to expect. Evelyn. These fucking bastards. So listen to me. Listen to this. I've just had a marvelous plan that came to me in my head.'

Evelyn said nothing.

'Are you there?'

'Yes. I don't want to talk with you. This isn't right.'

'I want you to come home with me for Christmas.'

'What?!'

'AHA!'

'You're crazy!'

'Listen to this: I'll pay your way.'

'No! No!'

'I'll pay your way. Money in the bank.'

'No! No way!'

'Plus, I'll give you a thousand dollars.'

'A thousand—James, how do you make your money?'

I stared at the cracks in my wall for a moment.

'I steal pharmaceuticals from the hospital and sell them,' I said.

'Oh.'

'I'm good at it! JESUS FUCKING CHRIST, WHY THE THIRD-DEGREE ALL OF THE SUDDEN?! . . . Wait, wait! Don't hang up.'

'This is how fucked up you are. You're a whole different somebody than the guy I went to Long Island with.'

'You're crying, aren't you?'

'No. Why would I?'

'You're disappointed in me.'

'You hid so much.'

'All right, listen. Here's the plan. See, Tar—THAT FUCKER—he gets a lot of mileage out of having this girlfriend, Amy. He's in this NICE relationship with this NICE girl, and she takes the heat off of him.'

'So you want to use me as a buffer?'

'A thousand dollars!'

'No way. I have to go.'

'Don't hang up. Evelyn.'

'What?'

'I'm going to win you back. Even if it means having to change my life.'

'No, you aren't, James.'

And she hung up.

Sue Lopmeyer's Panties

Gary and I stood on the yellow curb. We were in the parking lot. The sun was warm. It was May. This was the end of our eighth-grade year. It was the last day we would ever have to go to Saint Ambrose. Good riddance, I thought. Gary and I balanced ourselves on the curb and looked at the others playing dodgeball. Gary put his arms out to his sides and tottered. He didn't play dodgeball anymore. Too many of the guys would aim for him, making a game out of who could knock his glasses off first. I wasn't *allowed* to play dodgeball anymore. This was a shame, as it was one of the few sports I enjoyed or had any talent for. If there had been a professional dodgeball league, I would have aspired to it as a profession. But Monsignor Abman said I had developed a mean streak. 'Dodgeball and sadists do not belong together,' he said.

Gary's face was covered with pink marks. He and I had been slap boxing. Slap boxing Gary was always a big risk. I could beat him easily. I was faster and taller and stronger. But if I was winning too much he would become enraged and try to strangle me. It was a thin line.

The two of us stood side by side on the curb. We tried standing on one leg (each), like a couple of storks. We did this for a few minutes, then we sat down on the curb.

'Eight years,' Gary said.

'Eight years of hell,' I said.

'Oh, it wasn't *so* bad.'

As Sue Lopmeyer thrust forward to throw the dodge-ball, the back of her skirt flew up and I could see the bottom of her underwear. Her thigh was muscular. I had been thinking of fucking girls most of the time lately. It had been over a year since I had done it with a black girl named Stacey Kees during summer-school science class. We did it in the forest, it only took a couple minutes, and was unremarkable. Now that I was thirteen I thought that I might like it a little more.

Gary seemed to have missed the underwear. He was looking at a spot on the pavement between his feet. His face crumpled a bit.

'What happens next year?' he whispered.

'Next year we fuck a lot of babes.'

'What if they're mean? What if the kids at school are mean?' Gary bit down hard on his lip and his face was shaking.

I knew what he meant. He meant Tar and Nancy and I wouldn't be there to protect him anymore. Tar wouldn't graduate for another year. The rest of us were all going to different high schools.

Hi, Mark, How Are You?

Mark Lipton looked like a nice guy. He was in his back-yard raking leaves. He wore a sweater with green stripes.

It was slightly chilly outside. The sun was beginning to set.

Tar and I tramped through the leaves. We were both jittery with some combination of fear and anger and anticipation. I never really knew where one started and the others ended. My hands were shaking.

'Hey. You Mark Lipton?' I said, though I knew full well he was. Walt Lang had pointed him out to us.

Mark smiled. He had short blond hair and perfect teeth. He was the same age as I was, sixteen, but he looked a lot older.

'Yeah, I am. What's up?'

I was biting on the skin of my thumb, a nervous habit I had in high school. I took my thumb away from my face.

'My brother and I were wondering why you were such a cocksucker,' I muttered.

Mark Lipton's face went slack.

'Whaaaaat?' he said. He mustered a confused smile.

'Nothing,' Tar said. 'He was just kidding. Can I see that rake?'

'What? Why?'

'I got one my mom makes me use and the little things, the tongs, keep coming off. That looks like a pretty good one. I just want to check it out.'

Mark Lipton looked at me, still with the confused smile. 'Why'd you call me a cocksucker?'

I shrugged.

'He's got a weird sense of humor,' Tar said. 'Come on, just let me see it for a sec.'

Mark Lipton hesitated. Then he handed the rake to Tar. Tar took it and inspected it. 'Hm,' he said. Then he began hitting Mark Lipton in the face with it.

Mark Lipton yelled and fell facedown into the pile of leaves. He tried to stand, but couldn't with Tar striking him on the back with the rake. Mark looked as if he was trying to swim in the leaves. That part was funny.

I kicked him in the ribs. I kicked him again. And then I kicked him in the face. I pulled the back of his hair and pulled him up closer to me. He was crying. My breath went in and out in small whines. He stared up at me.

'Why?' he muttered. Blood spilled from his mouth.

'If you ever touch Gary Bauer again, we'll kill you. Swear to fucking God. Come after us if you want, but you better kill us. If you don't, we'll kill you. I swear to fucking God, we'll kill you.'

Tar brought down the rake and it sliced through his ear.

I punched him in the face until my hand was cut with bloody gashes from his teeth.

'Gary's head!' I screamed, and hit him. 'Does not!' I hit him again. 'Belong in!' Something was lodged between my fingers. It was a tooth. 'A toilet!'

Mark Lipton's eyes rolled into the back of his head. Tar stopped swinging. He looked down at me. Hundreds of little holes were in the back of Mark Lipton's shirt.

'Is he unconscious?' he said.

I nodded.

Tar dropped the rake. I stood up. I held on to my ravaged hand and made my way to the car.

'Hey, wait!' Tar said. He crouched beside Mark Lipton. He pulled out the boy's wallet. He flipped through it. He held the money up to me.

'Eight dollars,' he said. Tar ran after me, clutching the money in his hand.

Love Song

Gary was slamming the top of his head against a telephone pole.

'What's he doing?' I said.

'Shit, he's going nuts!' Tar said.

Tar and I ran over to our friend like a couple of drunken Keystone Kops and pulled him away from the telephone pole. Things like this had been happening a lot lately to one of the four of us, Gary most often. Two weeks before he had gotten angry with himself, rubbed lighter fluid on his left nipple, and lit it on fire. This was nothing compared to that, but, still, it wasn't good.

'Gary! Look at your head!' I screamed. 'Goddammit!'

Blood was falling down from his hairline, covering his face. Gary looked around dizzily. He began crying.

'Girls hate me!' he said. 'They hate me!'

'Tar, go get Nancy.'

'Yeah,' Tar said. 'She's a girl.'

Tar sprinted back up to the house where the party was still happening. It was mostly dicks in letter jackets and betties in Izods with peroxide hair. I had walked out on the lawn to smoke a joint with my brother. I didn't want to be at the party. Those kinds of people hated me. Plus, they had already run out of booze. Luckily Tar and I had been drinking since noon rec at the U High.

'Gary, girls don't hate you.' I put my arm around him. We led him down the street, where there weren't so many other teenagers. 'They just think you're a little weird. They're afraid of someone who has enough intensity to slam his head against a telephone pole. They know they get a guy like that in the sack, and it means the big O. Chicks our age are afraid of pleasure.' I sat Gary down on a curb. He pressed his fists against his eyes.

'Why am I still a virgin?!'

'You're only fifteen. Pace yourself, man. Me, let's admit it, I'm the freak. Not you.'

He clutched my shirt.

'Nancy lost hers too!' he cried.

'She's five months older than you. Now you have five months to catch up. You're upset just because Nancy got porked?'

Gary dropped his head in my lap and sobbed.

'I'm drunk,' he said.

'That's definitely no reason to cry.'

'I miss being alive.'

'You're alive, believe me.'

'I hurt all the time.'

'Hey. Shh.'

I rubbed my fingers through Gary's hair.

Nancy stopped in the street by our side. She held a beer with two hands. She was wearing her pink pants.

'What's wrong?'

Tar bent down into Gary's face. He was frazzled, like he always was when any of us became upset.

'Look, Gary, it's Nancy!' Tar said. 'Look! She's a girl! Nancy, do you like Gary?'

'Yes,' she said.

'See? Girls don't hate you at all!'

'What's wrong?' Nancy repeated.

'He's down,' I said. Gary was holding my hand. He moved his eyes without moving his head and looked at Nancy.

'Hi,' he rasped. 'I'm sorry I'm stupid.'

'You're not stupid, Gary,' Tar said. 'You just feel things more than most people. Because you're better than them.'

'Scoot,' Nancy said to me, and swatted my shoulder. She sat down beside me on the curb. She pulled Gary over so that his head was in her lap and the rest of him was in mine.

'Where's your handkerchief, Gary?' she asked.

'In my pocket.'

'Tar, get Gary's handkerchief out of his pocket,' Nancy said.

Tar scrambled down to Gary's pocket and reached inside.

'Don't grab his dick,' I said. 'Heh-heh.'

'It's going to be all right, Gary, really,' Tar said. He pulled the white handkerchief out of Gary's pocket and handed it to Nancy. Gary and Tar and I had all decided handkerchiefs were cool and had started carrying them.

Nancy went to work on Gary's head, wiping away the blood that covered his forehead and face. Tar knelt down in front of Nancy's knees and pulled back Gary's hair so she could get the harder spots.

Stewart, the big lug that had been fucking Nancy, stood behind us in his stupid public school jacket.

'What's going on with *him*?' he said to Nancy.

'He gets like this sometimes,' she said.

'Somebody in the party said he was fucking hitting his head on an electrical post.'

'Gary's got his own way of doing things.' She smiled at Gary.

171

'I'm embarrassed,' Gary said.

'You gotta be kidding me,' Stewart said. He started laughing. 'Come on, Nance, let's get out of here. Leave the freak be and let's go do something else.'

Tar's eyes clouded over. He looked up at Stew. He stood. The top of my brother's head barely reached Stewart's chin, but he got in close, just a few inches away. He stared up into Stewart's eyes.

'Hey, *Stew*,' he said. 'Hey, *Stew*.'

'What?'

'Go back inside.'

'What? Why?'

'Because if you don't I'm going to call your mother and tell her you're having premarital intercourse with Nancy.'

'*What?*'

'You heard me.'

Tar took a step back. He flipped his arms up into fists. He bounced back and forth, bobbing and weaving, making little strikes at the air.

'Come on, Stew, man of the ridiculous name, let's fight,' he said.

'Don't touch him, Stewart,' Nancy said.

'You're totally smaller than me!'

'Yeah, but my brother will jump in and we'll beat the living crap out of you. You've heard the stories. Come on, make your move.'

'Shit! Maybe I'll go inside and get my friends!'

'*Whoo!* Go on, let's do it! Bring out the lunkheads! Come on, Stewart! You only get to call Gary a freak one time! You're worth one billionth of him, you big letter-jacket crewcut Moose-from-Archie faggot!'

'Jesus, oh man, you're a fucking nut!' Stewart said. 'Nancy, are you coming or what?'

'Fuck off, Stewart,' she said. 'I'll call you tomorrow.'

'You guys are fucking weird. You're like I've heard.' He pursed his mouth, shook his head in disgust. He walked away.

'Feeling any better, Gary?' I said.

His hand squeezed mine. Nancy wiped the last of the blood from his face.

'Thanks, Jimmy. I'm sorry I'm such a pain. I feel better now.' Gary was staring straight up into the sky. He smiled. 'Look at all the stars up there.'

The other three of us looked up. Huge constellations of stars whited out chunks of the black sky. It shone down upon us, almost as bright as day.

'Pretty,' Nancy said.

'It's beautiful,' Tar said. 'It's the most beautiful thing I've ever seen.' Tar let himself fall slowly to his knees in front of Gary's head.

Gary's head was an important thing to all of us. It held secret paths to beauty, like the sky it had just shown us. It held tricks to play on people, and a kind of undying love, and vast geographical knowledge, and ideas I was sure no one in the history of mankind had ever thought before. Sometimes it would go underappreciated. But I saw everything it meant to me now, and I didn't want it to block its pathways anymore.

I brought my lips down close to Gary's ear.

'We love you,' I whispered. I had never said anything like that to anyone before, but at that moment it seemed necessary. Nancy kissed Gary's clean forehead. My little brother, our protector, placed his hand over Gary's and mine. Gary gripped tightly to both our hands, and then Nancy set hers on top all of ours. Nancy squeezed.

There was only one good thing in the world, I thought. The other three would always be there when one of us started to go. In this way we were a perfect machine.

Wednesday, December 21

A fat man sank into a sofa. I could see him down the hallway, in the living room. His boxer shorts were spotted with faded blue diamonds. But for a wisp of thin white hair the man was bald; he had lost a lot since we last met. The light in the room was dramatic. The lamps were off. Narrow slats of sun came in through shuttered windows. Mostly the TV ignited the room. Its colors lit the man from below. Looking closer, though, something besides the lighting took hold of me. In the man's thick arms was a baby doll. He rocked it back and forth. The doll's face was almost a clown's; thick black eyelashes, cherry cheeks, gray eyes, and a look of glee. The fat man's eyes were also gray, a silver gray. But his expression was more devoted than gleeful. He twirled his fingers through the doll's hair. On the TV, an old courtroom drama. The TV lawyer was handsome with dark locks and grace. He stood silent in front of the jury, slowly rising his hand. The fat man was also a lawyer. He was a personal-injury lawyer, recognized by many in Saint Louis from his TV commercials. Now here he was with a baby doll. He rolled his finger over the baby doll's cheek. The tenderness stung. Strange that a piece of molded plastic could elicit this love, perhaps for the very first time.

*   *   *

Tar and Amy both reeked from the long car ride. They looked like late-phase heroin addicts, purple shadows beneath their eyes. Their ugliness was a comfort to me. I exited the rented Taurus, slammed the door shut. The top of my neck pulsed with nicotine, caffeine, white crosses. I swung my loaded bag over my shoulder. This tilted me pathetically to one side. I looked up at my parents' house. Sometime during the past five years they had painted it from yellow to brown. Tar forged the path up the driveway. He carried three hard cases. Amy carried a single tiny duffel.

'What's the matter, Ame, afraid you're going to break a nail?' I said.

'James, I'm fed up with you,' she muttered.

I had been voicing opinions about Amy's taste in music, Tar's wheezing while he slept, and other blemishes. Admittedly I was a bit angry; they had told me they would pay for the rental *under condition* I didn't drink. I hadn't had a drink anyway, not since the night I offered Evelyn a thousand dollars to come home with me. But that I was changing my life wasn't any of their fucking business.

Amy leaned over and whispered to my brother as they walked toward the front door. This is how they had been expressing their resentment, through secret whispers. The Sensitive Ones, I liked to think of them as.

Above the house the sun was barely visible behind the pinkish clouds. My parents' front lawn was covered with frost. The cold filled my nostrils. Troll Court was empty. Still the street was as reassuring as I had remembered. Maybe it was the reassurance that I missed, that convinced me to come home for Christmas. Or perhaps it was the reason I had given: that I was sick of my mother's nagging on the phone.

The Delgesses' dog Lennon went limping around the circle of grass in the center of the court.

'Hey, Lennon!' Tar yelled. 'Lennon!'

But she didn't hear. Deaf, I guessed. The old girl moved stiffly from bush to bush. She squatted.

Tar opened the front door without knocking. Unlike me, my brother had ventured home every year. The last two he had brought Amy.

In the living room at the end of the hallway our father was sitting on the couch. At first he didn't see us come in. All the lights were off except the TV. In his arms, a baby doll.

?, I thought.

My father turned toward us. His face became bright.

'Ha-ha hey!' he said. He lumbered up the hallway to embrace us. He carried the doll with him. I shrank beneath his large arms.

'Jimmy, Jimmy,' he whispered in my ear. 'I'm so glad you've come back.'

'Yeah,' I said. The doll was wedged between our shoulders. It and I were staring face-to-face. A lawyer was sermonizing on the TV.

'*And Tar!*' my father said.

'Hey, you old swindler!' Tar said.

'Ha-ha,' my father said. They embraced. This had become second nature to them.

The baby doll wore yellow pajamas. On the pajamas, a duck. The duck's head was black. It was quacking at a smiling star overhead. My father hugged Amy. He kissed her on the cheek. I pointed at the baby doll.

'Dad, what the hell is that?'

Tar kicked me with the side of his foot. My father looked down at the doll.

'Well, that's . . . uh . . .' he said.

My mother came trampling down the stairs.

'Well, hello!' she said. 'Hello!' My mother hugged me in her prim way. Behind her, my father was holding the doll like a real baby.

'Well, let's look at you,' she said. 'Five years!'

'Yeah, well, I've been busy.'

'Five years is too long.'

'Oh, give the kid a break, Lynea,' my father said.

'Hey, Mom, Dad's got a baby doll. What's the deal with that?'

Tar kicked me again, hard. He glared at me.

'Kick me one more time . . .' I said. 'Will somebody tell me why my father is carrying around a doll?'

There was a moment of television music.

'It's something Karen asked me to do,' my father said.

'I don't know who Karen is.'

'That's your father's therapist,' my mom said. 'Billy is a new kind of therapy.'

Bill was my father's name.

'Billy?' I said. 'It looks like a girl.'

My mother clapped her hands together.

'Okay!' she said. 'Jimmy, pick up your bag. We're going to put you down in the basement, if you don't mind.'

'I don't mind. But . . .'

'Good,' my mother said. 'Come on. We fixed it all up for the return of the prodigal son.'

She walked down the hallway. I looked at my brother. He winced at me and shook his head sadly in disgust. I looked at Amy. She was distracting herself with a cabinet of Hummel figurines. I looked at my father. He wouldn't meet my eye. I walked out of the hall. After five years I should have known I'd be left out of things.

*   *   *

I set my bag down on the orange carpet. The basement had been subdivided and carpeted since I moved away.

'Man,' I said. 'I still think of it the old way.'

'It's been a long time since you've been home,' my mother said.

A futon sidled one wall. The rectangular windows at the top of the wall now had shutters. My mother opened one of the dresser drawers. She zipped open my bag.

'I'll unpack myself, Mom.'

'No trouble.' She picked up a handful of my underwear. 'About Billy.'

'The doll.'

'Yes.'

My brother and Amy's footsteps padded overhead into the guest bedroom. The TV's volume got louder. My mother placed my underwear in the drawer. She stood straight. She pushed her glasses up on her face. She looked at me.

'I would appreciate it if you didn't tease your father about him. He's been sensitive lately.'

'Well, I don't see why. There's no reason a grown man should be sensitive about carrying around a doll.'

'Stop it. His psychologist prescribed it . . . prescribed Billy. She thought it would help your father regain some of the nurturing he didn't get as a child.'

'That I don't understand.'

'It's what's called his inner child. That's why his name is Billy.'

'Oh, no. Oh, Christ, Mom. That's just plain fucked up. And spooky, it's spooky.'

'The language,' my mother said. She bent toward my bag. 'Maybe it will be helpful. I have to admit he's been better around the house.'

She picked up a handful of my socks.

*   *   *

My father weighed more than three hundred pounds. When he joined AA and quit drinking he gained even more weight. Although I was embarrassed by his carrying a doll around the house, I had to admit to Tar that night: 'You know, I always did think our father was putting on all that weight because for some reason he was ashamed of his skeleton. Like every jut that showed through was something he had to layer over until it was gone.'

'Hm,' Tar said. 'That's a weird theory, man.'

'I know. That's why I haven't said it until now. But speaking it out loud now makes me even more convinced that it's true. I bet there's millions of real psychological maladies that psychiatrists haven't thought of yet. And shame of the skeleton is one. Maybe the baby doll is like his skeleton, and paying attention to it helps him to lose some of that. Does that make sense?'

'No.'

'Maybe I didn't word it right.'

'Yeah. I'm going to sleep.' Tar walked into his bedroom and was gone.

Thursday, December 22

Shortly after the doorbell rang, Tar stood at the edge of the kitchen table. He wore a silk shirt. I could see the sunlight in the hallway coming in from the open doorway. Tar nodded toward it.

'The door's for you,' he said.

Nancy's face was the same: pretty from the appropriate angles, streamlined nose, brown hair, eyes a bit close in a cute way, large incisors. She had her hand on the door-frame. Nodding. Grinning. My pace slowed when I saw her.

'Whoa. Jesus. Nancy.'

She laughed. 'That's me. I came to see if you could come out and play.'

'That's about what you were doing the last time I saw you.'

Nancy laughed. She was very thin in a tan sweater and jeans. She had lost the bit of weight she had gained last time I saw her. Behind her the various-colored houses streamed up on both sides of the hill.

'Christ, you look all right,' I said.

'*All right*. Oh, gee, thanks.'

'Well, you know what I mean. Good. Real good. Healthy.'

We looked at each other and nodded for a few minutes. She stood straight.

'A hug?' she said.

'Yeah, yeah.'

We parried a bit back and forth. Finding an in, she brought her arms up around my neck. She squeezed me and shut her eyes tight. We rocked back and forth for a moment, gradually slowing to a stop.

'Hey, darling,' I said.

'How long? Five years?'

'Five years.'

I let myself close my eyes for a moment. When I opened my eyes I saw the gentle curve of her ass in her jeans. The hug, the warmth, and the view surged blood down below my stomach. Nancy dipped back, looking up at me. Her face was inches from mine. She brushed her knuckles over my whiskers.

'When'd you get this?'

'It comes and goes.'

She smooched me on the chin. She brought her head back down into my chest and squeezed me again. Nancy felt more like home than either my parents or their house.

'Oh, God, I still think about you all the time,' she said. 'I wonder what you're doing. I imagine you at the top of the Empire State Building.'

'That's where I spend most my time. Usually I got a little tiny person in my hand and helicopters are shooting at me.' I pushed her back. 'Hey, Nancy.'

'What?'

I pointed down the street at what used to be the Streckers' house.

'See those bushes down there?'

She nodded.

'Let's go back down there behind them. I'll show you mine if you show me yours.'

'*Ha-ha-ha-ha-ha!*' Nancy said, the same horsy loud laugh. She cupped her hand over her mouth. But her laughter was too strong. With ease it burst between her fingers and punctured distant hearts.

Tar, Amy, and I watched my father through the kitchen window. He carried a shovel across the front lawn. He wore an orange thermal hat.

'What're those things called again?' I said.

'Papooses,' Tar said.

'Oh, yeah.'

On my father's back was a papoose with the baby doll in it. He cracked the frozen ground around a tree, circling it.

'Somebody's gonna see that papoose,' I said. 'They're gonna say old man Gunn's gone loony.'

'I think it's kind of sweet,' Amy said.

'Bananas smell sweet when they start to go rotten.'

Amy spooned up some Fruity Pebbles. I set my cigarette in an ashtray on the table.

'Mom says he makes her baby-sit it when he goes to work,' Tar mumbled through a mouthful of cereal. 'He says it's a baby, somebody has to take care of it all the time.'

'Does she do it?' Amy said.

Tar shrugged. 'She says she does.'

'You know she doesn't,' I said. 'You know Mom just sets it on a shelf somewhere then when she sees him in the driveway she picks it up and starts making googly eyes at it.'

Tar raised his eyebrow. 'What exactly are googly eyes, James?' he said.

'Hm, well, they're the same kind of eyes you make while you're fucking Amy in the ass.'

Tar dropped his spoon in his cereal and glared at me. Amy's mouth opened. She stared at Tar.

'You told him,' she said.

'Hey, nobody told me anything. I just thought you've been walking a little funny lately. Heh-heh.'

Amy punched Tar in the arm. I took a sip of coffee to hide my smile.

'Nothing to be ashamed about, Ame,' I said. 'Everyone needs a little heinie-fucking now and again.'

Tar reached up over the table and flicked me in the temple.

'Ow! Fuck,' I said.

I picked up my lit cigarette from the ashtray. And I threw it at him.

'Uncool, James! Oh, shit! Oh, shit! Where'd it go?' Tar started to stand up. He was patting his torso and his legs looking for the cigarette. Amy scrambled around him trying to find it.

'Heh-heh-heh.' I sipped my coffee.

'Ow! I'm getting burnt! Oh no!' Tar jumped away from the table. With a panicked expression he picked it off himself. The cigarette had gotten caught in a fold on his shirt. Next to his chest pocket was a brown hole. Amy kneaded the hole between her fingers, shocked.

'Goddammit, that's a fifty-dollar shirt!' Tar said.

'Not anymore.' I sipped my coffee. He stood still, muscles taut. His eyes darted over the surface of the table. They stopped on Amy's bowl of cereal. I moved slowly back.

'Hey, Tar . . . don't,' I said.

Tar grabbed the rim of the bowl. I started to get up from

my seat. He threw the cereal on me. Little Fruity Pebbles stuck all over my suit. Amy laughed hysterically.

'Great.' I grabbed my coffee cup. I tossed the coffee on both Tar and Amy. The Sensitive Ones screamed. Coffee dots on their clothes. Amy snatched up a saltshaker.

'Oh, please please please, Amy,' I said. 'Don't throw salt on me. Please, anything but that. Heh-heh-heh.'

Amy chucked the whole shaker.

'Ow!' I said. It bounced off my forehead. I touched the spot where it hit.

Something cold was streaming over my face. I turned around. Tar was pouring a bottle of Coca-Cola on my head. I grabbed the bottom of the bottle and tried to wrestle it from him. Coca-Cola sputtered everywhere: us, the table, the drapes, papers stuck to the refrigerator with magnets. Tar and I tumbled to the ground. Neither one of us was able to gain control of the emptying bottle. A farting noise. A yellow streak passed by my face. The streak landed in Tar's hair. Another streak landed on my nose. Amy was standing over us squirting mustard. I wrapped my arms around her knees and she collapsed. Tar laughed. I laughed. Amy laughed. Then my mother's voice came down upon us:

'What . . . the hell . . . is going on here?' She stood in the doorway in a flashy flowered shirt. Her hands were on her hips. It was a familiar pose, though not one I had seen in the past twelve years.

'Oh!' Amy said. 'We'll clean it up!' She was on the ground. Her hair was in her face. Her legs were stuck under Tar's ass. I was sitting on Tar's legs.

'Look at my refrigerator,' my mother said. 'My calendar.'

'Amy attacked both me and Tar, Mom,' I said.

'Yeah,' Tar said. 'We tried to stop her but she was going

crazy throwing everything all over the kitchen. She just kept saying, "I hate your mother, your mother is a bitch." '

'I did not! Mrs. Gunn, I didn't!'

'Who are you going to believe, Mom, this outsider or your two loving sons?' I said. 'Heh-heh-heh-heh.' I grabbed the wet pack of cigarettes from my shirt pocket.

My mother moaned. 'Just clean it up.' She left the kitchen, shaking her head.

'Ha-ha-ha,' we all said. Amy covered her eyes with her hand. I tossed a cigarette in my mouth. Tar looked up at me.

'Hey, James,' he said. 'There's something you might want to see.'

'Dan Occansion!' I said. Tar had led me into the storage part of the basement. Shelves crammed with boxes lined the walls. Dan was cupped in the palms of Tar's out-stretched hands. The red on Dan's helmet had faded. And some of the blue stripes down the sides of his body had been scuffed away. On his back he still had the black spot. But besides that the old fellow looked pretty good.

'He hasn't aged a bit,' I said. 'Where'd you find him?'

'I was looking for my high school diploma in one of the boxes back there.'

'Why the fuck would you want that?'

'I don't remember.'

'Who's Dan Ocanjan?' Amy said.

'No, OCCANSION, you silly cunt,' I said. 'He's Dan the Stunt Man.'

DAN/DAD

In Dan's most famous stunt we tied his foot to a kite. Since I could tie knots the best I was the one to do it. Gary and I argued over who got to hold the spool. Tar didn't care; he climbed the gutter to the rooftop. He wanted to see this stunt up close. The kite was black with two big green eyes. Green streamers flew from its tail. This was a day of extreme wind. Nancy's mom had checked the weather channel on the radio for us.

'Yes,' she had said. 'It's certainly a blustery day.'

Up the kite went, higher, higher. As it moved across the sky, Tar darted across the top of our house.

'Don't fall!' Nancy cried.

Dan hung from the kite by his foot. He spread his arms wide.

'I am the greatest stunt man in the world!' Dan yelled. 'Evel Knievel can suck my dick!'

Gary hooted, clapped. He brought his clasped hands below his chin. I unraveled the spool and let Dan go higher. Tar reached out to touch him over the edge of the roof.

Frickles Fireworks stocked giant bottle rockets around the Fourth of July. They had them in the back. A sign warned,

It is illegal for anyone under eighteen to be in this part of the store. Neither Frickles nor any of the members of his fireworks staff paid any attention to the sign; sometimes God is good. Most of the giant bottle rockets we bought, Gary and I threw at each other. Only once did either one of us have to go to the hospital (Gary). The largest and most powerful rocket was called the SuperBuzz. We only had one, which we made sure not to use. It was reserved for Dan Occansion.

'Are you sure he's not gonna explode?' Nancy asked.

'Dan says he can do it,' Tar said.

We knew we could trust this. Tar had the greatest rapport with Dan. Instead of string we used wire to tie Dan to the SuperBuzz. We tied him with his back to it so if he did get burned his face wouldn't be harmed. We planted the bottle rocket's stick in a pile of rocks. Dan had the same smile he always did before a stunt. Some might call this stupidity, but we recognized this for the daring it was. I lit the wick. It flared, sparks flying to our feet.

'Bye, Dan,' Nancy said.

'Dig this!' Dan yelled. 'I'm taking a trip to outer space!' The SuperBuzz arced up into the air.

'We love you, Dan!' Gary screamed.

'Geez, Gary, get a life,' Nancy said.

At the highest point in the sky Dan's rocket exploded. Then it plummeted into the subdivision under construction next to our neighborhood.

'Oh, shit,' Tar said.

We didn't know where it went. We hadn't planned on having trouble finding it after it landed. The four of us traveled into the construction zone. It was Sunday, deserted. We searched the dirt lawns. We searched the roofs of houses already built and the interiors of houses only begun. Gary started into his nervous breathing.

'Don't worry, Gary,' I said. 'We'll find him.' I placed my hand on his back.

When it got dark we went back home and got flashlights.

'It's too late to be going out there,' my mother said.

Tar started to cry.

'But Dan's gone!' he said.

'You can find Dan in the morning,' she said.

'By then he might be dead!' Tar cried.

'What?'

'Somebody might take him by then, Mom,' I said.

'Who would want your little person?'

'Kids *die* for stuff like that, Mrs. Gunn,' Nancy said.

Tar cried louder.

'We'll be careful,' I said.

My mother gave in. It usually went that way when Tar cried.

Once outside the door Tar looked at me and smiled. His hands were in his pockets.

One of the houses under construction was only a wooden frame. We hadn't inspected it very well the first time around. I was looking in the gutters on the corners of the house when Nancy yelled, 'Oh!' I peered inside. She was on her hands and knees, looking down a hole in the floorboards going into the basement.

'I think I found him,' she whispered.

I walked into the house and climbed down into the hole.

'Is he alive?' Gary said.

Dan's whole body was black and charred. He was tied to the cardboard husk of the bottle rocket. He was hardly breathing.

'Yeah, but he's messed up,' I said.

Walking back to the house was sad because Dan was so fucked up. In the utility room we tended to his wounds.

We gave him a shower in the sink. To our surprise, almost all the black washed easily away. Dan regained consciousness.

'Hey hey hey!' he said. 'Nothing's wrong with me, baby!'

Only a small spot remained on his back. Gary grabbed my shoulder and squeezed, grinning.

Another time Dan took the wheel behind a buggy. He drove it off the roof and into the inflatable pool. Everyone cheered.

Tied with wire to the rear bumper of our mother's car, Dan Occansion held on all the way to our grandmother's house. Tar introduced our grandmother to Dan.

'Oh,' she said. She slid her finger over the top of her ear.

'The Bible says, Tar, it says to beware false idols,' she muttered. She looked at our mother uncertainly.

'It's not a statue, Grandma,' I said.

'Well. It's not the most appropriate thing in the world.' Again she looked at our mother. She said under her breath, defensively: 'Lynea, it's true. You just don't understand. And looking at me like that won't help. *It won't.*'

'Come on, guys,' our mother said. 'Go on downstairs, play.'

Our grandmother's basement was old, musty, and the lights were dim. In a glass case stood her dead cat, Socks. He was stuffed. He stared above us, a bit cross-eyed. His eyes were a very different color green than they had been when he was alive. A small plastic turntable that my grandmother kept for us sat on the floor. Next to it, a cardboard box of children's records. I put on a record called *Sing Along Circus*. Dan sat with his legs out straight on the record label as the turntable revolved. Tar looked out of the corner of his eye at Socks.

'Beware false idols,' he whispered in a high-pitched voice. We giggled nervously.

Then Dan said loudly: 'If you cats don't mind me saying, that old broad is half off her rocker.'

Tar and I put our hands over our faces and laughed hard. That day we invented a dance called *The Crazy Lady*. It involved sliding your fingers over the tops of your ears while wiggling your butt.

We strapped Dan Occansion to the back of a duck.

In a touching moment Dan admitted that his parents didn't love him. All of us were shocked to see him crying. It was touching, but uncomfortable. What do you say in a situation like that?

Unlike most action figures from that period, Dan Occansion's knees could bend.

Hey you cats, come here. I got something to show you. It's gonna blow your minds. Come on over here, through these trees. That's right. Look out for that root sticking up. Okay. You ready? It's this. Ha! Bet you didn't expect me to show you a dead squirrel! Man oh man, look at that! Its eyes have rotted away. Look, you can see its ribs. Whoo boy, it smells too. Get down close and smell it. What's wrong with you, Gary old boy? Afraid of a dead squirrel? Afraid it's gonna jump up and grab you? Ha! That'd be something. Man oh man. What do you mean you're gonna be sick, Nance? What's wrong with you? Hell, it's only a squirrel. A DEAD squirrel. Hey, babe, where you going? Get your bony butt on back here. Come on now.

I'm gonna figure out a stunt to do with this dead squirrel. Quit calling me that. Come on, Nancy. Come on back. We'll figure out something really cool. Maybe I'll stick my head through its skin, between its ribs. It looks soft enough. Of course it's disgusting. A disgusting stunt is a certain category of stunt, like people eating goldfishes. I am the master of ALL stunts if you don't recall. You think I can't do it? I said quit calling me that. My name isn't Jimmy. It's Dan.

William Gunn was from a Saint Louis family of lawyers, so Irish and so cloistered that after two generations in this country they still had a hint of a brogue. He started drinking heavily at the age of fourteen, and didn't stop for twenty-five years. William believed himself to be a ladies' man, but, nervous and Catholic, he only ever fingered one slit and that was his wife's.

William married Lynea Chylnek on a beautiful summer day, and it went downhill from there. William was drunk when his first child, James, was born less than a year later. He pressed his hand against the nursery glass. He wept and said his boy was the most handsome baby he had ever seen. His second son was born less than a year after that. The second son's name was Joseph, but because his skin was so dark at birth William called him Tar Baby. It was a nickname that, shortened to Tar, stuck, and the toddler later refused to be called anything else.

William was frightened around the children. He didn't know how to touch them. He never held one in his arms. He was usually at work, so much so that the two boys were essentially raised in a single-parent home. Even when he was present he wasn't present, his nose buried in a newspaper or staring at the TV.

But, oh, when he was drunk. When he was drunk,

William would stay up late with the children. They would ride on his back as he pretended to be a monster, a pony, a dragon. He would prop his hands on his head like horns on a moose and run repeatedly into the furniture, sometimes breaking it. His children would laugh. He'd snap towels at their bottoms. He'd pretend to eat them. He'd fill the tub with water and drop them in like bombs.

In the morning they'd jump on his back to play again. But William would be hungover. He would throw them aside with force, and once the younger son's finger was broken in this way.

William was given to violence. At nineteen, he was arrested for repeatedly slamming a man's hand in a car door. At twenty-three he threw a fifty-five-year-old insurance agent through a window. He'd slap or punch or kick his sons because he couldn't get them to shut up any other way. He hit his wife twice. This was well worth it to his entire family because he was incredibly nice and humble for a full two weeks afterward.

'I wish he'd hit Mom every two weeks,' James once said.

'Or, if he's too busy, I'll do it for him,' said Tar.

Friday, December 23

'I'm not sure where Tar went,' I said. 'I think to the Science Center with Amy.'

'You didn't want to go to the Science Center?' my father asked.

We were sitting across from each other on the couch.

'No. No. I think I'm going to do my own experiment in the basement. To hell with the Science Center.'

'Your own experiment?'

I leaned back in the couch, staring at the TV.

'Yeah. I'm going to make a robot, Dad. I might as well tell you. Soon the world will know.'

'What? A robot?'

'Yeah. A very huge robot. It will frighten you.'

'*What?*'

I stared at him.

'Nothing,' I said. 'Never mind.'

My father looked at me for a few seconds then turned back toward the TV. Two men were sweeping the curling stone from one end of the rink to the other. Curling is the greatest sport in the world because although I don't know what the hell they're doing it looks like a sport janitors would be terrific at, and I'm all for the little man.

The baby doll was in my father's arms, forgotten in the

excitement of curling. I sucked in smoke. There was beer in the fridge but I was doing my best to stay away from it. Nancy and I had made plans to hang out that night. I didn't want to be drunk when she came by to pick me up. The curling team in the red fumbled the stone.

'*Oh*, he lost it,' my father said. 'He lost it.'

'He screwed up,' I said. 'All the other curlers are going to make fun of him.'

'They're going to take away his broom.' My father laughed.

I looked at my father and watched his whole body shaking.

'Heh-heh. Hey, Dad. Let me see that doll.'

My father was cautious.

'Don't do anything to it.'

'Naw.'

He handed me the baby. I held it up in front of me under its shoulders. I lifted it gently up and down, felt its weight.

'That's not such a bad-looking kid,' I said. 'Nice PJs.'

I looked at my father. He had a slightly goofy smile and his eyes were watering up.

'Thank you, Jimmy. Thank you for being nice.'

'I'm just looking at it, Dad.'

Nancy and I were distanced by years. Experiences were the splayed fingers of God between us. She was flanked by men more important than me: an ex-husband and a little boy who's name I had forgotten. And cocks had filled orifices that had been shrouded around me since the first pubic whiskers. But in the right light her face was a mirror of my own. Maybe she missed the same things, the mystery, the magic. Of course it's impossible to reclaim the old world. But maybe fooling ourselves was enough.

In the old world we put on plays for our parents.

*   *   *

A small scar curved along the wrinkle next to Nancy's eye. Both the scar and the wrinkle were new additions, and I considered whether they fit. I shouted over the music: I asked her where she had picked up the scar.

'A ring,' Nancy shouted. The jukebox was up so loud she had to shout. The song was '96 Tears', so I had problems concentrating on Nancy. I hadn't heard '96 Tears' in a long time. We were in a bar, a secret Irish place named O'Corrigan's; everything in it was green or dark wood. Outside the bar the Mississippi flowed by, which always reminded me of thick chocolate spilling down a funnel in the Hershey's factory. Nancy and I were sitting on stools side by side. Nancy was wearing brown corduroys. They were tight, and they started me thinking things I shouldn't have been thinking about the oldest friend I had. Having the baby, whatever its name was, hadn't destroyed her thighs. I guided my tongue between my incisors and pushed out part of the chicken dinner we had earlier. Five years. It was better being home than I thought it would be.

'I got it from a ring,' Nancy said.

'That's a mysterious answer.'

'Jerry's ring.' Nancy took her right hand and gave herself a slow motion crack across the jaw. It was a funny smile she had on. This was the way she took everything life dealt her.

'He knocked you around?' I asked. A little bit of surprise came through my face.

'*I'm gonna cry ninety-six tears.*'

'We knocked each other around,' she shouted. 'But he had the girth.'

'Fuck. You want me to do something to him? I will. I want to.'

Nancy snickered. She sipped at her Long Island iced tea. She shook her head and looked up at me.

'I didn't think you were doing that to people anymore, Jimmy.'

'I'm not. It's an exception. To help you.'

'It didn't help Gary. It's not gonna help me.'

'Gary,' I said. I pushed that bastard's stupid face out of my head. Just in time, a couple of sorority girls came in the front door to distract me. They were doing a little dance with their hands up by their sides, their wrists bent back. They had on many bracelets.

'*I'm gonna cry, cry, cry, cry.*'

Nancy was sucking on the tiny straw. She looked up at me and held my eyes. Her eyes were dark brown, bloodshot, somewhat shriveled, but enchanting. After a moment she asked me why I had come back after being gone for so long.

'I left something here,' I told her.

'What's that?'

The bartender slid a quarter into his palm from the bar. I averted my eyes from Nancy's.

'*Ninety-six tears.*'

'Childhood,' I said. She made an attempt at a laugh. I wiped my mouth with my wrist.

I ordered a beer.

Nancy had learned to knock them back.

'You drink like this often?' I gestured toward her glass. Lipstick imprint on the rim.

'My mother says I'm going to end up like you if I don't slow down.'

I made a puzzled face. 'Every Picture Tells a Story' came on as '96 Tears' ended.

'There are stories about you,' she said.

'Yeah? What about?'

'Jail stories. They say you're bitter, you're squandering your life.'

'All scenes have been dramatically re-created.'

'I suppose.'

'But I guess those stories are better than no stories at all,' I said.

'Some people think that way.'

A *GQ* guy with coifed hair was leaning on the sorority girls' table. '*Moi?*' I overheard him say.

'I want to murder that guy,' I said. 'I want to torture him hard.'

Nancy asked me if I wanted to smoke some grass.

I didn't want her to leave. We went into my parents' basement. Nancy said: 'This is freaky how everything down here is so different.'

She removed the one-hitter from her jeans jacket. Then she stared at the figure on the lamp table.

'Dan Occansion,' she said. I tossed her a beer.

'Yeah. He's kicking back.'

Nancy ran her fingernail down Dan's chest.

'Too much,' she said. 'Dan Occansion. I think I used to have a crush on him.'

'Everyone has a crush on Dan.'

'Remember that once you grossed me out in the woods when you said he was going to stick his head in the dead squirrel?'

'Maybe.' I walked into the bathroom my parents had added on.

'Where'd you find him?' Nancy yelled to me from the other room. My urine was splattering in the toilet. For a moment it went on the edge.

'Tar found him in the basement,' I yelled back. 'We found a kite too. I think we're gonna take him out on a stunt tomorrow.' I shook off the excess piss.

Nancy was taking a hit as I came out of the bathroom.

'You're kidding,' she rasped.

'No, no, we are.'

'Can I come?'

'Tomorrow's Christmas Eve.'

'Screw it. If Dan does a stunt I want to be there. Remember when we tied him to the back of a duck?'

'Yeah, yeah. Tar and I went through all of them today. Amy said I should write his biography.' I toked off the one-hitter.

'Can I come?'

I shrugged. 'Sure.'

'Gimme that pipe.'

I handed it to her.

'Hey, Nancy, remember what it used to be like?'

'What what used to be like?'

'When we were kids.'

'Yeah, like what, you mean like wanting to be grown up all the time and never being able to?'

'No, hell no, Jesus, I never wanted that. I mean being able to imagine anything and having it almost be true. There was belief. Remember when Tar was crying because Oscar Jr. was dead?'

Nancy stared at me.

'Yeah,' she said. She lowered herself onto the couch.

'Well, Jesus, that was like everything to me,' I said. 'I remember looking down and seeing brains coming out of the back of Ellen's head.'

'Shit. Ellen. Damn.' I imagined that Nancy was about to shed tears now over the death of her friend. Maybe she was.

'But, shit, James. When you get older you get to see that stuff for real.'

'Well, I don't feel it anymore.'

'Don't you work in a hospital?'

'Yeah.'

'You see anybody die?'

'Yeah. But it seemed more real back when the people were plastic.'

Nancy said: You remember that? We'd steal your mother's makeup and dress up Brendan like a girl. He'd be the flower girl. I heard he's a transvestite now, I really did, I think. Gary'd be the best man usually. I don't know what the fuck Steve and Corey did. You know I could never really tell one from the other. You could? Wow, I couldn't. I think we made them servers. They were Methodists, so they thought that was some sort of real important position. Man, how much beer have we drank? Hold on just a sec. I have to go take a piss.

Ugh.

Nancy said: Tar would always be the priest. Always. He'd cry if we didn't let him. God, he was a little shit sometimes. While you guys would set up the altar and everything, Kelly and I would braid wreaths out of daffodils for your and my heads. Remember those? Those were for . . . Jesus, I'm drunk, what is it around you I just forget I'm a mother? . . . Kelly and I thought the bride and groom wore wreaths, for some reason. Maybe we saw it in a Disney film. I think we did. Then we'd do it, Jimmy. First you'd come out slow with your hands folded in prayer at your chest. You'd stop and wait for me at the porch, the altar. Then Robert'd be my father. He'd walk me out. I'd see you looking back at me, looking all serious, little wreath on your head. God, it was great. Tar had that humongous Bible and he'd read some nonsense from it. Then he'd ask us the familiar questions and all that. I DO. I DO. Then at the end you'd kiss me. A real pucker. Gary would clap. God, it'd be great. You know, I think I liked doing that even more than the dinosaurs.

No, I'm not kidding.

It's all a mess, really. Nancy was lying back, slumped down on the blue couch. Her knees were slightly parted, the thin V of her crotch curving down. Nancy's eyes were closed. The eyeliner on her lids was blurred, dim in places. My grandfather's obituary was framed on the wall behind her. I was on my knees. I held Nancy's hand. I held Nancy's hand in both of mine. My face was side down on the couch. Vinyl upholstery, smell of vinyl and lint. A dot of spit beneath my mouth.

'Marry me,' I said.

'Ha-ha.'

'No, really, I mean it. Marry me. We can drive to Las Vegas tonight.'

'Jimmy!' Nancy giggled and yanked her hand away.

I plopped back on my ass.

'We've already hitched up thirty or forty times,' I said. 'What's once more?'

Her elbow was over her eyes, blocking out the fluorescent light.

'I'm drunk,' she said.

'Maybe we should get married.'

Nancy propped herself on her elbows. Her eyes were red. Her eyes were scrunched.

'I've got a kid.'

'Oh, yeah, that's right. I forgot about that. I take everything back. Almost fell into a bad scene for a minute there.'

Nancy swung one of the couch cushions into my head. It made a slapping sound. The metal zipper stung the side of my eye.

'What's wrong with kids?' she said in a way that revealed her own insecurity on the subject. She swung the cushion into my head again.

'Nothing. I just don't want to have one.'

'Why not?'

'I don't know. One thing is I'm always afraid I'm going to want to fuck it. That'd suck, right? You'd have this kid, this cute little sexual animal, it'd be running around. You'd have to hug it and kiss it and sit it on your lap but not fuck it.'

'That's disgusting.'

'You haven't been around me. I get more and more disgusting every year.' I looked at her. Cheekbones probably get to me more than anything else and Nancy had them. She lay back on the couch. She was staring at me. I was staring at her. We didn't say anything for a few moments.

'What?' she said.

'Hey, Nancy.'

'I just said what.'

'Remember what I said yesterday?'

It took her another moment to answer. 'What?'

'I'll show you mine if you show me yours.'

Nancy's shirt was stretched tightly over her breasts. They rose, then fell, then rose, then fell, quickly. Her shirt was tan. She stared at me. Her mouth was slightly open. The fluorescent light was a shiny white squiggle in her lipstick.

'All right,' she said.

'Okay.'

She continued to stare at me.

'You're serious,' she said.

'This is the new world. Anything is possible.'

Her breath quickened, churned. In a counterrhythm

mine did too. Nancy slid up a bit on the back of the couch.

'Okay,' she whispered, almost inaudibly, a little weep of sound. 'But you first.'

'Yeah. All right.'

My fingers went to my belt. They flipped open the buckle, slid out the leather. It was undone. The zipper made a scratchy noise as I pulled it down. I lowered my pants, my boxers beneath my hips. The tip of my penis popped up. The helmet was inflated with blood. As I pulled my pants down farther Nancy stared with eyes at half-mast; I watched her from the corner of my eye. The shaft came up, quite large, a proud mammal between us.

'Oh God,' Nancy said. She covered her face with her hands. Her neck was flushed. 'Jimmy . . .'

I had to fight the impulse to touch my cock.

'Your turn now,' I said. 'Old buddy.'

'Old buddy, uh-huh. Yeah. This is ridiculous.'

'Your turn.'

Her hands trembled. She undid her belt. She unbuttoned her pants. This took a long time. I could see the elastic band of her panties, gray-black. She stopped for a second.

'Okay, okay,' she said.

While looking at the ceiling she wiggled and yanked down her pants all the way. Again she covered her face. 'Jimmy . . .'

She breathed in deeply. She sat up. As she put her thumbs in her panties' waistband our eyes connected.

'Here we go,' she said. 'I don't know why . . .'

She pulled them down. She removed one leg. The panties collapsed around her foot. Her legs were fairly close together. Still I could see. Her black pubic hair was shiny wet. Just a little bit of the blooming red was visible.

'Nancy,' I whispered.

Her hand was clasped firm over her mouth. I reached out. I grazed her knee with my finger. She nodded, closed her eyes.

'Okay, okay, all right,' she whispered.

My fingers moved to the top of her pubis. I brushed the moistness. This loosened the scent. Her smell struck me like the first step into a flower shop. I pressed down on the bone there. Nancy's sigh vibrated. My fingers trailed down through her pubic hair, working their way between the thick curls. One finger moved up the side of her lip. Nancy shuddered. The tip of my finger lightly touched her clit. Her knees splayed wider.

'Oh God, oh God,' she said. Her elbows snapped back behind her. Her hands gripped tight the vinyl. I was shivering. A drop of pre-come spilled down the side of my cock. I dropped my head between her legs, my mouth wide open on her vagina, my tongue emerging, and upward. My tongue brushed up over her distended hole and over her clit.

'Oh Jesus!' Nancy yelled. Her hands sank into the back of my head. They pulled me in harder. My tongue crossed her clit again, again, again. 'Oh Lord! Oh fuck! Oh Jimmy! I'm coming! Jesus, here it is! Coming!' A great flood of juices into my mouth, into the spaces around my teeth. She pushed on my forehead with the heels of her hands, pushed my head away. Her head fell back. The blush on her neck was almost mauve.

'That was quick,' I said (with heavy breath).

'No, uh-uh,' she muttered. 'Not quick. We've been having foreplay for twenty-five years.'

I grabbed her elbow. I began to arrange myself on top of her.

'Jimmy and Nancy sitting in a tree,' she whispered. She wrapped her fingers around my cock. She towed me toward the grotto, brown, pink, red, and wet with bliss. Barely had she moved her hand along my penis when the torrent of white splashed upon the inside of her thigh.

And soon after, inside. Nancy lubed not only me, but also the couch and the crevices between the cushions. She shouted. Her eyes were closed. Her teeth grit. I brought myself up into her with increasing fervor. My hands traveled down around her back, pushed up against her lower spine. My finger circled the nub of her coccyx. Nancy curled her body inward. Her hips positioned so that I could go in deep. Her forehead against my chest. Her stomach thinly folded. Her mouth and teeth gnawed my nipple. Her spit soaked my chest hair, ran down my stomach.

'Jimmy, Jimmy, Jimmy.' Evelyn's sweet song again; Nancy knew all the words.

'Don't let me die,' I whispered.

Nancy grabbed the sides of my head. She folded down my ears, brought her mouth to my cheek. She whispered:

'Dollhouses and wreaths . . . on . . . our . . . heads . . . and all through high school then wondering if we should but not . . . didn't because of Gary . . . oh God . . . Jimmy . . . you do this better than . . . Dan Occansion ha-ha . . . oh . . . oh ah ah.'

And I slammed hard enough to push us back through time. A tunnel around us of memories, going backward, blasting through every experience and year that separated us. Destroy yourself, I thought. Destroy the New World. Push us back to the core of magic. I will fuck her. And through fucking recapture. The gritty silk of her cunt is all I need. My fingers bent and slid over her sweaty skin.

I told her I loved her. I told her I loved her so much. The

tears fell from my face into her mouth. Her nails tore at the flesh on my hips.

'I'll show you mine if you show me yours,' she said. 'I'll show you mine if you show me yours I'll show you mine if you show me yours this is mine this is mine this is mine this is mine this is mine, oh God, Jimmy, you bastard, we're married, I'm coming.'

Saturday, December 24

I pulled my arm from under Nancy's head. The clock over the bed ticked loudly. The little hand pointed at four. The long hand was on six. Drunk and raised on digital, it took me a minute to translate this as 4:30. That meant it was after six in Philadelphia, I thought. Six was morning to some people. I sat on the edge of the bed. I held the pillow against my chest like armor. Liquid pain pulsed around my eyes. I looked down at Nancy's face, asleep, slightly splotched. She hummed through her nose. Fucking her had been like having dreams ripped from my insides. I'd have done it more, but there were too few dreams left to rip.

'Nancy,' I whispered.

She didn't stir.

'Friend,' I said.

She was still. Asleep, she seemed to belong, something soft among the sharp angles. After all this time, we had finally consummated what had been there between us as children. I wondered if I had fucked up, if I had plundered the last innocent thing in my life. I wondered if she was going to want anything out of me beyond Christmas. Then I pushed the thought aside as absurd. She no more wanted me than I wanted her. In an alternate universe maybe. A world where she was my wife, where we fucked every night like mad tigers. A world where she didn't have a child, where I wasn't attracted to women shorter than her, where I didn't care that she didn't know who Kandinsky was. I pushed myself up from the bed; a painful jolt at the top of my neck. I staggered toward the phone on the lamp table. Dan Occansion lay on the table next to the phone. He always had a real smug look on his face. It could piss you off sometimes it was so smug.

Lift the receiver. Dial. Ring. Squint. Rub my head.

'Hello?' said a woman on the other line.

'Hello. Is Evelyn there?'

'She's asleep, of course. As was I. Who is this?'

'Um, James.'

'James. It's five-thirty in the morning. You'll have to call back later.'

'Oh, sorry. I thought it was a different time than that. I'm calling from . . . Japan.'

In the background a man said sharply: 'Who is it?'

'Evelyn's friend, James,' the woman said.

'It's five-thirty in the morning!' the man said.

'He's calling from Japan,' she said. 'Go back to sleep, Leo.' Her voice louder on the phone: 'Call back later, James.'

'All right.'

'Okay.'

'Mrs. Mako?'

'What?'

'Have a merry Christmas.'

'Yes, James.' She hung up.

I set the receiver back in place. I wiggled my toes in the carpet. They went in and out of focus. Nancy was sitting up in the futon watching me. She was mostly hidden in the dark. Her small breasts hung limp.

'You felt guilty, so you had to call her, huh?' Nancy asked.

'Something like that.'

'Her name's Evelyn?'

'Yeah.'

'Dammit. I would have never slept with you if I knew you had a girlfriend.'

I rubbed the cigarette filter over my lower lip.

'Ah, malarkey. You would have too. We've been waiting too long. It had to happen sometime. Now we just got it out of the fucking way. Besides, she's not my girlfriend. Not anymore and not yet.' I stared at the circles-within-diamonds pattern of the wallpaper. 'Hey, Nance, I was thinking. Is there anything else besides time that can move in only one direction?'

'What?'

'A truck can move in many directions. The universe shifts in all different directions. Thought patterns, they're malleable, right? The imagination can move in any direction it wants.'

The shutters' slats were filled with the day's first dim light. Nancy held her legs against her, her cheek against her knee.

'You just equated time, the universe, thought patterns, the imagination, and *trucks*. 'Trucks' doesn't quite meet the same standards.'

'Says you. I have acquaintances without imagination. But where would we be without garbage pickup?'

Shortly thereafter Nancy rode me, bouncing, pressing her thumbnails into the soft upper sides of my elbows.

I told Nancy about my father's baby doll.

'Take me to see it.' She toked on the one-hitter.

'You want to see the baby doll?'

She nodded. 'Yeah. Will they wake up?'

'That can be the adventure,' I said.

Nancy and I tiptoed up the stairs. On the stairwell wall

was a photograph of me as a child. A photograph of Tar as a child was next to it. We wore matching outfits. My parents' bedroom door was open a sliver.

'Come on,' I whispered.

Nancy's hands were clasped tight under her chin. I pushed the door open. My mother slept on her back. Her nostrils looked large and pinkish. My father was in the fetal position. They both snored loudly.

'It sounds like a car factory in here,' Nancy whispered.

A bassinet was beside my father's side of the bed. A streak of sunshine from under the curtain cut across the baby doll's face.

'There it is,' I said.

Nancy put her clasped hands against her mouth.

'A crib,' she said.

'It's sleeping soundly.'

'Go get it.'

I stared at her.

'You want me to go get the baby doll?'

She nodded while staring at the doll.

'Why would you want me to do that?'

'It looks so real.'

'That's your reason?'

'Shhh. I just want to see it up close.'

'Whatever,' I said. I walked softly over the carpet. The baby doll's big eyes stared nowhere in particular. I snatched it by its foot and darted out of the room.

'I think this guy might be a little bit retarded,' I said.

The baby doll smiled dumbly. It had gums, no teeth, a rose blush on its cheeks. No movement in the eyes. Its brown hair, though, was real. Over the yellow pajamas a lace bib hung around its neck. I dangled the baby doll in front of me by its hair.

'Hey, Billy, you little fucker.' I lit a cigarette.

'Your dad must have changed a lot since we were kids,' Nancy said. 'I never imagined him as the type to have a doll.'

'Yeah, well. Sobriety bends a man over and fucks him in the ass.'

Nancy pressed her finger between the baby doll's legs.

'No dick,' she noted.

I shook the baby doll up and down.

'Hey, Billy, what's up, man?' I said.

Nancy laughed. She was packing the one-hitter, her chin holding the bag of sinsemilla against her chest.

'Hey, Nance, watch this.' I spoke to the doll: 'Hey, Dad, can I go to the Roller Castle tonight with the other kids? *No?*'

I chucked the doll across the basement. It smacked against a bookshelf and knocked over a wooden chicken. Together they toppled to the ground.

'Heh-heh-heh.'

'That's mean.' Nancy had a wicked smile.

I walked beside the baby doll. It looked up at me like an idiot.

'Hey, Dad, remember when I stole that pack of gum? Remember when you hit me afterward? You do? Oh good.'

I jumped on Billy's skull.

'Jimmy! You're gonna break him.'

I was laughing. I picked the doll up by its foot. Its head was caved in.

'No, look, Nance, it'll pop out.'

I squished its head. The face slowly puffed back into shape.

'Let's go put it back,' Nancy said.

I held the baby doll upside down. I took a drag off my cigarette.

'Dad. Dad, I'm glad to have you here. I've been meaning

to have this little talk with you. How do I say it? Well, some of the things you say, they hurt my feelings. Like when Tar and I were riding the Big Wheel at the same time, and you said cut it out because we look like a couple of fags. Remember?'

I pitched the baby doll across the room; *thwap!* against the wall. He fell facedown on the ground. I walked over to him.

'Hey,' I said loudly. 'Hey, Dad! How's it going? Let me show you this new move I just learned. You can use it on Mom.'

I kicked the baby doll. He ricocheted off of the wall and came back to my foot. I kicked him again. He bounced off the ceiling, flipping up one of the corkboard panels, landed on the floor across the room.

'Jimmy, stop it now.' Nancy's arms were crossed. I laughed.

'Watch this, Nancy.' I cupped my hands around my mouth. 'Hey, Bill! You okay over there? Good. Good. Because there was one more thing I wanted to ask you. *I was wondering if you could tell me what it felt like being such a big fucking asshole!*'

I ran toward the baby doll. A yard away I jumped. In midair I wondered if this was such a good idea after all. My feet landed on the baby doll. A shattering crack. The chest gave way.

'Oh shit,' Nancy said.

I stood on the flat yellow pajamas. They stuck to my feet as I stepped back off the doll. Seems his torso was made of a harder, more brittle plastic than the head, arms and legs. Inside the pajamas, a thousand shards.

Sitting in Nancy's car outside the Toys 'R 'Us waiting for the doors to open at eight o' clock. My throat was raw with too many cigarettes, too much weed. The car was clouded with smoke.

'We were loud last night,' I said. 'We might have kept my parents up. That means they'll be sleeping late.'

Nancy's hand was flat against her hairline. The rings around her eyes had aged her fifteen years since the beginning of the night.

'I don't fucking believe you,' she mumbled.

I like to believe she said it with affection, love, fond remembrance.

'No, I don't know what brand of doll it is,' I said.

I held the baby doll's head in front of a manager's face. He stood behind the customer-service counter. He was putting figures in a book. He had barely glanced at the doll head.

'But it's very important that I get one just like it,' I said. 'Exactly the same.'

The manager's face was punctured with blue-rimmed pockmarks. He smelled like Vitalis. Behind him a woman shot prices onto game boxes. Click! The manager looked up. His voice was monotone.

'I don't know what kind of doll that is either, sir.' He aimed his pen down the store. 'All the dolls are in aisle eight.' Then he went back to his figures.

'Listen. Man. I need your help. Now you may think you're doing something important with that book there, but it isn't every day you meet a son who's smashed his dad's inner child. I need to find this doll before my father wakes up.'

'I'm sorry, sir. I don't have the time right now.' He dashed off something else in his book.

'Excuse me.' I propped my hand on the counter to help my balance. 'Listen. I've been outside since six o'clock. *Six o'clock.* Now with all that waiting time I think I've earned the right to have every employee in the store looking for THIS DOLL.' I shoved the doll's head in close to the manager's nose.

Again he looked at me, his face slack.

'Let me guess,' he said drolly. 'Intoxication.'

'What is that supposed to be? Some sort of joke? That must be the sparkling wit you used to rise to your lofty position of *toy store guy.*'

The manager's eyes were steel blue.

'Watch it,' he said.

'All I wanna *watch* is *you* helping *me . . . find . . . this . . . doll.*'

He muttered: 'It seems to me I've already told you twice. I've never seen that doll and I can't help you find it.'

'This is *Toys 'R 'Us*! People buy *dolls* here! *That* is what *you're here for! You're the manager!* IF NOT FOR YOUR DOLL-FINDING ABILITY YOU WOULD HAVE NO USE!'

He placed his pen on the pages of the book.

'There's one thing I can help you find,' he said. 'And that's a fat lip.'

'*That's fine. That's fine. There's only one problem. I'm not looking for a fat lip. I'M LOOKING FOR THIS DOLL!*'

The girl shooting prices stopped to watch me.

'It's the day before Christmas, pal,' the manager said. 'I don't have time to be matching up doll heads for maniacs.'

I shouted and hurled the doll head at his face. He winced and lifted his elbow to block it. The head ricocheted off him and into the girl's lap. She moved back from it as if it were a dead bird. The manager brought his fist down on the counter. His face was flushed. I stood still, breathing heavy.

'In a second I'm going to come out from behind this counter, and then you're not going to be so loud,' he said.

'*Oh yeah. Right. Scary Lego man.*'

Nancy's voice: 'Jimmy!'

I turned. She was standing halfway down the store. She held a green-and-yellow box out in front of her like a game show hostess.

'Here!' she said. 'I found it! Come on!'

The doll's pajamas were blue instead of yellow. But besides that it looked the same. Thank God is what I thought. I heard the manager and the price-click girl muttering about me behind my back. I plunged my hand in my pocket for money.

'Fifty-seven dollars for a plastic doll. That's ridiculous.' I stripped the new doll naked. Nancy drove past the familiar neighborhood landmarks. Although it was morning, most of the houses hadn't yet turned their Christmas lights off. I put the new doll's foot in the yellow legging.

'It's eight twenty-seven,' Nancy said.

I sauntered inside. I wiped the inside corner of my eye with my finger. The new baby doll was crammed under my arm. My mother stood in the kitchen doorway. She was holding a box of Bisquick in one hand at her side. Her face was grim.

'What are you doing with the baby?' she said.

'Nothing I was, uh . . . just taking it with . . .'

My father was on the couch. His elbows were on his knees. He was watching the TV. He wouldn't look at me. His lower lip was tucked into his face.

'You were just making fun of me,' he said. 'Is what you were doing.'

'*No. No.* Nancy, she just wanted a doll, she had to get

one for her niece, hell, the party's today. So I said, I said, Hey, my dad, he's got a cool doll.'

'Stop it,' my father said.

'I showed her Billy here. Nancy went, Wow, I want one just like that. She said that.'

'Stop it.'

'So I took it to Toys 'R' Us. 'Cos Nancy wanted an exact copy of this doll. And we found it. I mean, you don't have to worry about Billy. I took care of it and all. Talked to it.'

My father stared at the TV. The video images reflected in the tears rolling down his cheek. His chin was shaking. I turned my head and blew out air.

'Dad,' I said.

My mother stomped up next to me.

'When are you going to grow up?' she growled. She wrenched the doll from under my arm. She handed the baby doll to my father. He took it gently from her without looking up. He positioned it in his lap.

'I didn't do anything,' I said. 'What did I do?'

'You've become a loser,' my mother said. 'It's obvious why you've kept yourself hidden for five years.'

I stared at her. My mother set the Bisquick box on the kitchen counter.

'Yeah, well fuck you both,' I said.

The doll was hidden in the darkness of my father's flesh.

My coat was unzipped, but I was too drunk to zip it. I had tried, believe me. Now the wind swept under my arms and was cold. From the roof of my parents' house I could see most of the neighborhood. There were seven types of houses, their colors different, their shapes repeated. My parents' was a two-story, the largest of the seven models. As a child this was a point of pride, to have had a home larger than most my friends. Now as I sat on top of the roof I felt pride again. It wasn't because of the size of the house, though. It wasn't because of my talent or my looks or the women I had slept with. It wasn't because of anything. My pride was self-sustaining. My mind felt enormous as I peered down on the neighborhood, as I looked down on the tiny people and tiny cars I had left behind. I came back the King, I thought, the King of Troll Court. My subjects were all around me.

It took me a long time to tie one of the kite's streamers to Dan Occansion's foot. Through perseverance I succeeded. Dan's body was hard. Most of its old energy seemed to be gone. But it would come back, I thought, when he was up there doing a stunt, it would come back again. The kite was painted like flames. The wind was wild and heavy. I stood up, wavering. The incline of the roof was steeper than I remembered it being. I set the kite down on the edge of the house, poking over the gutter. I ran toward the other side. I lengthened the string, unrolling the spool little by little. Instead of flying, the kite was blown down over the side of the house.

'Shit. Let's try again. You'll fly.'

The sky was gray. I tried running across the roof again, from the opposite side. The kite went into the air for a moment. But I couldn't keep it flying. I ran back and forth a few more times with no luck. Once I slipped. I had to catch myself on the chimney so I didn't fall.

A woman yelled from her driveway: 'Is that you up there, Jimmy Gunn?' It was Mrs. Delgesse. She was next to her mailbox with a handful of mail.

'I am trying to fly this kite,' I yelled to her.

Mrs. Delgesse stared at me blankly, then she walked inside her house. Old cunt had always hated me.

Again I ran from one end of the roof to the other. This

time the wind caught the kite. It whipped upward, red and orange flames against a gray sky. The kite twisted from side to side with Dan Occansion's weight. I unrolled the spool letting the kite float farther away from me. But the energy didn't return. Dan Occansion was only a little piece of plastic hanging from it. Again I slipped. I slammed down on my ass and slid toward the edge. A shingle skated down over the gutter and onto the porch. The kite careened down into a large tree in the backyard.

Fuck.

I yanked. I yanked again. The kite became punctured and impaled upon a tree limb.

'Hey, get down from there,' I heard someone say. I looked down. Tar stood in the driveway staring up at me. I leaned over the edge.

'Dan's doing a stunt,' I said.

'You're wasted. You're going to break your fucking neck.'

'Tar. Mom called me a loser.' I began to cry.

'Come on, Jimmy, get down here.'

I shimmied down the gutter pipe. When I was near the bottom I fell into mud and dead rose bushes.

'What'd you do with the doll?' Tar said.

'Nancy and I were using it as an example,' I muttered. I pulled myself up using the bricks on the side of the house.

'It has different-colored eyes. The old doll had gray eyes, the same color as Dad's. You gave him a doll with blue eyes, James. It's a different fucking doll.'

I breathed in deep. I shrugged lightly.

'Who knows, Tar? Maybe a miracle happened. Iris transubstantiation.'

My back was to the wall.

'What's your fucking problem?' Tar said.

'Get out of my way.'

'No. I'm not going to get out of your way. I always get out of your way. I want you to answer me.'

'I got nothing to say. Move.'

Tar's body was tensed. He was staring at me.

'Quit trying to look tough,' I said. 'You don't know what tough is. You're a pussy.'

'Fuck you. Why are you such a prick all the time?' My brother poked me in the shoulder. I backhanded his finger and began to move away. Tar grabbed my coat and pushed me back against the bricks. Again I knocked his arm away. I snapped my fists up in front of me.

'Come on, Tar. You want to fuck with me? Is that it? Come on.'

'Get serious.'

I punched him in the chest and he staggered backward.

'If you're so tough, Tar, come on. Come on. I've tangled with guys ten times you.' I swiped him in the lip. I hit him in the shoulder.

'*Come on,*' I said. '*All of you want to fuck me up, that's all you want to do. Well, fuck you.*'

Mrs. Delgesse was standing on her porch behind us.

Tar's eyes were teary and enraged. I hit him.

'Cut it out,' he said. His fist came up into my neck. This made me cough. I tried to hit him but he blocked me.

'Cut it out.' He slammed me in the stomach. He struck me hard in the mouth. I was stumbling. He was throwing his body into me.

'Cut it out.' He punched me in the ear and I fell down. He came down on top of me, hitting me repeatedly.

'*Cut it out,*' he yelled. '*Cut it out! Cut it out! Cut it out!*'

I tried to get up. Blood was spilling down onto my shirt. Tar's fist came down upon my nose. I heard and felt a sickening crack. Different-colored moons clouded my vision. I fell down onto my side, my arm bent beneath me. Tar backed away. He was sobbing.

'*Every time, all these years you just hurt everybody,*' he cried. '*Everything that happened to you happened to me! But you use it—you use it as an excuse to be selfish and plain, just plain fucking abusive!*'

Tar moved quickly away over the lawn. I heard the front door close. I pushed grass out of my mouth with my tongue. I was trying to stay conscious. I rolled onto my back. I lay there, spinning. I heard singing. Somewhere in the neighborhood Christmas carolers were making their way from door to door.

God rest ye, merry gentlemen, let nothing you dismay
Remember Christ our savior was born on Christmas Day
To save us all from Satan's power when we have gone
  astray

The sight in one of my eyes was blurred with blood. The wind was forceful on my face and neck. It whistled in my ears.

O tidings of comfort and joy, comfort and joy
O tidings of comfort and joy

Grabbing hunks of dirt and grass, I pushed myself to something like standing. I stumbled away from my parents' house and down the white streets.

Nancy stole cash from her mother's wallet, and I used it to board the first Greyhound to Philadelphia. I was there before the first light of Christmas morning.

More Fun in the New World

Gary Bauer had lived a life on the lower end of luck. The other children around him harassed him in the way children do to those who are weak or unusual. He had been spit on and beaten. He had had his glasses stolen and thrown over his head. He had been snickered at by girls who found him ugly. Gary's parents loved him and even doted on him. But they were saddened by the way he had matured. He was plagued by visions and strange ideas. He had peculiar rituals. He was not an attractive boy, and, by the time he turned sixteen, his face was awash with acne. About this acne, I thought: If there is a God, he should be mercilessly tortured.

Our phone lines led to Gary, were attached to him, and he would reach us by them every day. Regularly he would be frustrated because of something he had overheard someone say about him, or a girl at school who had the prettiest eyes, or anonymous Clearasil advertisements left in his locker. Sometimes he would sob.

'We're helping him work his way through adolescence,' I said to Tar and Nancy. 'For us it's easy, even fun, but Gary's not going to hit his stride until college.'

Nancy would be at Gary's house every other night. They would watch TV and he would lay his head in her lap.

Tar would take down the names of those who had hurt him and seek out revenge.

I would hold Gary in my arms and he would cry.

'I'm trying hard to push it all out,' he said. 'But it won't leave, won't go. For months I've tried to get out the pain.'

Let me say that our friend was not a burden. He was what made our lives different. He was the one who let us feel.

On a Saturday morning in April of our seventeenth year, Gary called me and told me that he loved me. His voice was low and quiet. He had me put Tar on the phone, who received a similar message.

That's why it should have been no surprise when Gary's uncle called later that afternoon and told me that my best friend had just blown off his own head.

Tar and I drove our Buick the two blocks to the Bauers' home. There were police cars outside, and an ambulance.

'A motherfucking ambulance,' I muttered.

Tar and I entered the house without knocking. The same porcelain Virgin Mary was on the wall facing us, but it looked somehow different. More evil. There was a different soundtrack to it, for one thing. Sobs of Gary's extended family came at us from the direction of the living room. If there had been a contest on who could be the loudest and sound the most despairing, Gary's mother would have been the winner. 'Shh, Momma, shh,' Mr. Bauer said. It was strange that he used the word *Momma*, considering. Noticing something, Tar began to cry.

'He's still out there,' he said.

Beyond a piece of wall and part of the kitchen we could see a section of the back porch. The sliding glass door was open. A pair of skinny legs was lying on the ground. It was a position no sleeping body would have chosen, with one foot bent inward. The blue jeans were soaked in blood. A cop stood in front of the legs, writing something down or sketching something.

Tar wailed. It was as angry as it was sad. I felt his wail in my chest as if it was my own. There is a superhero in Marvel Comics called the Banshee, who can destroy things with the power of his scream.

Mr. Bauer must have heard my brother's voice and remembered us and how this would affect us, because he began to weep loudly at the sound. He was always a man to react to the living more than the dead.

The cop saw us coming toward the porch. He pointed to us with a pencil and said something to another cop who was hidden from our view. The other cop came skipping around the corner. He was a bloated man with an uncaring face. He was doing his job, cleaning up dead teenagers. He put his fingers on my chest.

'Okay, son, we have to keep you outside for a minute,' he said.

'I'm warning you,' I said. 'Do not touch me.'

'Okay, son.' He didn't take his hand away. 'Come on now.'

Tar screamed again. He looped around the cop for the back porch. The cop with the pencil jumped out, blocking his path. He pressed the palms of his hands on Tar's shoulders, stopping him. Tar screamed Gary's name at the top of his lungs.

As we were being escorted out the door, Nancy entered. Her clothes didn't match. Her face was pallid and wet, streaked with red. When she saw me, her mouth opened wide but she didn't make a sound. She grabbed at my neck, almost strangling me for a moment, and then collapsed against my chest. She repeated the word *No* many times. She hit me on the arms with her fists. I crushed her there against me and I wept because no matter how hard I tried I couldn't stop it from coming.

'Now, if you guys don't mind, just stay out here on the porch until we get things straightened out,' the bloated cop said. 'It shouldn't be long.'

The cop left.

'Around back,' Tar said.

Upon reaching the backyard, we stared up at the deck porch. It was twelve feet above the ground. I was sure that Gary had shot himself up there because it would be easier to clean up. You could just take a hose to it. The cops didn't seem to be up there any longer. We jogged over to the supporting braces and shimmied our ways up. My head peeked over the bottom of the deck and I saw the soles of Gary's shoes. I became sick to my stomach. I almost turned around and left, but didn't.

Tar was first up. He clutched the front of his T-shirt in one hand, and moved in close to the body.

Gary's chin was the only intact part of his head. It was slightly unshaven. Beneath his chin, at the top of his neck, was a large wet red crater. Above his chin, where his face and the top of his head were supposed to be, was a scooped mass of bone and blood. His hips were twisted in a way that looked painful. His father's shotgun was tangled in his arms. His body was covered in pieces of itself. Gary had placed the muzzle directly under the chin, so that his insides splattered straight upward and plummeted back down upon him. He had knocked every inch of anything out of himself.

'No,' Nancy whispered.

No is the perfect word in the face of an unwarranted death. It can be a denial, saying, No, this is not true. I'll scream and shake my head and it will go away. It can be a condemnation of the situation, as in, No, this is wrong, Gary shouldn't have done this. And it can be a universal condemnation, as in, No, there is nothing good, there is nothing just, there is nothing beautiful about this world.

I knelt by Gary's side. I gripped his ear and turned his head toward me. Juices from inside of him came sluicing down onto my hand and between my fingers. Senseless, empty matter. Gary had swept himself away without knowing how much we needed him.

Tar clasped at Gary's body, picking him up beneath his arms. He was muttering something about how it might be okay if we could get him to the hospital. He started to drag the body across the deck. As he did, Gary's face fell toward me even more. More of his insides fell out onto my arms and legs. Nancy grabbed Gary's shoe and dropped her head there against it.

'No!' she cried.

'No!' Tar screamed.

And I said it too, as in reason number three:

There is nothing good. There is nothing just. There is nothing beautiful about this world.

A Day at the Parlor

The community, upon hearing that Gary Bauer had died, commonly believed that the Gunn brothers would destroy some things. Instead we were very quiet, at least until the day of the wake.

Our mother cried for two days. She cooked food, massive amounts of it. She would send it down to the Bauers', who would do away with it in favor of food by the other, better cooks in the neighborhood.

'Are you okay?' my mother would ask Tar. 'Are you sure you're all right?'

My brother would nod.

'I'm fine,' he would say.

I would say the same thing when she asked me.

She was afraid we were two of the types like the serial killers, who had no feelings at all inside. But it was just that we didn't want to think about it. Tar didn't want to think about it for his own reasons. I didn't want to remember the gunk from Gary's head on my hands. People have no idea.

Gary was in the closed casket. His father told me he was in his bow tie.

'The red one with the ducks,' Mr. Bauer said. He

lurched forward, which frightened me. He grabbed the lapels of my suit and began crying. I poked his arm.

'You're a good boy,' his father said, drawing away from me. He placed his large hand on my cheek. 'You're a good boy.' His hand slid away from my face. He walked, slumped over, to the other side of the room.

I looked at the casket. That was nice of his parents, I thought. They never liked him wearing that thing, but still they buried him in it, because they knew he would want it. That was nice. I knelt down on the kneeler and stared at the swirls in the wood grain on the casket. They wouldn't have let us see the body, of course, because it had no face; it would have made everyone sick.

Nancy knelt down next to me, wearing perfume. She had on a teal blouse and a pleated black skirt. She also wore nylons, which I never remembered seeing her in before. There were a lot of people milling behind us having conversations. Intruders, whom I hated.

'How are you?' Nancy asked.

'Good.'

'*Good?* James.'

'Nancy, I kind of fucked up.'

'Fucked up how?'

'He so much as told me yesterday on the phone. I could have gone right over.'

'That's dumb, really dumb, that you think that,' she told me. But she said it with all love, and she put her hand on my back and began weeping.

Tar grew more furious as the day went on. He was a person who wanted to destroy things. He was holding it in. He was wearing a blue-and-red-striped tie.

There were three round tables in the rear of the funeral parlor where food was laid out. Tar was cutting

an apple into thin slices on a paper towel. When he was
done he set them in a line. He made no move toward
eating them.

'Cocksuckers,' he whispered to Nancy and me. 'All
these people from his school. All they ever did was make
fun of him.' Tar exchanged the last slice of apple in line
with the first slice.

'They feel guilty, Tar,' Nancy said.

'Fuck their guilt. Everybody's laughing, telling stories.
As if it were some fucking Super Bowl party. Yuck it up.'

'Tar, you're drunk, aren't you?' she said.

'Stoned. James is too.'

Her eyes darted from Tar to me and back.

'You guys are both stoned?'

'What's a Super Bowl party without pot?' I ate one of
the apple slices.

'Jesus,' Nancy said. She was staring at my hands. Her
cheeks had risen in disgust and disbelief. Her eyes welled
up with tears. Tar looked at her and he began to cry too.
He knew she probably felt abandoned.

'Sorry, Nancy,' he said.

'We didn't smoke very much,' I said, and ate another
apple slice.

Mr. Hampton was a longtime friend of my father's, and I
suppose he and Gary had crossed paths somewhere along
the way. He was having a conversation with Joe Collins,
Gary's older cousin, behind us. Joe was explaining to Mr.
Hampton about how he was doing some landscaping
work while he tried to find a job that had something to
do with his degree. Mr. Hampton asked him what he had
gotten his degree in.

Tar looked at me as he began to cut up another apple.
We were both listening to this conversation.

'See?' Tar said. 'What the fuck does that have to do with anything?'

Joe said his degree was in business. Mr. Hampton told a joke about how many business BA's it took to screw in a lightbulb. It only took one, but they needed a whole crew to sort through the eight thousand résumés! Mr. Hampton and Joe laughed.

'A joke,' Tar said, a little more loudly than he needed to. He spit out a laugh and then choked on it. 'Who are they to even be here? Gary's dead and then all of a sudden it's okay to tell jokes? I'm really getting pissed off, Jimmy.'

Mr. Hampton said he might know someone who could help Joe, a man by the name of McIntrey who worked at Maris Publishing House. They needed somebody who was bright and young to keep track of all their records. It wasn't a great job, but, hey, it was a good start.

'Really?' Joe said, enthusiastically.

'I thought I had his business card on me somewhere,' Mr. Hampton said. 'Oh, here. Here it is.'

Tar made a throaty, squealing sound, and swirled around toward them. Mr. Hampton was in the process of handing Joe the card; they both had their fingers on it. They turned and looked at my brother. He was wheezing. His jaw muscles were twitching.

Tar grabbed the card in his fist and yanked it from them.

'Hey!' Mr. Hampton said.

Tar tore it once and then again and then again, and he threw all the pieces at them. A piece landed on Mr. Hampton's eyebrow and stuck there. Tar stared hard at him.

'Hey now, boy! What are you—?'

Tar spit on the man's shirt collar. Mr. Hampton was totally confused. He looked around the room for some sort of support. Perhaps it was that pitiful expression that caused Tar to grab Mr. Hampton around the neck and thrust him backward. The man fell into one of the tables of food. The table collapsed and a bowl of dip and some cold vegetables splattered onto the carpet. Tar jumped onto Mr. Hampton's chest, sitting there, and brought his fists down into the man's face. There was a sound like a champagne bottle popping its cork, which was Mr. Hampton's nose. Tar was wailing and growling and sobbing. I watched, still chewing on the apple, tensed and waiting to see when I would be needed to jump in. So far, Tar had Hampton under control and everyone else seemed too surprised to do anything.

'Tar! Stop!' Nancy screeched.

Mrs. Bauer saw what was happening. She brought her fingers to her face. She wailed like an old-time siren.

Joe Collins made his move. He scooted in behind Tar and grappled his head. He plunged his fingers into Tar's eyes and tried to pull him off. That was my cue.

I wrapped my arm around Joe's neck and yanked backward, removing him from my brother.

'Let go!' Joe Collins rasped.

I squeezed harder to shut him up and I didn't stop. His face became a shade of purple I had never seen before. As I pulled him backward, knocking over a table of cheeses, my fury swept away logic. A vision took me in its grip and wouldn't let go. Maybe I could cut off Joe Collins's connection to this planet, cut him off entirely. It would only be justice after what happened to Gary. It would be a strike against the evil God, throw one of his own back at him. He wanted a war? I squeezed harder, with both arms now, trying to crush Joe Collins's esophagus and break his neck. His eyes rolled up into the top of his head. His hands were flapping at his sides as if he were trying to swim to the surface of the water. I hollered as loudly as I could. Every bit of hate I had in me was on him. A crowd of people was pulling me off and Nancy and my father were pulling them off of me.

People thought it was in bad taste that Gary's father asked Collins and Mr. Hampton to leave but told Tar and me to stay. (Well, actually, Hampton had to leave. He had to have his nose set at the hospital. He brought suit against my father, because of Tar, but lost since the only witnesses to how it began were Nancy and myself, who both perjured ourselves. Joe Collins refused to testify.) Mr. Bauer brought us into the bathroom for a conference. He leaned forward on a sink, gazing down into the drain as he talked to us. You could see the top of his bald head in the mirror in front of him.

'Gary loved you boys more than anything else in the world. So out of respect for that I'm not going to ask you to leave. Hell, I guess I should have expected it.'

Mr. Bauer looked up at us in the mirror.

'I know Gary wasn't somebody that everybody automatically loved. I knew they gave him a hard time . . . And I know that you two spent your lives protecting him. But you have to get used to the fact that he's gone now, get over it, and learn that the only ones you need to learn how to protect now is yourselves.

'Claris used to say that you didn't really care about our son. She said you used Gary to rationalize your predilection for violence. But that's only half true, I know. I know that, boys. You wouldn't have done everything you done if it wasn't somebody you loved.'

Mr. Bauer nodded while looking down at the drain again. He turned. He patted Tar on the shoulder as he passed him. Tar was looking down at the tile and sniffling.

Gary's dad plodded toward the door. When he had opened it partway, he turned to us. He had a small sad smile.

'The doctor gave me some medicine to help me sleep,' he said. 'I told him, hell, going to sleep at night, that's the easy part. Waking up in the morning, now that's something I'm gonna have to get used to.'

Mr. Bauer's smile had turned bitter.

'Shit,' he said.

He turned away from us as he walked out the door, down the hall and back into the funeral parlor.

Tar was staring at one of the urinals. He seemed to remember something. He turned toward me.

'*Orl Caatu*,' Tar said. He laughed and his eyes teared up at the same time. 'That means, "Life is really fucked without Gary." In French.'

Chipmunk

1. I Acquire the girl

Saint Gabriel the Archangel was large and impressive, a stylized structure in a mod early-'70s style. That period of architecture brought back memories of the educational films they would show in grade school, films about car crashes and littering and the horrible things drugs could do to your body.

I hadn't been in church for a long time.

A row of windows lined the top of Saint Gabriel's. From each window a dusty sunbeam jutted down, selecting a random parishioner. Above the altar was the Christ: an enormous, wire-frame, welded god, dripping frozen metal. His neck was twisted back. God was screaming.

'We're born of God,' I once said to Tar. 'Your temperament is based on his mood, I guess. That is my new theory. Often, God yawns, and very boring people come out. Other times he is chatting away to some angels, and some of those people who can't shut up fall out from between his teeth and down into the bodies of fetuses here on earth. On one day God was screaming and my life flew off the tip of his tongue. That's why I'm filled with rage and sadness.'

'That's pretty sentimental,' Tar said. 'And melodramatic.' He was swishing a straw around in his glass of diet Coke.

'Filled with those things, too.' I put another french fry into my mouth.

I arrived early. Saint Gabriel's was already close to standing-room only. I dipped my fingers in the holy water as I passed it, and stabbed out the sign of the cross. I staked out a place in the last pew. All the sinners and scourges sat in the back, I supposed. My kind.

I wiped the holy water from my fingers onto my pants. An old woman in a black dress sat beside me. 'Merry Christmas,' the old woman said to me. She propped her cane against the back of the pew, but it fell and began rolling away. I caught it with my foot and helped her to find a place for it. The old lady touched my wrist. Her hand was blue and purple.

My broken nose was covered with tape. Dark circles surrounded my eyes. Nancy had taken me to the emergency room before I left Saint Louis, where they informed me I had a slight fracture. Old Tar had thrust me into a state of public humiliation. Parishioners checked me out. A raccoon person, a wounded geek, a beaten man, a pussy.

At eleven thirty-two the Mako clan arrived. Evelyn came waltzing down the aisle: my heart in makeup and a green dress. Her bones shifted around in the material like chiffon. I scooted back behind the old woman so that I was hidden from Evelyn's sight.

My love's father was a feeble man with an Ethiopian bloat. He wore glasses. He had spots on his face. Mr. Mako placed his hand on his daughter's back as she slid into the aisle. Evelyn's mother was of average height, dark and thin, with a worried face. Deep lines were etched beneath her eyes. She had had troubles. Evelyn's brother was also dark-haired. Ectomorphic, buck teeth, a bit of Gary Bauer around the mouth. I rubbed my thumbs on the back of the pew in front of me.

One section of the church held the chorus. They wore gold gowns and red robes. Great gold pipes ranging in size from a pencil to a factory chimney ran up the side of the church wall. Organ music blared, flushing over the crowd. The chorus began to sing. It made me dizzy. I apologized to God for fucking up my family, for smoking pot and smashing up the baby doll. In the row before me a small child was munching Cheerios from a plastic container.

The priest's homily was about how it had become a cliché to put down the attention given to presents at Christmas and to say that presents and Santa Claus and et cetera had nothing to do with the true meaning of Christ's birth. Christmas is about love, the priest said, and gift giving is an attempt to communicate that love. And that is beautiful.

I wondered what my parents had gotten me for Christmas. I wondered if they were going to send it to me, or just take it back to the store.

I fucked up the words to 'Hosanna in the Highest.' The old woman next to me probably thought I was one of those Catholics who only went to church on Christmas and Easter. I played with the tape on my nose, acting as if I was distracted by the pain.

The old woman used both hands to shake mine during the sign of the peace. A fat man shook my hand firmly. He smiled. He probably had some turkey and gravy waiting for him at home. The mother of the child with the Cheerios looked sorry for me because of my bandaged nose.

I went to communion. I tried to talk myself into believing the wafer was the body of Christ, but it was pretty much just a little tasty thing. Evelyn didn't see me when I walked past her. She had her forearms on the row in front of her, her chin on her wrists, a strand of dark hair hanging in her face. She was checking out what was going on on the other side of the church.

Snow attached itself to us as we filtered out of Saint Gabriel's. People were happy. It was Christmas. Don't believe what you hear about the suicide rate going up: It's an urban legend. Evelyn's back was to me. Her bony hips poked corners into the green dress. Her family and another family had formed an exclusionary circle. They exchanged tales of the past year.

'Look at Tim,' said a man who unfortunately had one eye positioned lower on his face than the other. He grabbed his son's head and pulled it backward. He forced open the head's mouth. Braces. 'Tim got a new car inside his mouth this year!' the man said. The kid gagged and tried to get loose.

I approached stealthily.

'Evelyn,' I whispered. I hadn't completely made up my mind not to dart back to Manhattan. 'Evelyn.'

The girl turned around. As you might imagine, she was astonished.

'James?!'

'Yes, it's me. I know I look ridiculous. Don't laugh.'

'Oh, God. Oh, my God. Why are you— Oh, my God, why— What happened to your face?'

'Oh, well, see, we fought. Got into a fight.'

'Who? Who'd you get into a fight with?'

'My brother. Yes, Tar.'

'That's horrible!'

'Yes, and the worst part is he won the fight.'

Evelyn lifted one hand into the air, still in the phase of astonishment.

'But why are you here?' she said.

'Well, that has to do with you.'

Evelyn stared at me, blank-faced.

'What?' I said.

'You are so weird.'

'I am. And I'm not going to drink. I promise. I have finally learned my lesson.'

'You aren't going to give up.'

'I'm not. Are you moved?'

'Moved?'

'Because somebody rode a thousand miles on a noisy bus full of people with various smells, having Evelyn Mako in their head the whole way.'

Evelyn giggled. She looked up at me. I looked down at her. Snowflakes sprinkled her black hair like beautiful dandruff. The tip of her tooth was sticking out over her lower lip. Her brown eyes glinted in the cloud-filtered light. Her beauty was breaking my heart. I reached out and caressed the side of her face.

Evelyn's eyes welled up. She smiled, sadly. She reached up and took my hand.

'We could try, I guess,' she said. 'Especially considering the stinky people on the bus.'

'You mean okay?' I said.

She nodded. 'Okay,' she said.

'Okay?'

'Yes,' she said. 'Okay.'

'As in okay?'

Evelyn nodded. As in okay.

There were a thousand trumpets around me.

Evelyn's father trotted up beside us.

'Chipmunk, we have to get a move on.' He had a very gruff voice for such a frail-looking man. 'The family's meeting back home in fifteen minutes.' He smiled at me and offered his hand. I gave him mine.

'I'm Leo.'

'I'm James Gunn, Mr. Mako.'

He shook my hand with both of his. I did my best not to intimidate him with my superior size and strength.

'Ah, James Gunn. The five-thirty-in-the-morning caller. Very good, very good.'

'Yes, I suppose I must apologize.'

'What happened to your nose?'

'My nose?' I looked at Evelyn. She made a little face.

'I'm twenty-five years old, and you would have thought I'd have decided I didn't want to learn how to ride a skateboard already,' I said. 'My little cousin had this contraption. He called it the mean machine. The word *mean* should have tipped me off, eh?'

'Ha-ha! Well said. Have you ever heard of windsailing? I'll tell you a story sometime that will knock your socks off. Well, James, we have to go back to the house so that my wife's relatives can rape us of our food and rummage through our drawers when we're not looking.'

'Ha-ha!' I said, and pointed at him.

'You're welcome to stop by, of course.'

Evelyn was kicking the toe of her shoe on the pavement.

'I think I'd like that very much, Mr. Mako.'

'Terrific. I'm going to put you on post, though, make sure my in-laws don't steal my jewelry!'

'I know a few people like that.' I waved my fist around next to my head. 'And I know what to do when I catch them. You don't think I really got this nose from *falling off a skateboard*, do you?'

'Ha-ha. Very good, very good.' He touched Evelyn on the shoulder. He gave her a happy little nod in approval. I had played her father as easily as 'Chopsticks.' On some days, I could play them all.

'Hurry up now, Chipmunk,' he said. 'And, James, you're coming, all right?'

'Yes, sir.'

'Good.'

Evelyn and I walked together toward the Mako-family van. Her father slid open the big door for us.

'Go on in, Early Riser,' he said to me. 'I think I'll call you Early Riser.'

'Strangely enough, that's my confirmation name.'

'Ha-ha! Very good.'

Evelyn moved a wrapped gift aside in the backseat. I sat down beside her. Evelyn's mother turned around and glanced at me, then back up at the windshield. Quickly, she turned around again, making sure that she really saw me there.

I waved.

'Hey there.'

2. On consummating the relationship

My finger slipped between the top of Evelyn's pantyhose and hip. Her mouth was on my neck. Her tongue wiggled there. Her hands traveled up under my shirt over the skin of my back. Evelyn and Evelyn, oh Evelyn!

*   *   *

We were in the room her parents had kept for her. It was Neapolitan ice cream, brown and white and pink. Evelyn was sitting on the edge of her desk, her knees bent up. I was standing between her legs. Her feet rested on the rim of my belt, her big toes snug against my hips. The desk chair was on its side beneath me.

'I love you,' I said. 'I love you.'

She said it twice back to me. Her eyes were closed. Her hands were bent up at the wrists. The heels of her palms beat a crazy little rhythm on my back.

'James.'

As I kissed her, I considered these items: That I wanted to be grown up now, okay, I was ready, it was sad. I'll miss all that solitude behind me. But I was ready to surrender. I moved my mouth up to the tiny saucer of her ear. We were both crying, all these things pouring out. My beautiful Evelyn.

'It will be good, okay?' I said. 'It will be good between us.'

But she wasn't thinking straight. Her face was all screwed up with the acceptance of our situation. My finger was inside her pussy.

On the other side of her door we could hear her relatives. They were yelling and laughing. They were thanking their Kris Kringles for their presents. One of them adored a tie somebody named Susan bought him.

Evelyn looked down and grasped for my belt. She unbuckled my pants. She shoved her arm into my underwear and grabbed at my testicles. The tip of her finger ran up the underside of my cock.

'Oh!'

Evelyn brought my head into hers. Teeth scraping teeth. Our faces mashed together.

'Ouk,' I said.

Evelyn's eyes opened.

'Your nose?'

'My nose.'

'Poor baby.'

'I'm a man now, okay? I'll be one, Evelyn.'

'Okay. That's good. You know what?'

'No.'

'There's a lot of people right outside the door there.'

I snapped out my arm and locked the door.

Evelyn stared at the door. Beads of sweat freckled her forehead. She was thinking, weighing options.

'We can wait though, Evelyn. We can wait if you want, of course.'

Evelyn smiled at me. She shook her head no. The communion wafer must have worked; it gave me magical powers. I grabbed Evelyn's buttocks and lifted her off the desk. She giggled as I carried her to the bed. We fell onto the bed. We flipped over. She was on top of me, wriggling over my body like a wonderful little animal. She pulled off my pants and threw them against the back wall. The clasp of my belt clattered on a picture frame.

On the other side of the door a woman cackled.

Still in her underwear, Evelyn's crotch ran over mine, rubbing it there. I slid myself up the bed, pulling myself out from beneath her. My penis flapped against my stomach. I grabbed Evelyn around the waist and set her on her back. I kissed my way through the tiny, taut muscles of her abdomen. I pulled her panties off over her thin legs, her black-as-oil pubic hair. The scent filled my nose and head. I set my mouth down upon her hole. Evelyn bucked her hips and put the pillow over her head to block her squeals. Her thigh was against my cheek. My tongue was up inside her, it was my favorite place I had ever been in all of life. Evelyn squeaked more loudly. She grabbed the headboard with her hands behind her and raised her hips.

Somewhere two countries warred. Somewhere a killer mutilated a child. Somewhere a man lay curled up in the death throes of starvation. Somewhere a hurricane ravaged a town and everything the people there had spent their lives working for. But none of it mattered, because here Evelyn was coming. She was coming in my mouth. It coursed throughout my body.

Evelyn screamed, and her screaming was the universe. She clamped her hand over her mouth. Her face was red.

'James Gunn,' she said. She grabbed my arm and started pulling. I kissed her mouth, her juices a film over our tongues. I looked into her pupils and saw her tender naked core. I almost backed away, it was so helpless. But instead I cradled her head in my hand and began to slide myself inside her. The wet clamp around the tip of my cock blinded me.

Evelyn's hand came down around her vagina.

'Wait!' she said. 'Wait! No babies! Condom!'

'No pill?'

She shook her head.

'Oh,' I said. 'Oh.'

My cock was just outside her now, so close. A strand of her pubic hair entered the hole of my penis. The bristles tickled the sides.

Evelyn's hair was a mess. She pulled me by the hand through the crowd.

'Evelyn,' her mother said. She was holding a large glass of wine. She had a goofy grin and was slurring her words. 'Where've you been? You didn't even open your gift from Carol.'

Evelyn's lipstick was streaked across the side of her face.

'I've been . . . uh . . . James had to see some stuff. I showed it to him.'

'What stuff?'

'Stuff, Mom! We have to go!' Evelyn pulled me. I knocked through a couple of her cousins.

'Yo, sorry,' I said to the cousins.

'Go where?' asked Mrs. Mako.

'Mom! We have to go somewhere! It's Christmas! Where are the keys!'

'In my purse, on the kitchen table. Have you been drinking?'

'I don't drink, Mom. You do enough of that for all of us.'

Evelyn pulled me into the kitchen. Wrapping paper crinkled beneath my feet. She dumped the contents of her mother's purse onto the kitchen table. She scooped up the keys. The key chain was a fuzzy-wuzzy guy with big feet.

'Come on,' Evelyn said. She leaned up and kissed me.

'Yes, condoms,' I told the fellow at the counter of the 7–Eleven. The store was empty except for me. I looked outside where Evelyn was parked by the curb in the green Chevrolet. Exhaust fumes rose from the back of the car.

'It's Christmas,' he said.

'Yes, merry Christmas to you. I'll take the Trojans ribbed.'

'No, I mean it's Christmas. What are you going to do with condoms on Christmas?'

'You're kidding.'

'The baby Jesus lies in the manger. That's the focus of Christmas.'

'Give me the goddamn condoms.'

'I'm sorry, I can't do that.'

'You're kidding.'

'No, I'm not kidding.'

'They're right there on the wall behind you.'

'I know where they are.'

'You won't sell me some condoms?'

'I'm a Christian.'

'*Give me the fucking condoms!*'

'Now that you use that tone with me, I especially won't give you some condoms. I wouldn't even sell you some beer nuts.'

I turned and saw, through the 7–Eleven window, Evelyn waiting in the car. She widened her eyes at me. She was beautiful. I tried to smile at her. I turned back to the man.

'I'm gonna remove your throat from your fucking neck,' I said.

'I'm calling the police.' The man took a couple steps over and picked up the phone. He began dialing. 'I know the number by heart.'

'Oh Jesus!'

I pushed the front door open. I walked over the sidewalk. I opened the door to the green Chevrolet.

'You didn't get them?' Evelyn said.

'Step on it.'

There was another 7–Eleven about a mile away next to a Taco Bell. I thanked God there was an Indian behind the counter.

The Taco Bell was closed. Evelyn drove the car around back, to the parking lot, and stopped. A large metal trashcan was beside us. Evelyn kept the engine running. The heat was on. It was warm. We began kissing and were immediately back into a frenzy.

'I'll put the condom on,' Evelyn said. 'That's now considered an aspect of foreplay.'

'All right.'

I sat back in the seat. My pants were in a heap next to

me. Evelyn ripped open the Trojan packet and pulled out the condom. She took my cock in her hand and tried to roll the condom over the tip. The condom just mushed down my penis.

'The condom's upside down,' I told her.

'Oh. Oh.'

Evelyn slid the condom onto my penis. It was taut and a bit constricting. Our mouths came together.

'Baby,' I said.

Evelyn removed her underwear completely and crawled onto my lap. She used the rim over the passenger door to balance herself. She lowered herself onto me. She grabbed onto my neck. We both made little noises upon entry. Her knees were splayed out wide by her sides.

'You're limber,' I said.

'I was in gymnastics all through junior high and high school.'

That was something I had never known.

Evelyn's shirt was open, her bra pushed down below her breasts. Her nipples stuck out straight. They brushed through the hair of my chest as she moved up and down. We were staring at each other. It was strange and sometimes embarrassing.

'Can we move to the side a little?' she asked. 'The heater is burning my butt.'

We moved to the side a little. We kissed softly.

'I'm in love with you,' she said. 'I knew it for sure when I saw you in the church parking lot.'

I nodded and smiled.

'Is it okay that we go slow?' she asked. 'I want to go slow.'

'I want to go slow too.'

But it was impossible for long. Pretty soon I was pulling her down hard onto me, pushing her forward, running my tongue up the bones of her chest and then into her mouth. Evelyn's hair clung to the front windshield. She thrust her hips against me with as much force as she could muster. All the muscles in her body were standing out, the palmars, glutei, semitendinouses, peroneals, radial extensors, each and every precious little deign of movement. Her fingernails buried into my shoulder and my back. Her face seemed to be in pain. Evelyn was hollering. I grabbed her ass and slammed her down even more quickly onto me. I crushed my face into the crevice of her neck. And I was pouring it all into her, twenty-five years without love.

3. Rules of the girl

Evelyn lay on her stomach on the bed. I had sneaked into the room after her parents had gone to sleep.

I gave her a massage. Pretty soon I slid my hand between the cheeks of her ass and between her legs. I cupped her vagina in the palm of my hand. It was exceedingly wet, the sheets beneath it were soaked. She said my name.

After putting on another condom, I crouched behind her. I slid myself inside. Evelyn bent her forehead into the pillow. Her shoulder blades stuck up. I focused on the two lanes of downy hair on the back of her neck. I rubbed her back. I reached my hand around to her face. Evelyn bit my finger.

On Evelyn's bottom there were some red spots and goose bumps. I didn't like looking at them. And there were freckles on her shoulders, something else I didn't like. I stared forward at the wall. The sex felt good, but not as good as it had earlier in the car.

I had probably been pushing too hard. My pursuing of Evelyn had been too relentless. That's what I must do with all the career ambition that Tar has, chase after toys and these women. That which you collect, you control. Sometimes, the more I can't have something, the more I think that I love it—her, that is. I hoped that I hadn't made a terrible mistake, committed myself to something that I had no way of sticking to. I thought of three stories: that of Faust, that of Midas, and that of *The Monkey's Paw*.

Evelyn orgasmed first. She shouted that she loved me.

Since I had been thinking about other things, I wasn't close to coming. I started moving as quickly as I could, slamming. Evelyn's buttocks were a powerful force against my groin. She reached her hand back and grabbed my wrist. I came into her, hard. I imagined something as I did: My sperm shot through Evelyn's whole body, came out of her mouth, went all the way around the earth, and landed again in the base of my spine.

The alarm rang at six o'clock in the morning so that I could leave Evelyn's bedroom before her parents awoke. Evelyn slithered up on her belly to turn off the alarm. Her eyes were puffy and crusty with sleepers. The sheets fell away from her, exposing her breasts. I lifted up the sheet and covered her again. She turned on her side to face me. Evelyn smiled.

'Good morning, honey,' she said.

'Good morning, sweetheart.' I smiled.

Evelyn slid on top of me. She kissed me. Her tongue went inside my mouth. It moved around a bit. I swirled my own around it. Her breath wasn't as horrid as it could be, but I didn't like it in me much.

Evelyn closed her eyes and lay her head on my neck. Her arms and legs clutched my body, as if pinning me there to the bed. I looked at the ceiling.

'James, tell me how much you love me.'

'I love you very much.'

'Tell me all those things, about how you thought of me while we were apart.'

'I thought of you lots.'

'Tell me . . . let's see . . . tell me what my best feature is.'

Ceiling.

'Evelyn, I have to get a cigarette. I haven't had one for more than twelve hours and my lungs are going nuts.'

'Oh, okay. We can go outside.'

'It's cold out. You don't have to go with me.'

'No, that's okay.'

We put on some outfits, socks, shoes, and our coats and we walked outside. Evelyn lay her head against my chest while I smoked three Marlboros in succession. She locked her arms around me. I looked out over her backyard. A neighbor's collie was passing through. The dog stopped, turned to look at us, then went on. Pine trees swayed in the wind. I blew smoke out of my lungs, and gently brushed my hand through Evelyn's hair. I looked down at her as she snuggled her face against my chest.

'Brrr!' she said. She kissed my shirt.

I had made a very big mistake.

4. A potted plant

On the Wednesday after Christmas Evelyn brought me a potted plant. It was a fern of some type, which are supposedly harder to make die. I had never had a plant before. Evelyn was standing in the doorway. I hadn't seen her for three days, since I had to leave Philadelphia before her. She had on a thick tweed coat. She looked quite pretty.

'I thought you and Bill might want something alive around all these robots.'

'I thought Bill and I were alive.'

'Well, in a way,' she said, laughing. She stood on her tiptoes and kissed me on the mouth. Her face backed slowly away. Her face stared at me.

'Have you been drinking?'

'No. A little.'

'Oh.'

'My dispatcher bought me a couple beers after work.'

'Oh.' Her eyes darted around the room. 'Where do you want the fern?' she asked me.

'I don't know. Wherever's cool. Just make sure that it's not touching one of the metal toys. The moisture might rust them.' Then I added, 'Thank you for the plant.'

'You're very welcome!'

I sat down on the edge of my mattress. Evelyn carried the plant with both hands over to the corner next to Bill's side. The plant looked heavy.

'Here okay?'

'That's a pretty good place for a plant.' I pulled my cigarettes from my pocket and lit one. I scratched my nose. We had gotten a new batch from the pharmacy that afternoon. Some of them were Methedrine, which I had never tried in pill form before. My skin was itching all over. I scratched under my arm. Evelyn looked at me from the corner of her eye.

She sat the plant in the corner of the room, then stepped back and eyed it. She wiped the dirt from her gloves.

'That looks good.' She took off her coat and laid it on the mattress. She sat next to me. She stared at me as I continued to smoke. She grabbed my chin and pulled me to face her. She lowered her head and looked into my eyes.

'Is there something wrong?' she said.

'No.' I looked across the room at a mirror Bill had bought while I was gone for Christmas. It was strange to see myself walking around the apartment all the time now.

The purpleness around my eyes was gone, but my nose was still dark and swollen.

'Where's your tongue?' Evelyn asked.

'In my mouth,' I said.

'Why isn't it in mine?'

I kissed her. We messed around for a few minutes. I began to get heated up. My hand was down the back of her jeans, inside her underwear. She was squirming beneath me. Then I backed away. I knew I had to tell her. It was going to be hard enough without having had sex with her first. Boy, I'd seem like a real jerk doing that. I sat up.

'What are you doing?' she said.

'Sitting on the edge of the bed. Now I'm rubbing my eye. Look, see?'

'Why did you stop?'

'Because I thought maybe we could see a movie tonight.'

'You're in one of your moods, aren't you?'

'What's one of my moods?'

'Your down moods. Come on, you know what I'm talking about.'

'I'm tired from work.'

'Tired . . . James.' Evelyn winced. Her body went loose.

'What?'

'It's just a little disappointing, you know. I've been going nuts in Philadelphia waiting to see you. And then I come home and you're like this.'

'I've just been thinking about some stuff.'

Long pause.

'You've been thinking about some stuff?'

'Yes.'

'What are you talking about?'

'Listen. I've been thinking about us.'

Evelyn's face crumbled; actually, it looked more like it was caving in.

'You fucking bastard,' she said.

Her fists were clasping onto my bedspread. My bedspread had pictures of Astro Boy all over it. One of her hands was squishing up Astro Boy's face.

'I'm sorry.'

'You asshole. I can't believe. *I can't believe*,' she screamed. She jumped up from the mattress. Her hands were out to her sides, slightly raised. Her fingers were spread out taut like claws. She paced. Tears were streaming down her cheeks. *'This is exactly like the worst thing that I could imagine would happen, exactly why I didn't want to be with you.'*

'We've hardly even gotten back together, Evelyn. We've had sex two times, that's all.'

'That isn't all!' She continued pacing. *'This can't be real! This is all a set-up, like something you'd do just to hurt me. How?'* She was sobbing.

'I don't want to hurt you, Evelyn. I swear. I swear to God.'

Evelyn shrieked in frustration. She swung her head swiftly to the side and looked at my robots lining the wall. She breathed heavily. Her eyes widened.

'I'm going to destroy your toys!' she said. *'I'm going to destroy your toys.'* She stomped over to the robots, her face in a red, teary growl.

'Don't do that, okay?'

Evelyn kicked the robots. She shrieked loudly. The toys bounced off the walls and she kicked them again. Saturn's head cracked open and the wiring was exposed. The batteries popped out of his back and rolled toward me.

'No!' I said.

Evelyn kicked more of them. I sat frozen, my hands on my knees. I couldn't seem to move.

'Please. Don't.'

'This is what you did to me! You're a bastard! YOU'RE

a robot, you're so fucking cold! You tricked me!' Evelyn fell to her knees. Her head was lowered. She heaved for air. Her body quaked. Bits of plastic and robots' appendages surrounded her.

'See,' I whispered, not looking up. 'This is one of the reasons we should reconsider our relationship. It makes you destroy my things.'

'Fuck you! You're demented!'

'I know. I'm sorry.' I forced myself up and tottered toward her. I crouched down behind her.

'Evelyn.' I set my hand on her shoulder.

Evelyn swung around quickly and knocked my arm away. She swung at me again with the side of her fist. It landed square on my broken nose.

'Oh no!' I yelled. I brought both hands to my face and fell over. Blood spilled from my nostrils over my arms and onto the floor. 'Oh Christ.'

Evelyn punched me two more times in the back of the head. Then she stood and kicked me in the ribs. Evelyn wailed. I heard her trotting toward the door, scooping up her coat. I heard the door slamming behind me, and her sobs trailing down the hall.

There was enough blood that my pants were soaked red. I stood and walked toward the dresser. I took two more Methedrines. I looked at myself in the new mirror. I was a strange and demonic-looking guy. I made some faces. I tried to make myself cry as I watched myself in the mirror, but I just looked pitiful.

I walked to the kitchen. I filled a towel with ice and held it to my nose. I made my way down the stairwell and to the street, where I could hail a cab to the hospital.

I Become a Nightmare

Bill and I were waiting for Lou and Pennywhistle in Central Park. They were very late. Bill sat on the Alice in Wonderland statue. I sat on a park bench, which was covered in drops of hardened tar. Bill's lips were parched and flaking as if he had been in the desert. He licked his lips rhythmically.

'That only makes matters worse,' I said. 'The licking.'

He ignored me, continued doing what he wanted, ruining his life.

Even though it was late, some little black kids were playing soccer beside us. The soccer ball flew out of bounds, and rolled beside where I was sitting. I picked it up, and got ready to throw it back to the kids.

'Hey, man,' said the kid, eight or nine years old. 'Throw me the ball.'

'How about some manners?' I said.

'What?'

'I was about to throw you the ball, but you can say please. You order me like your slave. Maybe now I'll keep it for myself. I need a soccer ball.'

'Give me the ball, fucker!'

I stared at the kid for a moment. Then I threw the ball at his face as hard as I could. It slapped him hard. He shouted in pain and collapsed to the ground. His friends all ran over to him.

'Dude!' Bill said.

'What? He called me a fucker!'

Bill shook his head in disbelief.

'It's just a little kid,' he said.

We decided that Lou and Pennywhistle weren't going to show. Bill slid off the Alice in Wonderland mushroom and started walking away. I followed him. All the little black kids stared at me angrily as I passed them. Their friend was crying. His nose was bleeding.

I followed Bill out the park and down the sidewalk. After a few minutes, I felt bad.

'What?' Bill said, referring to my sad face.

'I shouldn't have smashed that kid's face up. He was probably just afraid I was going to take his soccer ball.'

'Dude, sometimes I think you're the meanest person I've ever met.'

I started to cry.

'Don't cry,' he said. 'Just stop being mean.'

'Bill?'

'What?'

'I still love Evelyn.'

'Oh, man.'

'I made a mistake, Bill. I made a mistake. I should have waited just a little bit.'

'You were scared of intimacy,' Bill said.

'What?!'

'You were scared of intimacy.'

'That's too easy, Bill!'

'What?'

'The intimacy thing. I don't believe any of that! Fuck all of that stuff, man! You sound like my fucking Twelve-Step motherfucking brother! And you're drunk!'

'My philosophy is that I may be drunk, but you're a little drunker than me. That's my philosophy.'

'So what?'

'So that gives me the right to give you a helpful diagnosis. You know what else? You cry so much when you're drunk that it's got to be a sign of some deeper problem. You become a nightmare.'

'Yeah, well, you're a speed addict.'

'No, duh.'

'You can't tell me these things, Bill!'

'Yes, I can.'

'You're as screwed up as me! More!'

'I can. I just did.'

'Fuck you!'

'Fuck you.'

I punched Bill a few rapid times in the chest.

'Hey!' he said, trying to block himself with his hands.

'Get away from me,' I said.

I stomped down the sidewalk. A fat Latino was in my path and I told him to get the fuck out of my way. I stomped by the storefronts. I thought about how presumptuous Bill was to tell me what my problems were. I stomped down the street, getting angrier and angrier. And when I got angriest I thought of Tar, of how we had fought and now we hadn't spoken for over a month. I thought of how pitiful my father looked when I came home with the new baby doll. I thought of how angry my mother had been. I remembered the contorted enraged expression on Evelyn's face when she was beating on me. I thought of Gary. I thought of Gary. I thought of how I had lost them all, every single last one of them, and I began sobbing.

I turned around. Bill was standing a block and a half behind me, hunched over with his hands in his pockets, confused, staring.

I raised my arms high over my head. The sobs came catapulting up from my chest. I cried out to the hunched figure of my friend.

'*I'M SORRY, BILL!*'

Bill wandered up the street toward me. He glanced sheepishly from side to side.

'Dude, I used to kind of get bummed out when you quit drinking. But now, you know, I see why you did it.'

I grabbed the sleeve of his shirt.

'Bill, you can help me,' I said.

Bill shrugged.

'We can go talk to Evelyn. You can help me.'

'All right,' he said. 'No prob.'

Evelyn's apartment building had one glass door, and then another glass door beyond that. The first door was open, but to get inside the second you either needed a key or to break the glass or someone in one of the apartments could buzz you in. The apartment-livers were listed on bronze plates with buzzers next to each. Evelyn had never put her name over the name of the former occupant. It was one of those things you could put off forever.

I couldn't remember Evelyn's exact apartment number. She was somewhere on the seventh floor.

'Is it Seven-J?' Bill said.

'Oh. That sounds right.' I pressed the buzzer. No one answered so I pressed it again. A gruff man's voice came over it: 'Hello?'

'Who is this?' I said. 'Where's Evelyn?'

'Evelyn? It's twelve-seventeen at night.'

'I bet he has a digital clock,' Bill said.

'*Who the fuck are you?*' I shouted into the intercom.

'Get off the goddamn buzzer, you!'

I let go of the buzzer. I turned and looked at Bill.

'I don't think that was the right apartment,' I said.

Bill rolled up his lower lip and shook his head.

'Try this one,' he said, pointing to 7A.

I repeated 7A several times in my mind. That had to be it, I decided. Evelyn's apartment had to be 7A. I pushed the buzzer. I pushed it once to be polite. Evelyn's voice came out from a tiny black speaker. Her voice was like a finger on the soft of my brain. My darling baby. I felt weak. She was mumbling as she woke up.

'Hello?'

I pushed the intercom button.

'Evelyn.'

No answer.

'Evelyn! Can you hear me?!'

'You have to lift your finger off the button for her to speak,' Bill said.

'Oh.'

'—don't want to talk to you,' she said.

'Evelyn, I'm sorry.'

'I don't want to talk to you. Go away.'

'Evelyn, I screwed up. It was a mistake. Evelyn, I was drunk. Wasn't thinking clearly.'

'You're drunk now.'

'Evelyn, I'm sorry. Evelyn.'

'I'm going back to sleep. If you ring again, I'm not answering.'

'No! Wait! Bill has to talk to you!'

I pulled Bill over in front of the intercom. Bill pressed the talk button. I used his shoulder to balance myself while he did.

'Evelyn?'

'Bill, take him home.'

'Um, Evelyn, James still really likes you a lot.'

'Get off the intercom. I don't see the logic in all of this, James, I really don't.'

'Uh, why don't you come down here and talk to him. He's in a—it's totally hurting him, right? Because he made a mistake. We all make mistakes, right? He's a good person.'

'I'm going to sleep now.'

'No,' I whispered to Bill.

'Evelyn just—wait—hold on a second.'

No answer.

'Evelyn?' Bill said.

No answer.

'She left,' Bill said.

I pushed down the button and yelled into it, '*Evelyn!*'

No answer. I pushed the button down again.

'*Evelyn!*'

Static, no answer.

'*EVELYN, COME BACK. I'M SORRY!*'

I turned and looked at Bill. 'She can still hear me,' I said. 'She's up there and she can still hear me.'

'I've never been up there,' Bill said. 'I don't know the layout of the apartment to know if she hears you or not.'

I turned away from him.

'*I'M SORRY, EVELYN!*' I screamed.

Nothing.

'*EVELYN! EVELYN! EVELYN! EVELYN! EVE-LYN!*' I alternated rapidly between the buzzer and the talk button.

Bill walked out of the small foyer and onto the porch outside. He sat down on the thick concrete railing there and lit a cigarette.

She'll *have* to answer if I keep screaming, I thought. She'll have to come downstairs. She might be in her robe. She'd have to, but she didn't.

257

People began hollering down from their windows for me to shut the fuck up. Bill poked his head inside the door and said, 'Get outside now, dude. People are going nuts.'

'*EVELYNNNNNN!!!*'

Eventually I slunk out onto the porch. People yelled down names at me. Someone threw a candle at me. This increased my sourness. I swirled around and stared up at them. I told them to fuck off. They yelled various things back at me, their little pink heads sticking out of the windows. They had become a team.

'Come on down, you fuckers!' I screamed. I walked backward, stumbling toward the street. Bill was pulling my arm.

I bent over, clutched my stomach, and vomited onto the dirty street. When I was most the way finished, I looked back up at them. They had gotten quieter.

'Come on down. I'll take you all on!' I screamed. 'Not one at a time, but all at the same time, you motherfuckers! I have broken bones, I have snapped legs and seen the bone pop through the skin, I have smashed heads on brick walls and *now I will do this to you! I will smash your heads on this cement thing next to me! You hear that?*'

I was about to faint. I turned toward Bill. His face was filled with sorrow.

We arrived home. A message from El Hombre Fitzgibbon, a friend of Lou and Pennywhistle's, was on the answering machine. Lou and Penny had been arrested, he said. Neither one of them ratted us out; sometimes loyalty is where you least expect it. Our friends were both most likely going to do some time. Our salad days, as bleary as they were, were over.

The Greatest Toy in the World, Part II

On the subway, a woman sat across from me holding a naked infant. The baby had a flabby, dimpled ass. The woman's eyes were the color of a muddy stream, with little black flecks like tadpoles. She changed the baby's diapers.

A loud scream came from somewhere. I looked around quickly; perhaps I could help; perhaps I could get in a fight with some perpetrator, defend someone—an old woman, a small, insecure man who had never learned his way with his fists. I leaned forward in my seat to see through the window down into the next car. Only a couple people were in the car, and neither one seemed to be screaming. I looked at the woman.

'Did you hear that scream?'

'A scream?' she said.

'Mm.'

'No,' she told me.

'Oh. Maybe it was the wheels scraping on the tracks. Wow.' I grabbed onto the bar next to me. It was covered with a thin film of slime from other people's hands. I didn't want to touch it, but I needed it to stay steady.

The woman was wearing old, frayed Nikes.

'That is a very small baby,' I said. 'How big is—How old, I mean?'

She stared at me. She was wondering, I knew, if there was some way I would be able to use this information against her.

'Three months,' she said with a phony smile.

'I don't remember being that old. He loves everything, I bet. He lets loose in his drawers and somebody comes and takes care of it for him. I would like someone to do that for me.'

'What?'

'Be taken care of, is what I'm saying.'

She nodded.

'What's that guy's name?' I asked.

'Larry.'

'Larry. Larry the little tiny person. May I hold him?'

'I'm sorry. No.'

'Eh, all right.' I looked down through the window at the other end; nobody looked like they had just screamed down there, either.

'It's not that I mean to be rude,' she said.

'That's okay.'

'I mean, have you had a lot of experience with children?'

'I haven't held a baby for eighteen years. That's not including dogs.'

Over the woman's head was a placard, an ad for an abortion clinic done up in pink, with flowers surrounding the text. It creeped me out, and for a minute I considered walking up to the next car, getting away from this conversation, perhaps looking for whoever it was who may or may not have screamed.

The woman stared at me, reconsidering. Perhaps I looked harmless.

'I guess you could hold him. For just a moment.'

'A mere moment, yes.'

The woman crossed the aisle. She sat down beside me.

'You have to prop up his neck, like this,' she said.

She handed me Larry carefully, and I took him carefully in return. I cradled him in my arms. He had a tiny head. It seemed a miracle that so many babies lived for more than a year with such small, fragile skulls. You'd think they'd all get crunched somewhere along the way. All it would take was one millisecond of forgetfulness jumping over to change the channel. I couldn't even remember all the toys Bill and I had stepped on when we weren't paying attention. And a lot of those were made out of metal. A white bubble came out of Larry's mouth.

'I am never going to have a baby,' I said. 'Because I'd probably step on his head.'

'What?!' the woman said. She leaned in toward me, as if about to take him away.

'He's a cute little animal, all right,' I said.

The woman stayed on edge next to me, ready to lurch for the child. I stared at him.

Larry's little brain was just being formed. I wondered what things had already invaded his head. All the information that had to be going in there: cop shows, his parents fighting, the smell of bums' urine in the streets, Disney characters, his father worrying about money, how pitiful his mother's shoes are, sports of all types, goo-goo baby talk, the sound and feel of subways, jam boxes everywhere, honking, the hot New York sun when in a stroller, electronic billboards, people impersonating Groucho, the sound of modems connecting, pit bulls, shock jocks, thunder, religion, country music, halitosis, tetanus shots, bad children's books about giant dogs and people drawing doors with giant crayons and walking through them. I felt the bones in Larry's back. His eyes looked up at me but didn't see shit. I ran my fingers over the fuzz on his head.

I looked at the woman.

'Does it take a lot of money to take care of a baby like this?' I asked.

'You wouldn't believe. You would not believe.'

'Here,' I said. I handed her the baby. She took him gently. I reached into my pocket and pulled out a couple fifty-dollar bills.

'Here, take some of this money,' I said.

'Oh no,' the woman said.

'It's not for you, it's for him. Buy him some big . . . some big stuffed animal. Go to the FAO Schwarz.'

The woman looked at me.

'Go ahead,' I said. 'This is a thing that I do. I'm independently wealthy. I go around drinking and doing good deeds. I don't know what else to do with my life.'

The woman smiled. She took the money.

'Thank you,' she said. 'Thank you very much.'

I nodded. I took my handkerchief from my pocket and wiped my nose. I stared straight ahead. The woman turned and smiled at me again.

'It really is very kind of you,' she said.

I smiled. I continued looking straight ahead. I watched the graffiti on the subway walls out the window. I shook my head slowly.

What the fuck had I just done? I thought.

I looked at my reflection in the darkened window.

You stupid faggot, I thought. You need that money to buy a robot! And there you are, showing off, playing a game!

I turned toward the woman. I opened my mouth to tell her to give me back the money. She smiled at me. I stared at her. I nodded.

Eat it, I told myself. I turned back and stared out the window.

You fucking loser.

*　　*　　*

Charlie was arranging comic books behind the counter. He was wearing the same stained red T-shirt he always wore.

'James, old man!' he shouted.

'I got to get something here.'

'What's that?'

'A robot.'

'Sure thing. How's old Eva doing?'

'Evelyn, stupid.'

'How's old Evelyn doing?'

I raised my hands over my head and shrugged.

'Jesus, you're really polluted, aren't you?' Charlie said.

'They haven't called me Jesus for two thousand years.'

'Jesus, you are polluted.'

'Shut up.'

'This is my store. Don't tell me to shut up.' Charlie continued to arrange the books on the counter.

'Charlie. It's Evelyn, not Eva.'

'As you told me.'

'She told me she didn't love me.'

Charlie stared at me. 'Oh, geez, I'm sorry, kid.'

'Charlie, I drink too much.'

'Yeah, well, me, I just have a beer every now and again.'

'And these pills. They're fucking my head.'

'Well, just say no.'

'Charlie, you ever been in love?'

'Ha-ha. Shit. I don't know. Maybe. I guess I thought so at the time. But I had things to do, you know.'

'I'm sorry it didn't work out.'

Charlie nodded. He was sad and fat.

I wandered up the aisle. I braced myself on the corner of one of the cabinets.

'There'll be another fish in the sea come walking along,'

Charlie said. 'For both me and for you. Of that I am bona fide sure. And you got nice clothes. Ladies like that.'

'They probably like that red T-shirt, too, Charlie.'

'No! This? I don't think so!' Charlie laughed and shook his head.

'Charlie.'

'What?'

'I only have three hundred dollars left. This is all I have.' I pulled the three hundred bucks out of my pocket. I held it toward him. 'What can you give me?'

'If it's all the money you have left, I'd give you advice not to spend it.'

'I don't want advice. I want a fucking robot.'

Charlie shrugged. He came out from behind the counter.

'I can't say I have too many great deals on robots. But I did get one thing you might be interested in.'

'A robot. A robot, Charlie. Is the thing I want.'

'Oh, you ain't seen this. Come here.'

Charlie's keys hung from a silver chain on his belt loop. He flipped through them. He walked toward an enormous and ornate wooden cabinet with closed doors. It had Egyptian hieroglyphs carved into it. Strange: I had been in the store a thousand times and had never really noticed the cabinet. Charlie unlocked its doors. He pulled out a box.

The box read: SCRUNCH 'EM, GROW 'EM DINOSAURS.

'This is what you were looking for, wasn't it?'

I nodded.

'It's in the original box,' Charlie said. 'Some actor who just moved here from Minnesota came in with it and a bunch of other stuff that was mostly junk. I saw this, though, and remembered it was you told me about it, how you wanted it the first day we met. I had only seen it the once.'

Charlie handed it to me. I stared at the cover. Brontosauruses, pterodactyls, woolly mammoths.

*Put the cubes in the Energizer Machine and WATCH
'em transform into DINOSAURS! Then scrunch 'em
up again in the DINOSAUR PIT! Endless Fun!!!*

I set it on the counter. I removed the top. Everything was
there, the colored plastic cubes and the red machine and
even the directions.

*DO NOT put the blocks in a conventional oven. DO
NOT eat the blocks. DO NOT touch the wire surface while the unit is turned on.*

'Oh,' I said. 'I can't believe this.'
    'Ha-ha,' Charlie said. I looked at him. 'I'll give it to you
for a C note,' he said. 'I have no idea how much it's worth.
Ain't listed anywhere.'
    I nodded. I took out two fifties and handed them to
Charlie. He shoved them into his pocket. I put the lid back
on the box and pulled it against my chest.
    'Thanks, Charlie.'
    'Don't mention it. Go home and sleep off that drunk
you got on.'
    I nodded. I walked toward the door, then stopped. I
turned back toward Charlie. A plastic Tinkerbell hung
from a noose over his head.
    'Charlie. I just wanted to tell you something.'
    'What?'
    'That these toys are all I can find that's beautiful.
They're all I can find.'
    I pulled the magic box closer to my chest.
    Charlie didn't say anything.

I moved quickly out the store. A bell jingled. Sunlight, street, a million bums passing, whether in tattered sweat-pants, tie-dyes and jeans, or gray business suits. They counted me among their number.

A Dexies canister was on its side. It was empty. A vodka bottle stood beside it. It was a quarter full. The rest of the vodka and Dexies soared through my bloodstream and clawed at my stomach. They alit my mind like a hundred thousand helicopter searchlights panning over the ab-sences inside me. And my liver hurt.

Once Tar had exclaimed: 'Let's pretend that our beds are pterodactyls and that we're riding on their backs.'

Now I pinched the small green pterodactyl in my fingers. I flew it over the folding table.

'Good fly,' I muttered. I drooled.

The sunlight shone between the window bars and onto the Greatest Toy in the World. An empty chair stood across the folding table. I could see the chair through the clear dome atop the red machine. The dome distorted the chair's shape, curling it, fitting it into my world. It was comforting. Tar's face, fresh and four, appeared in the chair.

'Which . . . hey, Tar . . . which dinosaur . . . should we do next?'

I guzzled some vodka. I slammed the bottle back into its place on the table, knocking some dinosaurs onto the floor.

'The orange one?' I asked him. 'The orange one's a triceratops.'

I picked up the orange cube from the table. I slid open the door on the clear dome. I dropped the cube inside. The mesh was red hot; the machine had been on for a while.

Nancy came to my side. Seven, I thought. She had a

hunk of her hair between her teeth. She looked out of place: a smooth elfin creature against the backdrop of the beer bottles, ashtrays, clothes, and chicken potpie trays.

'Hey, ugly,' she said.

'Nancy, I got the good thing back.' I motioned toward the red machine. She touched my arm.

'Look, it's growing,' she said.

The horns and the helmet of the triceratops were sprouting.

'Mm,' I said.

I fell asleep for a moment, then awoke.

I went to touch Nancy's face. But of course my hand passed straight through her. Still, everything was becoming more real by the second.

Footsteps passed by the front of the table. I looked up. Gary.

He was pale. His bow tie was pink. It was spotted with little swords, the sort with which someone would pierce an olive.

Sounds came out of Gary's mouth, but he sounded like he was speaking underwater. He waved his hands around, trying to get my attention.

'What? I can't . . . there's no understanding you,' I said.

Gary's body quivered like the string on a bow after shooting an arrow. He widened his eyes. He shrugged. And then he was gone.

Nancy was sitting on the edge of my mattress. She lifted up her skirt. It was her vagina, a hairless line. She smiled. She liked showing it to me.

'Heh-heh-heh.' I dropped my hand into my own lap. I tried to grab my zipper, tug and pull. But the zipper was too minuscule and I couldn't keep a grip on it. 'I'm too fucked up,' I muttered.

'Look, Jimmy,' Nancy said. She lifted her butt off the

mattress a little. She stretched open her vagina with her fingers. It was red inside.

'Heh-heh,' I said. 'I used to hate when you did that. Now, though, it isn't so bad.'

'Look at the triceratops,' Tar said.

The triceratops was fully grown. I grabbed him. I flung him to the ground.

'Which one next, Tar?'

No answer.

'Anybody?' I announced. I was alone for a moment.

'Any of you can say what . . . which one we do next. Come on, anybody, an idea.'

The room was empty. I was slumped over in the chair. There was a digital clock on Bill's dresser, the type where the numbers flip over. The first number was permanently broken. The upper half of the eight set in the bottom of the clock's window.

'Put your hand on it,' somebody said. I looked up. It was Gary Bauer again. But I didn't see how he was able to speak. Most of the roof of his mouth was missing. I could see the gums and teeth on one side. There was a large red hole in his neck, too, surrounded by flaps of skin.

'Put your hand on it, Jimmy,' Gary said.

'Leave me alone, dead guy.'

'Chickenshit. Is that what you are? Hah-hah!'

Gary's head swung backward as he laughed. I could see up into his skull.

'I can see your brains,' I said. 'You don't look so smart.'

'Chickenshit!'

'I'm not the one afraid to climb down into holes to go get Dan Occansion, buddy.'

'Then put your hand on it.'

I clamped my face tight. I shook my head.

I did not want to. I did not want to at all.

It was a hallucination. He was dead.

But he still kept taunting me after all this time.

I hated him.

'Put your hand on it.'

I looked into Gary's single eye.

'I can do anything,' I said.

I backhanded the clear plastic. The dome cracked. I struck it again. It snapped off the red machine, and clattered to the floor. The wire mesh glowed red. I placed the whole of my palm on the mesh. For a moment it didn't hurt. Of course, I thought. They wouldn't invent something this dangerous for a child.

Bolts of pain shot up my arm and through my shoulder and neck. The skin on my palm was burning, melting like the army men. Tears flowed from my eyes and down my face. But I kept it there. My hand wanted to come up but I wouldn't let it.

'Fuck you all,' I said. 'Fuck all of you.'

As I went to pull it up, I found I couldn't. My skin was stuck to the metal. I screamed. I ripped my hand away. Smoke rose from the wire mesh. Touches of glop were attached to the wire mesh, touches of glop that used to be part of me. I held my hand in front of my face. I stared at it. It was a bloody hole. Rivulets curled down around my arm.

The acid of vomit struck the back of my throat. I placed my fingers over my mouth to block it. The vomit gushed out. It streamed between my fingers, shooting out six feet or so in different directions. It splashed on the Greatest Toy in the World, my clothes on the floor, my mattress. There was more smoke, a sizzling sound. The red machine sparked.

I tried to stand up from the chair. I pushed my fingers down on the table and half stood. My legs buckled. I fell to my knees. One hand cradled the other. I looked around the room. It was empty. Gary, Nancy, and Tar were gone.

'Toys,' I said. I stood again and stumbled toward the robots against the wall.

I kicked the toys, finishing the job that Evelyn had started. I kicked Rom Spaceknight until his chest was crushed. I kicked Captain Future Superhero and Interplanetary Spaceman into shards. I kicked them all until they were bits of plastic and crushed tin, even Bill's toys. Especially Bill's: He was the one who had gotten me started on this collecting stuff. That's what started everything. I destroyed Ralph Malph, knocked off David Soul's head, and smashed Laura Ingalls Wilder's sternum with one swift kick. I turned around and knocked Scrunch 'Em, Grow 'Em Dinosaurs off the folding table. I lifted it over my head. I hurled it toward the wall, but because it was plugged in and the cord wasn't long it swung down and smashed against the floor. The red metal popped off the machinery beneath.

I gathered together the dinosaurs and the colorful cubes and moved toward the bathroom. I stuffed them down the drain of the sink. My blood covered them. I turned on the water. I gripped onto the edge of the sink and started to pass out, but I wouldn't let myself fall. I looked in the mirror.

God giving man life and taking it away is not nearly so bad as God taking away childhood and giving him life.

'Amy, put my brother on the phone.'

'Jimmy, listen, Tar wants to talk to you, I know he does. But I really think it'd be better if you called back tomorrow. When you're sober.'

'Tar. Put him on the phone.'

'Listen, Jimmy, I'm just trying to help.'

'Your help is like . . . it's . . . it's horrible! Get my brother!'

Amy paused.

'Hold on,' she said.

I heard her walk away. They conspired in the background. The phone picking up.

'Hey. What's up?'

'Tar. I fucking killed it.'

'What'd you kill?'

'The dinosaur game. I killed it. After all this. This waiting. I killed everything. Everything in the apartment is dead. Agh. I was their father, Tar, and I killed them. The fucking robots. But I just couldn't fucking take it anymore, all this.'

'You killed your toys?'

'Oh, Bill's too. That bastard.'

'Are you okay?'

'My hand.'

'You hurt your hand?'

'A big bloody hole. I could drown in all this gunk.'

'Do me a favor. Go to the medicine cabinet in your bathroom. There's some Neosporin in there, I saw it. Rub some on your cut.'

'Ha-ha-ha. Neosporin? All right, Tar. Jesus.'

'Will you do it?'

'Need fucking three or four cans of Neosporin.'

'Just do it when you get off the phone.'

'Ha-ha. Oh certainly, Tar. Oh certainly.'

'Why'd you call?'

'I thought of something.'

'What?'

'We should have gone over there that morning, right after he called us.'

Tar was quiet for a moment.

'Come on, Jimmy. We don't need to talk about this now.'

'If we would have just gone over there, you know what I'm saying, that morning. He just as well as told us. But we were thinking about other things. Stupid things.'

'You've said all of this before.'

'It was a moment that would have passed, I think, Tar. Straight there and he wouldn't be fucking— he wouldn't be fucking dead. It's true.'

'Wrong. Wrong.'

'No, yes.'

'We couldn't've known. Why the fuck are you bringing this up again? It's over and over with you.'

I started crying.

'He was my job, Tar.'

'He wasn't your job.'

'He killed me with him, Tar. He killed me with him.'

'The fuck he did!'

'He did. I'm dead. My hand is fucking bleeding.'

'Listen to me: You're not dead. You're alive. And you've got to be thankful for that.'

'*Oh, what bullshit! Gary Bauer fucking shot his face off and what's thankful about that! You're standing there dragging him all over the fucking porch, Tar! You picked him up and started dragging him all over the porch, trying to get someone to help!*'

'This is getting so old, Jimmy. I was in shock. It's a real, medical state. I've had to listen to this for ten years, do you realize that?'

'He was my friend.'

'He was my friend, too. But that doesn't mean you have to fucking kill yourself over it. And that's what you're doing, man. You don't see it. But every fucking night, every fucking night I'm afraid I'm going to get a call.'

Tar was crying now.

'Oh you and your fucking AA minions.'

'Oh, yeah. Well, listen to this, Jimmy. What about me, huh? You were all I fucking had. You didn't just take care of Gary. We all took care of each other. In fact, you—you took care of all of us. And then Gary's dead and you're gone too. It was your job to take care of Gary? What about me? Where's all the great responsibility there? I was your brother. I didn't have anybody else. What about me, Jimmy?'

I didn't say anything for a minute. There was a small fire in the corner of the room. The sparks from the red machine must have caused it.

'Neosporin,' I whispered.

'Good night,' Tar said. 'Just go to sleep, all right?'

'I gotta put some of that stuff on my hand. It's really— there's blood everywhere.'

'Put a bandage on it and go to sleep.'

'Oh yeah. Good night.'

'Mm-hm. Good night.'

I hung up.

I stumbled into the bathroom. I squirted an entire tube of Neosporin onto the wound. I wrapped a whole roll of toilet paper around my hand. But in seconds the paper was drenched with blood. I leaned against the wall. I looked down at my arm. It was turning white. The veins around my forearm were more visible than usual. It was interesting to me that I might die. I had no feeling in my skin or tongue.

I stumbled out of the bathroom. I moved through the apartment, out the front door.

I dragged my hand along the hallway wall, leaving a fingered streak of blood behind me. I stopped and vomited again, a mix of blood and what seemed to be black bits of my lungs. The old alcoholic that lives down the hall passed me. He eyed me and quickly disappeared into his apartment.

Outside, I stepped onto the sidewalk. I almost stepped on a pigeon. The bird flew up and out of my way. It flapped its wing against my face. This probably hurt my eye, and I was grateful I couldn't feel it. I turned.

Bill was standing there, holding his keys. He was arriving home. He was staring in horror at my hand.

'What happened?!' he said.

'Bill,' I said, though I could barely speak. 'A black guy. He broke into our apartment. He broke into our apartment and he destroyed all of our toys, and then he did this thing, Bill, this terrible thing, to my hand.'

And at that point I collapsed, passing out.

'God, please,' Larry whispered. He was on the brink of unconsciousness. The tears pooled in his bubble helmet. 'My neck's broken. My spinal cord's severed. My spinal cord's severed, my friends are dead . . . Satanists are overtaking the earth.'

Gary, Tar and I watched as the little man squirmed helplessly in the grass. We looked at each other, wondering what to do. Tar stared at me. He stood up. He bent down and picked up the gun. Tenderly he set the gun in Larry's palm.

I felt myself being lifted. Bill was carrying me. He cradled me in his arms. Despite his amphetamine dependency, he was still strong.

'Look out!' Bill yelled at some kids in our way as he stepped off the curb and into the street. He was attempting to hail a cab. We were almost hit.

'Stop!' he cried at the cabs.

But they all sailed by. One, and then another. Zipping, cheerily. Their centrifugal force snapped my bloody shirt against my side.

'Stop!' Bill screamed again, louder than before. But the cars refused. We looked like a couple of fucked-up, drugged-out bums with a bloody hand. No one wanted to stop for us. No one ever had.

Bill carried me. He shuffled down the sidewalk. His face contorted into hideous worry. Panting. His arms strained. The veins in his neck distended into thick, pulsing squids. My neck draped back over his elbow. I gazed up at the purple sky and I started to lose consciousness. Bill eyed me.

'Stay awake,' he said.

I forced my eyes open, and I tried. I breathed. I concentrated on this breathing. In, out. In, out. Stay awake. I couldn't breathe. I lost the ability to breathe.

I breathed.

My organs sloshed as Bill tottered. My heart pounded. It flailed its sick red body against the birdcage of my chest. It was dying. My liver screamed, enraged at the torrent of alcohol drowning it, flowing down through my crotch, my hips, my sides. My nostrils pulled in the putrid New York City air. My parched lungs circulated this foul mix throughout my already polluted form. And this was what I was. This was all I was. I was flesh. I was pulp. I was stupid eyes and ugly face and nagging heart and nothing. And that, in the end, was my only kingdom.

'*Stay awake!*' Bill screamed at me. My ankles struck the passersby.

Bill carried me. He carried me past Uncle Charlie's Sandwiches and the newsstand on 49th and Tenth, past Lucky Lady's Adult Books and a Friedrich's Hot Dogs and a bum that slapped his thigh and laughed at me because he thought I was hilarious. Bill grunted. Sweat sat like tadpoles in the space beneath his eyes. His nose started to bleed from the exertion. The blood from his nose dripped down, spotting my cuff. Bill wheezed.

And then we were there.

The statue of Saint Dominic, staff in hand, gazed down at me. Like all statues, his pupils were two little holes. They bore through me, into me, and it wasn't without love.

Bill crumpled to his knees. The emergency-room doors flew open. Fluorescence bathed us in their forgiveness. The orderlies turned to face us.

Bill screamed, 'Help!' And he dropped his face into my chest and he started to sob. Because sometimes, you see, even your life means something to somebody.

'Stay awake,' Bill pleaded.

And I did.

A NOTE ON THE AUTHOR

James Gunn was born and raised in St. Louis,
Missouri. He is a writer, an actor, and a filmmaker.
Most recently, he wrote and starred in the
independent feature, *The Specials*. He also wrote
the cult classic *Tromeo & Juliet*, as well as
screenplays for Warner Brothers Studios,
including *Scooby Doo* and *Spy Vs. Spy*. With
Lloyd Kaufman he wrote the book, *Everything
I Know About Filmmaking I Learned from
the Toxic Avenger*. He earned an MFA from
Columbia University in 1996. *The Toy Collector*
is his first novel. He currently lives in Los
Angeles, California.

Read more about James Gunn and *The Toy Collector* at
www.jamesgunn.com

A NOTE ON THE TYPE

The text of this book is set in Linotype Sabon, named after the type founder, Jacques Sabon. It was designed by Jan Tschichold and jointly developed by Linotype, Monotype and Stempel, in response to a need for a typeface to be available in identical form for mechanical hot metal composition and hand composition using foundry type.

Tschichold based his design for Sabon roman on a fount engraved by Garamond, and Sabon italic on a fount by Granjon. It was first used in 1966 and has proved an enduring modern classic.